A Catalogue Of Redundancy

A Catalogue of Redundancy by: C. F. Collins-Hall

Third Printing 2023

A Catalogue Of Redundancy

By:

C.F. Collins-Hall

Disclaimer:

Unless otherwise indicated, all the names, characters, businesses, places, events, and incidents in this book are either the product of the author's imagination or used in a fictitious manner. Any resemblance to actual persons, living or dead, or actual events is purely coincidental.

Dedication

This novel is dedication to my wonderful husband.

David Hall, who listened to all my ideas and encouraged me to express myself in the written word.

To my daughter Samantha, who said "Mom go for it!"

To Melissa Brown who was in from the beginning, listening, and working with me to fine tune the final storyline.

To Neil Penney, who helped me get my novel to publication.

To all my family and friends, who listen to me, encouraged me and answered some of the weirdest questions!

Thank You!

Prelude

According to Canon Law of the Roman Catholic Church,

"The sacramental seal is inviolable; therefore, it is absolutely forbidden for a confessor to betray in any way a penitent in words or in any manner and for any reason."

This edict would haunt Father Micky for the rest of his life.

Part One

"WHERE DO I BEGIN"

Chapter One

"What this individual has told me, will haunt me for the rest of my life. She has come to unburden her soul at any cost. Yet, because of the seal of the confessional, she would be protected forever."

In his mind Father Michael reviewed his church teachings "where it is absolutely forbidden for a confessor to betray in any way a penitent in words or in any manner and for any reason." Then to himself, "How this edict of the Roman Catholic Church, would come to haunt me in the years to come!"

Father Micky went back to how his day had begun, Saturday, one of my busiest days at church, everyone had something to confess. They would come for even the smallest indiscretion. I believe they just want to feel better about themselves. So here on this beautiful day that would change my life forever, a blend of sky-blue and turquoise sea, with the Alosio winds blowing across the Island. I made my way from the presbytery over to our small, but very dignified church. I would love to go fishing, or for a walk in the village or along the shore to gaze out over the Caribbean Sea. Perhaps there would be no one in the church, I would sit for twenty minutes, and then leave, but as I passed through the door, over in the shadows by the south wall sat alone figure. My walk would have to wait.

Strange, it was not one of my parishioners'. Also, I did not recognize this person as one of the regular winter visitors. Best not to stare, just continue as I normally would do. I approached the steps to the altar kneeled down and whispered my prayers. The stranger still had not moved, I guess they were waiting for me to enter the confessional. As I quietly enter my compartment, I slipped a quick glance at the stranger, but whoever they were, they weren't looking my way.

As I sat down, I was so glad that I had made changes to the interior of the church to ensure that the breezes came through and the confessional did not become stuffy. This could have become a problem, because of the old wood, dampness and age would have given it a musty smell. However, I had it refurbished, the wood stripped and varnished, and screening vents in the upper areas of the walls. In this way the breezes always flowed through. As I sat in the confessional, the breezes carrying the scents of flowers in the garden passed through and I could easily go off into my mental reverie.

The church was aged, almost dilapidated, but maintained an old-world dignity. Money was sparse so any repairs would only be for safety. Nothing elaborated here, no gold leaf, just strong walls, a waterproof roof, large open windows with shutters. Sturdy benches, no kneelers, people either stood or sat during Mass. Most of the time, they stood. What we lacked in elaborate surroundings was quickly forgotten; when the music started, and the parishioners were singing, you would think we were in the grandest church on the continent.

As I sat patiently waiting for my visitor, I began to think about how I had ended up in such a pleasant, yet poor parish. I had spent most of my years as a parish priest in the hectic world of New York City, where you heard just about every story imaginable in the confessional.

After thirty years the stress and time had worn me down. When the Archbishop had offered me a transfer to a totally different Diocese, it was like the Holy Spirit had heard my prayers. I was delighted to move, hoping for a quiet parish upstate, small community, different problems, but hopefully manageable. To my utter surprise the deal the Archbishop had made for me was to go to a Caribbean Diocese as an exchange. At first, I wondered how I would manage the change in climate, summer all year round, a green Christmas, typical traditions but so ingrained into my person.

God always has a plan and his plan for me had worked out beautifully, my days were much easier, and the people were so glad to have me. Yes, they were very poor; I had never imagined that such poverty could exist. But it was a different type of poverty, not always sad faces, these were happy faces enjoying and making the best of each day. In a few short months I found myself falling into the rhythm of life and enjoying each moment. So different from New York, I found my outlook and health improving. I realized this was where I want to live out my life in service to God, and his children. I was so lost in my owns thoughts, I had not heard the person enter the confessional, until I heard the words "bless me Father for I have sinned."

With a start, I opened the curtain that covered the screen, the voice was quiet, that of a woman. I assumed that this would be over quickly, and I would be on my way. Then the lady said that it had been ten years since her last confession. One quick breath in and I said, "that is all right my child, God is always glad when we reach out to him."

What was to follow would haunt me for the rest of my life, this individual had come to unburden her soul at any cost, yet because of the seal of the confessional, she would be protected forever. I only knew it was a woman because of her voice, the screen dividing our two compartments was designed so that the penitent could see me, but I could not distinguish what they looked like.

With a deep breath taken in I said "Yes my child, please continue" with that statement I was to begin a journey of darkness beyond my imagination.

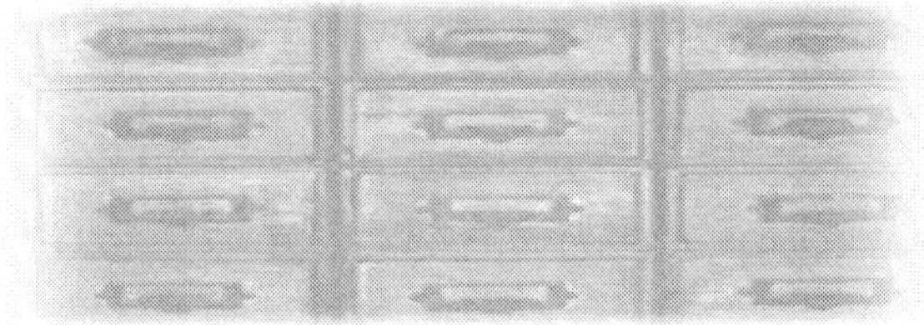

Chapter Two

An unearthly silence overtook the confessional, the woman did not speak. The island breezes seemed more intense, carrying with them the smell of the hibiscuses planted in the garden at the side of the church. Their aroma was so powerful that your senses were dimmed. What is she waiting for? How do I move this conversation along? For some reason I wanted to delay this confession. Was it second sight, a premonition, or the foolish thoughts of a priest unsure on how to proceed? "I never had this problem before with a penitent, why now?" Father Sweeney asked himself.

"Father, do you believe that good people can become evil under certain circumstances?"

With that question I quickly came to attention. What did she just say? How do I respond? This was clearly going to be a very perplexing confession. I was beginning to feel uneasy about what was coming, yet I must admit I was also becoming very curious as to what would be her next comment.

"Do you know Father that I worked my whole life, always trying to do the right thing, regardless of where I worked, no matter what my job was at the time. Yet for some of my employers it was never enough." The lady stated and then continued to say.

"The worst employers I ever had were those connected to our faith, because when they were callus it went to the root of my spiritual beliefs."

Then silence enveloped the confessional again, it was like she was getting control of her emotions to continue, time seemed to stand still. It was as if the breezes had stopped but the aroma from the hibiscus was now overpowering and stifling. Would she ever get to the point? "Don't be impatient!" Again, speaking to himself.

I had to break the silence.

"Yes, my child, often when we encounter those, with which we share the same faith and we feel as if they have let us down, it can confuse us about many things and make us doubt our own beliefs."

"No Father, it is much more complicated than that, it makes you question your relationship with God. It makes you question everything about your life! It enters that dark space that exists in every heart, soul and mind and begins to grow like a cancer, eating away at goodness and replacing it with pure hatred." She stated.

As I sat in shocked silence at these words, I now knew that I was dealing with a very troubled soul, could I really help them, make a difference? I needed to know more about her story, what made her tick so to speak.

The quietness of her voice was deafening, it carried such calmness, yet at the same time such despair.

"Father, I started working at a young age, I have had many jobs, and some would even say careers. All of them were in what you would call the secular world, so when people did unkind things, you were not surprised, disappointed yes, but not surprised." As this woman spoke, I was beginning to feel uneasy, not scared but definitely apprehensive. Again, she went quiet, was she thinking about past jobs, forgetting where she was, gone off into her own world. Now I wished that I had had a good breakfast, small pains of hunger were beginning to start, or was it my nerves.

"Do you know Father, my first job; I had to travel over one hour each way. I had to use public transit, until I met some people who travelled in the same direction.

I shared a ride with them every day, except when they were away, and then I used public transit. That first job was interesting, I worked hard, learned everything that was needed to be done, after my first year I was promised a raise by my boss. I had learned all the paperwork inside-out. I even did some of the forms for my boss. Then one day, management called us all in, severely criticized us for our work, they were blaming us for the world's financial disasters, but in fact it was their own underhanded business practices that were the problems. Father I was disappointed, but not surprised after all it was the secular world." "Then I quit with no prospects in sight, but I had to get out before I lost control of my emotions and what would have become a terrible verbal assault against them, after all I stilled needed a reference letter.

Again, silence enveloped the confessional, but this time briefly. Then out of the blue came a question, I could not have expected.

"Father did you always plan to be a priest, or did you start out in one direction and then change your mind?"

"What an unusual question my child, I must say, I would not expect to be asked that in the confessional."

"It is a valid question, Father; it helps me understand if my changing jobs, over the years was normal; if in fact, everyone has doubts about their choices."

"When you put it like that, then yes, it is a fair question. But I believe we are here to hear your confession, not my career choice."

"I agree Father, but I am too tired to continue today, goodbye, I will come again."

"But my child your sins, did you want to confess?" I asked.

"Don't worry Father, lots of time for that" was her reply, almost in a laughing voice. And with that she got up and left, leaving me to wonder what had taken place and why.

The quiet of the church and the gentle breezes where now being taken over by an odd piece of music I had heard in the movie theatre, that was the sounds of "Beethoven's Silence" composed by Ernesto Cortazar in my head and controlling my thought process.

Crossing the courtyard and going back to her car, the lady was in shock, here she was four thousand miles away from home and there sitting on the other side of the screen was her childhood sweetheart, Micky! "Will I be able to come back here and speak with him, so close, or should I seek out another church." Speaking to herself, "Don't worry Gwen it's been forty years, he probably doesn't even remember you." "A stolen kiss at the theatre hardy leaves a lasting impression." With that closing thought the mysterious lady continued onto her car.

Driving along the road back to her resort, more thoughts emerged. Gwen spoke to herself, "In profile, Micky still is handsome, but he looks much thinner, than I remember.

Chapter Three

"I'm tired, another day," did she just say that? I could not believe what I was hearing, after having spent almost an hour with this lady I still had no idea what her problem was or if she had one. Since, when had this confessional become the psychiatrist's couch? After a few more minutes I blessed myself and locked up the church. I desperately needed fresh air, but I was hungry, so I went back to the presbytery for my lunch. As always, my housekeeper, Isabel had left a sandwich plate in the refrigerator. What a great housekeeper, she is not nosy as some of my priest friends complained about their housekeepers, but quiet and respectful.

Everyday Isabel came early in the morning did her work, got my meals ready and left by noon. She had her family to attend to, and I knew she had a second job at one of the local hotels to make ends meet. That was Isabel, such a lovely person, so polite and thoughtful, just the right person to be my housekeeper. After eating I decided to walk to the beach and clear my head, there I found a quiet spot to sit and think. Again "Beethoven's Silence" played in my head, it was so eerie.

To say the least, I had not expected my day to go this way, dealing with such a strange person.

"Father did you always plan to be a priest, or did you start out in one direction and then change your mind?" What kind of question was that to ask me? Yet as I sat there the nuance of the question set me on a path of examining my own life. "Did I always plan on becoming a priest? Yes, it was what was expected of me, I had changed my mind, only once, but that I had always kept that to myself.

There I sat, Father Michael Philip Louis Sweeney, examining my past. My last name Sweeney represented my strong Irish American background. We lived in Boston, which according to my grandmother was the rock of Ireland in the New World. My parents were part of the first generations of their families born in Boston, and I was the second generation. But within the four walls of our home, it was like we never sailed across the sea.

Everything was the old way, and the sayings never left the mother tongue. Many of my friends when they came to visit me at home would say they felt they had stepped back in time as the conversations flowed. That was my home life, a struggle between the past and the present, the old and the new.

Even my name or should I say a combination of names was designed to set me forward on my current career path: Michael Philip Louis, really mother what were you thinking. Mom always had the perfect explanation, "Micky, we gave you those names to prepare you for the priesthood, one day you will become a Bishop or perhaps even a Cardinal and your Christian names will match your stature." "Micky, Michael means serious minded, a person who thinks things through and comes up with the correct answers to problems, Philip means peace and harmony, other fine qualities you need to have. Finally, Louis, Micky, means patient and willing to be of service to others. Live up to your names Micky and someday you will be one of the leaders of our church". Of course, when I asked if my younger brother Kevin could go into the priesthood, the answer was a resounding 'NO'; the oldest son becomes the priest, it is his duty.

So, I grew up in Boston, I studied and did everything that my friends did, but always in the back of my mind I knew what my future was to be, so much for being one's own person. In many ways I thought my family's ideas were to say the least, medieval.

Then came grade twelve, a new year, my last year at high school before I went off to university and then onto the Seminary. On the first day as I sat in my homeroom class, I looked up and there she was walking through the door, long reddish golden hair, swaying as she walked. The movement was as if she was gliding and the breezes of the ocean were carrying her hair into the sky, flashes of light dancing in her hair. I was completely captivated. Then she turned and looked my way, her eyes, oh my God it was like the sky and sea had come together and created magic. I fell hopelessly in love that day with a beautiful angel, Kathleen O'Hare.

I was so shy, I could barely speak that first day, but somehow, she sensed my feelings and opened up the conversations. Over the next few months, we had lunch together, talked and walked together, but I would not bring her home.

Then came the Fall Formal, I asked Kathleen to go with me and she said yes, now I needed to tell my parents, I did not want to become a priest, I wanted to marry Kathleen in the future. I went to the formal with her and felt like a prince with his princess, we were going to be happy ever after. I still remember going to the theatre on a Friday night, and when the lights had gone down, I had leaned over and given Kathleen a secret kiss, it was brief, but sweet. Even now I can still feel the softness of her lips on mine.

How my parents found out about my plans for the future, I had no idea. Their knowledge, swiftly put an end to everything. I never knew how, but after Christmas, Kathleen was gone from our school, and with her were my dreams of happily ever after. I finished high school went onto university and then the seminary. I was ordained in Boston and had been a parish priest there for ten years, when I was transferred to New York, another Irish hub. I was a parish priest there until I got sick, after a spell I found myself here in the Caribbean with a quiet parish to manage and lead.

Sitting under this palm tree feeling the breezes off the ocean, a wave of sadness enveloped me, I hadn't thought about Kathleen in over forty years. But today I am, and I wonder how her life turned out. She no doubt married, had children, and probably had grandchildren by now, they could have been our grandchildren, but it was not to be.

Let go Micky, the past is the past, no point going over what might have been, it didn't happen and that was that. Momentarily the breezes crossed over my lips and for some unexplained reason I thought I felt the softness of Kathleen's lips on mine. Nonsense Micky you are letting your imagination take over. The past is over, deal with the here and now!

With that final thought I got up and headed back to the church. Strange, how the comment of one stranger could bring up so many memories. Tomorrow I am going fishing; I need to connect to my current world.

Chapter Four

A few weeks had passed since my unique penitent had visited the confessional. It had been a quiet and amazing time for me. My island parish had only little sins. No big problems here or so I thought until last Saturday. One of my parishioners came into the confessional in a terrible state, it seemed she was pregnant again. It certainly would enlarge the family as she already had six children. Her husband seemed pleased at the idea and had even told me after Mass, that he hoped it was a boy to help out in the family business. However, the tale she was relaying moved the scale from a minor to a mortal sin. The baby was not her husband's.

All I could think of was where she had the time for two men, with six children in tow. My only advice was for her to keep quiet, say her penance. And we would talk later, "Say nothing to anyone", "are you still seeing the man"? "No Father, he has left the island, gone to the USA. He will probably never be back".

"Then my child, say nothing to anyone, do not break up your family over this, but never take another man to your bed again." Did I just tell someone to lie, yes, I did, and I am not ashamed?

If this wife knew how many children her husband had from other women, she would die from heartbreak.

Sometimes a little white lie can save many lives. That is the hardest part of my job, I know all the secrets of the confessional, but can never tell anyone else. If my compromise is a small lie here and there, so be it. In the larger picture I am trying to preserve this family. Such is the life of a parish priest, forgiving sins, forgetting what I am told and trying to keep the peace.

But today was quiet, no penitents, actually I had been sitting here for an hour and not a noise, just the gentle breezes coming through the windows and off in the distance the sounds of birds singing. One of my favorite pieces came to mind it was from "Pachelbel in the Garden' by Dan Gibson. The song Serenity was perfect for the setting, the sounds of birds singing and the musical notes reaching into the soul and lifting it up to the heavens. Somehow it gives substance to the quiet and seems to be part of the natural setting in which I reside. The very name suggests nature and I feel the strength of the music, but as in nature, you sense a deeper meaning. As I sat there in quiet reverie, I did not hear the church door open or anyone entering the confessional. Somehow, I had transported myself to a place of beauty away from all the cares of this world.

"Well, hello Father Micky" the voice spoke from behind the screen. I nearly jumped out of my seat.

"Hello!" Wait; get yourself, together man, focus. Ok what's next? I was thinking.

"I hope I have not startled you Father, I have been away for a few weeks and needed to think things through, before I spoke to you again. I have so much information to share with you Father about my sins. I am afraid one sitting will not suffice."

"I am sure you have not done that many things, shall we start."

"Yes, Father I have done more than you can imagine, but I think the best way to work through this is to go back to the beginning." "I hope you are a patient person Father."

Yes, usually I am a patient person, but I hate being played were the thoughts going through my head. Enough Micky, this is not like you, what is bothering you? Why this animosity towards this stranger? Blocking out these thoughts I gave myself over to the penitent.

"Yes, child let's begin" I said.

"I am not a child Father; I am a grown woman" was her curt reply.

"We are all God's children" "But you are right let's start at your beginning." I replied trying to relax the atmosphere. Then thinking to himself, 'why I was trying to relax the atmosphere?' I do not know, but my instinct was telling me, 'that's what I needed to do.'

"Well, I imagine that it would be best to go back to my childhood, that's where the root of all my anxiety started." The mysterious lady stated.

Are you kidding me, I thought, her voice sounded like she was in her fifties, how long was she going to take to cover five decades? Perhaps I will be pensioned off before we get to the real problems. Keep these unholy thoughts to yourself Micky and act in a professional manner. Why does this woman bother you, you don't even know her?

"Did you have a difficult childhood?" I asked.

"No actually Father I had a wonderful childhood, we lived in a large home, had servants and my parents were very much chumming along in the higher social circles" was her quiet reply.

"I am sorry, I am confused, what was the problem?" I asked in a confused voice.

She gave such a direct reply "Oh that's easy, my father was a crook, he had a position of power, he abused it and stole a lot of money" "All I can remember from the early years was my father saying, don't talk to anyone about what goes on at home."

Thinking to himself, 'Ok, now we were getting somewhere, I thought, but I wasn't sure where she was headed.'

"Was your father arrested?" I cautiously asked.

"No, we skipped town, changed our last name and moved to a new city" was her direct reply.

Oh my god, what a thing for a child to endure were the thoughts swirling through my mind, this explains why she is so hesitant in her speech. It's like she is testing me, to see if it is safe to talk.

"You know we are speaking in the confessional, so no matter what you tell me it remains here, no one else will hear about it." I tried to reassure her.

"Oh Father, I know that, but I was raised to be cautious when talking. I'm sorry, Father I need to go now. I will see you again soon. Oh, sorry I mean we will talk soon" the lady stated.

"Excuse me you seem to know my name; can I give you a hypothetical name?" I asked.

"Gwen; short for Gwendolyn; goodbye Father."

And with that she was gone; was this going to go on forever. Again, I heard "Silence". I desperately needed to get outside. I think I am going to go for a walk along the beach to clear my head.

An hour later I found myself walking along the beach, I felt the breezes and the scents of the ocean taking me back in time. Back more than forty years ago in Boston, walking along the shore hand-in-hand with Kathleen, sharing secrets and laughing. Every so often stopping for her gentle kisses and then her warm embracing hugs. Suddenly I was back on my Caribbean beach, no kisses, no hand holding and no embracing. Was my mind deceiving me, but Gwen's voice held hints of Kathleen's. No not possible!

Walking back to the church, a thought struck Micky, "She called me Father Micky, not Father Sweeney or Father Michael as was on the parish sign, Pastor: Father Michael Sweeney." Continuing on that thought process, 'such familiarity from a complete stranger, odd.' "Get over it, Micky, the world is becoming more informal, and this is an example of the new trends in speech."

As the days passed, I struggled to get over Gwen's visit; I had to know what was really going on. I went to the local library, asked to use a computer, and began my search for the truth. The librarian helped me with search engines, I tried everything, but there were no references to a family disappearing with a child named Gwendolyn in the USA in the 1960-1980's. She is lying, I thought completely astonished. Why would anyone lie in the confessional, the one place in all the world where all truths are protected by God's seal?

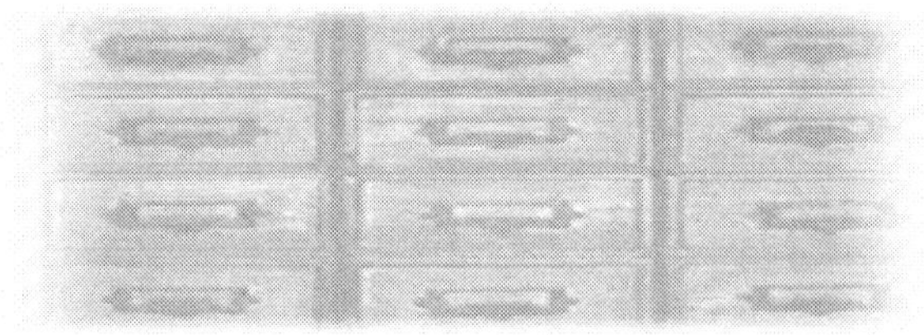

Chapter Five

A quiet week had passed, after my parish duties were handled, I found myself spending an incredible amount of time at the library. My new interest into searching out crime did not bother the librarian if anything she gave me ideas for searching out my quest.

There were no reports of a family disappearing with a child name Gwendolyn, so I needed to think of what else Gwen had said. 'We moved because my father was a crook.'

Trying to find disappearing crooks could last a lifetime, there had to be a way of being more specific in my search. Oh yes, she had said they were wealthy and travelled in better social circles, but where? In the USA or another part of the world?

I now was waiting for her next visit, not to hear her confession, but to put together the pieces of the puzzle. I could not believe at sixty plus years of age, I was pursuing private detective work. Perhaps I do have too much time on my hands. Somehow every time I thought of Gwen, I still heard the piece, "Silence" playing in my head. I need to bring this woman's visits to an end. I could not make a logical reason to myself for these thoughts, except my own instinct for survival.

Another week passed and no visits, then out of the blue on a quiet Saturday, my visitor returned.

"Good afternoon, Father, how have you been?"

"Hello Gwen, it is Gwen?" I asked.

"Yes, Father it is, interesting that you remember my name, perhaps I should have used a false name. She said with a light-hearted laugh.

In my head I was thinking, really how have I been? This is not a social visit, and yeah you did give me a false name. However, I kept those thoughts to myself.

"Well, you know Gwen, I have a small Island parish here, so I do get to know people's names and their voices. Not to worry you are covered by the seal of the confessional."

"It's not that Father, I guess I was surprised you remember, but yes, I realize that with a small parish you would recognize names and voices. That brings to mind how do you deal with coming face to face with the real sinners? Ha Ha! Sorry Father I did not mean to be so flippant; I am sure you have your ways of dealing with those awkward moments."

"Yes, Gwen, I am well trained to deal with such times. To quote Our Lord from the bible in Matthew, "Truly, I say to you, whatever you bind on earth shall be bound in heaven, and whatever you loose on earth shall be loosed in heaven."

"So as per the instructions, I make it my mission to leave in the confessional what I am told and let it go." "As they say, they are part of my priestly studies. Are you ready to continue with your confession?"

"Well yes Father, I am ready to progress in my monologue, I am afraid the juicy bits will take a while for me to get to, I hope you understand?"

Monologues are you kidding, again 'Silence', who turned on the radio, no it's not the radio, it's in my head, how do I bring this to a conclusion.

"Father are you still there?" Gwen asked.

"Oh yes, I just was distracted for a minute, I don't think I understand your comment about a monologue, what has that got to do with confessing to anything?"

"Did you have your lunch today, Father, you seem on edge? Maybe I should leave and comeback when you have more time."

"No, no it's alright, I had lunch thank you, lets continue where you left off. I believe if my memory is correct, you said that you were told to be cautious when talking to people, is that right?"

"Yes, mother and father often talked about his work and the deals that he had going on, most were about construction projects. Mother was always asking him if that would create problems for the family, he assured her it would not." "I guess he was lying to her, but I think he was also lying to himself. Dad would always pretend that everything was fine. He could not face the truth about anything." "Mom went along with him to keep peace in the home, but I think she also loved having beautiful things around her and a beautiful home to show off to the other ladies in the church council."

"Was social position important to your parents?" I asked trying to sound not too inquisitive.

"Of course, Father, social position, who you worked with, what you worked on, where you lived, where your children went to school, your political ties were the heart and soul of my parent's existence."

"Did you feel anxious about this as a child?" I asked in a lower voice to sound calming.

"I did not feel anxious until everything came crashing down.

Then our life as we knew was over and we were forced to become different people. That would be the definition of stress, yes?" At first her voice was calm but began to raise towards the end of her statement.

"Yes, I can see where that would create anxiety. I would imagine that moving and establishing a new life in a different

country could be difficult." I was trying to be soothing in my questioning.
"Actually, we did not move to a different country, just a different state, and a family name change to my mother's maiden name help out for a while." "But I must say our 'FBI' will chase a man down to his grave." I sensed the anger in her voice.
"I am sorry for your troubles" was all that came to my mind.
"Not to worry Father, water under the bridge so to speak, oh God I have to go, goodbye."

And with that I sat quietly in the confessional, confused, and irritated at the same time, and wishing that song 'Silence' be silent.
Remaining in the confessional to think, Micky spoke out loud, but only to himself, "God you have sent this woman to me for forgiveness and guidance, I only hope I am up to the task."

Micky waited another few minutes for another penitent, when no one came he went back to the presbytery, still thinking about what had transpired.

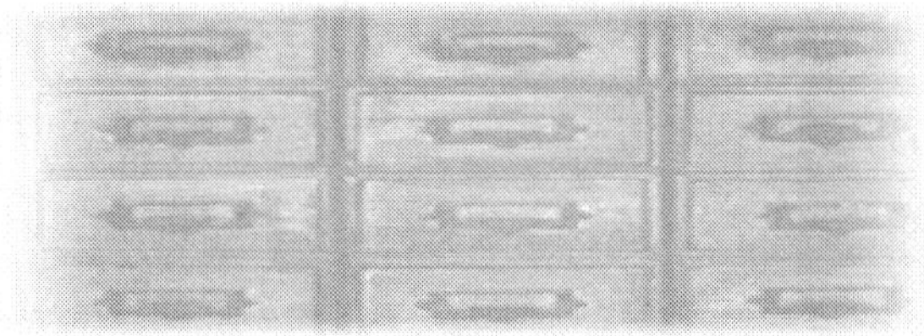

Chapter Six

I could not believe that again, she had left me with only questions and a sense of unease about everything. Yet not one answer as to why. I needed to eat and go for a long walk to clear my head. I needed to talk to ordinary people. As I walked down the main street of our village, I observed the various individuals, tourist and locals' alike going about their business. They all seemed to be smiling enjoying the bright sunlight, the gentle breezes off the Caribbean, the food, and the atmosphere. This really was a lovely island, not to populated, but modern enough to be welcoming to the tourist. Most of the tourists were from Europe, the UK and some Americans. Most of the Americans who came wanted a quieter setting for their holidays. Also, we did attract a few Canadians, but they usually stayed with friends who had bought homes on the island.

After walking around for an hour, I decided to stop for a coffee and a treat. Why not? It was Saturday evening and I had done my bit for today. We did not have Mass on Saturday night, just two Masses on Sunday, one very early for the people who worked at the resorts and a noon Mass for the rest of the parishioners and visitors. Thus, the evening was mine to relax and unwind. I had not felt this much tension since I left New York. It was expected to be tense in

New York, the confessional there was more of a shock box, than a place to confess and reconnect with God.

Now all of that stress was coming back to haunt me, and this mysterious lady was responsible.

As I sat at a patio table under the umbrella my mind was travelling in many directions, so much so that I was no longer taking in my surroundings. When the fog in my head cleared, I looked across the street and there sitting at a table by herself, was quite a striking woman. She had on a large hat with a wide brim that hid much of her face. She also wore dark sunglasses which seemed strange to me as the sun was going down, and sunset was only about thirty minutes away.

I tried not to stare, but I found my gaze going back to her, there was a strange familiarity about her, but I could not place it in my mind. That's enough my boy, back to the presbytery for you, and off I went.

Across the road the stranger had also noticed Father Sweeney but had made sure not to make eye contact. Gwen thought to herself 'seeing Micky, outside of the confessional is bringing up too many memories, he has aged, but even after all these years I would recognize him. I guess it was love after all.'

Chapter Seven

Gwen sat quietly at the table sipping her drink, thinking about the past. This quiet space and time opened up Gwen's mind to reliving her past and in her own mind voicing to herself the realities she had faced and overcome. Seeing Micky in person today brought back so many memories, she thought to herself. Those fun and lovely days in Boston, going to school and making new friends. Meeting Micky Sweeney had been the best thing of all, about the move to Boston. It was like a new life was opening up for me, the promise of a brighter future. After the year of upheaval, preceding the move, things had finally begun to look promising.

Kathleen Kennedy-O'Hare-Wahl the only daughter and child of the prominent construction contractor Conrad Wahl and his society darling wife, Mallory Kennedy-O'Hare-Wahl living the high life in Devon, Pennsylvania, one of the more affluent suburbs of Philadelphia. As a family we had it all, a beautiful home, fine cars, and spending time with the upper crust of Philadelphia. I went to a private girl's school and enjoyed all the privileges that went with the lifestyle. I would be entering my last year of high school, then onto a world-renowned college and university. Meet a young man from a good family and be set for life.

Yes, every detail of what my future was to be, was discussed with my mother. Mother would move heaven and earth to ensure that my social stature would be upwardly mobile.

My parents were so blinded by their ambitions for the future that they forgot to attend to the problems of the present. My dad's company was one of the construction firms involved with the 1976 Bi-centennial projects. Everything seemed to be going smoothly until in early 1973, questions were to be raised about cost overruns and missing funds regarding the project. I can remember mom and dad arguing about this, mom asking dad if he was involved. Dad stated that in no way was his company involved in any deceit. A couple of months passed, and my mother again asked my dad if he was involved in the missing funds. Dad said he would swear on a bible that he had nothing to do with the problem. But both mom and I knew from the sound of his voice that he was lying.

Then one evening when the maid was out, Dad asked mom and I to sit down, he needed to talk. "Things may get very difficult in the coming weeks; you will hear and see in the press a lot of negative stuff about me and other construction companies. Don't be afraid, nothing is going to happen to us, but you must not discuss these problems with anyone outside this house, not even the servants. We must pretend that everything is fine and that I have done nothing illegal." What a strange statement for my father to make, but I would do as he says, there was already enough fighting between him and mother, no point in me adding to the trouble.

Then two weeks later two FBI agents were at the front door asking to speak to my father.

Mother spoke with them and said Father was out of town on business and would be back on the weekend. I will always remember that day, Thursday, June 21, 1973, that was the day that our family's life came crashing down. When Father got in late that night, I could hear him and mother arguing again, but nothing was said to me. The next morning dad spoke with our maid Helen and informed her that her services were no longer needed. Dad would pay her two months wages in lieu of notice, but she needed to leave by noon.

After Helen left, Dad called both of us into the kitchen. "We need to leave tonight; I don't believe we will be back for a long time. You must pack only personal items and things you really need."

My mother was visibly upset "What about all of my china, silver, the pictures, family heirlooms, I cannot pack that in an afternoon." Father yelled at her "forget all that stuff, we would lose it all anyways if I am arrested." "Mallory I am guilty, I stole the money, get over it we need to escape now." With that shocking statement mother and I quietly went about packing up what we would need.

Father said, "we will pack the car after dark in the garage, I want to be on the road before midnight so that we can blend in with people coming home from various events and once we are on the open road it won't matter." Father seemed so cold and matter of fact, it was like he was on autopilot. Then mother asked him a question, "What about all of your paperwork, are we taking that too?" "No Mallory I have been destroying it for weeks, so there is no evidence for them to find." Mother finally lost it, "are you kidding me, you knew this was coming, you didn't tell me, you let me think everything would be fine, I am your wife did you not trust me?"

"I am sorry my dear, I could not trust anyone," "This way when you answered any questions your answers would be truthful as you had no knowledge of anything else, but your truth." "In time you will understand."

By nine-thirty the car was packed, we walked around the house, checking timers, windows and curtains, dad wanted it left as if we had gone away for the weekend and would be returning. His logic was it would buy us more time to settle someplace else.

So, at ten o'clock at night of Friday, June 22nd the Wahl family left Devon, Pennsylvania for what would be a weekend trip, but only they knew from one which we would never return.

In keeping with his criminal mind, dad had replaced the licence plates on the car with new plates, probably stolen. Smart move!

Chapter Eight

As the darkness deepened, I came out of my trance, looked around and realized it was time to get back to my hotel room. Well not really a hotel room, more like a suite in a small but exclusive resort. It was so hard for me to believe that after choosing this island, I should run into Micky. Strange indeed, but in reality, I finally found someone I could unburden myself to, and so far from home, he would never connect the details of my crime. I best be going, from here it would be a thirty-minute drive back to the resort and it was dark. One problem with these smaller islands, streetlights were few and far between. I was glad I had gotten a rental car while I was on the island, it allowed me to travel around, see things and people without anyone paying me the least amount of attention. Driving carefully along this semi-dirt road my mind began to wonder again to the past, which it seems is all that I have left.

It was so strange, as a young teenager I was driven everywhere, but once I could afford my own car as an adult, I felt so free. To be able to come and go as I please, answering to no one, nothing to explain, except for the built in GPS in the car, no one tracking my movements.

After leaving Pennsylvania, we were always looking in the rear-view mirror, trying to remain invisible to everyone, blending into the crowd, not drawing attention to ourselves. I felt like I had become a ghost of my former self. Except for my long flaming red hair and I did everything possible to blend in and not be noticed.

Friday, June 22nd, 1973, the Wahl family vanished from the face of the earth, and on Monday, June 25th, 1973, the Kennedy family arrived in Boston and rented a house in the suburb of Charlestown. What were three more Kennedy's in one of Boston's Irish hubs. Father had stashed a lot of cash in deposit boxes in Boston banks using the name Michael Kennedy.

This was to last us a lifetime, mother and I had no idea how much money dad had hidden and where, which proved to be a bigger problem within the year. I know dad thought he was trying to protect us, but looking back now I see that really, he was only protecting himself.

I still needed to complete high school, so my parents registered me in the local Catholic High School. The strangest thing is that they presented me as their niece 'Kathleen O'Hare'. Mom explained that my parents had died in a tragic accident, the family home had burnt down, and so all my records were lost. Whether the Mother Superior believed them or not, when the ten-thousand-dollar tuition fee was paid in cash, no other explanations were required.

Chapter Nine

That first day was strange, remembering to say that my parents were dead and that I lived with my aunt and uncle, but remembering not to give my classmates any other name but O'Hare. When I entered my home room, looking across the classroom was a very handsome boy. Did his eyes ever light up when he saw me. This year may not be too bad after all, I thought to myself.

Michael Sweeney, Micky for short, and I became quite good friends, spending much of our free time together. However, for some reason he never took me to his parent's home. I was fine with that, because I would not have to answer any questions about my family. Then came the Fall Formal and Micky asked me to attend with him, I was thrilled. My parents not so much, but not for the reason most parents would have, that being their only daughter going steady with a boy in high school. No, they were afraid, I might confide in Micky about our family. I loved my parents dearly, but I was beginning to find their isolation practices annoying. The Fall Formal was a success, but neither of us had sat down to a meal with the other's parents. What a strange couple we were. Christmas break was soon approaching, and I wondered if my parents were even planning on doing a traditional celebration.

Dad was becoming more distant and difficult to talk to, and extremely irritable. School finished on the Thursday, December 21st, when I said goodbye to Micky and wished him a Merry Christmas, I never realized it would be the last time I would see him. We talked about getting together over the holidays, but I was evasive. I didn't think my parents would let me go on a date, but so not to hurt Micky feelings, I said I thought we would be going out of town to visit family. "I'll see you in the new year" were my parting words.

Thank God, mom had done the grocery shopping last week, and the house was filled with food, because Friday, December 22nd our lives went from a pale version of our previous life to one of complete darkness, a living hell. It was after two in the afternoon, dad came into the house yelling and screaming about the banks and how they were out to destroy him.

My mother tried to get him to calm down, but nothing was helping. "Conrad, what has happened, why are you so upset?"

My dad's reply still haunts me to this date. "Mallory how stupid are you, where do you think I have been getting the money from for the last six months for us to live on, it's not mana from heaven, and it's the money I embezzled in Philadelphia. Remember those trips I took on business, it was here to Boston to establish banks accounts and safety deposit boxes under an alias, to the banks I am Michael Kennedy." He paused to take in a deep breath, "Today when I went to the first bank, they told me that the accounts and boxes were frozen, I was unable to access the money. Then I went to one of the other banks and the story was the same with no explanation. I don't know what is happening. I have about two thousand dollars in cash, that will not even cover our expenses for January."

Whether mom was in denial or not taking in all that dad was saying, but her comment enraged dad so much I thought he was going to hit her. "Conrad what does that mean to us?"

"Mallory are you dense, we are broke, and don't make any more ridiculous statements, my patience is wearing thin".

"Don't open the door to anyone, I expect the FBI will be here before the week is out." Dad came close to yelling.

Christmas Day came and went with no visitors, but also dad was unable to access any more money.

Then on December 27th, the doorbell rang. Dad went up to the attic, while mom answered the door. The gentleman spoke to mom "Mrs. Michael Kennedy?"

"No, my name is Mallory O'Hare, but we rent from a Mr. Kennedy." Mother replied.

Sitting in the living room, my thoughts were, “quick thinking mom, you surprise me, I didn’t think you could.”

“Can you give us the address where you send the rent cheques?” the agent asked.

“I am sorry, but my husband handles the household expenses” was mom’s reply.

“Is he home?” the second agent asked.

“No, he is away on business.” Mom’s short reply.

The police didn’t move, waiting to ask more questions, then a terrible sound came from the attic, it sounded like a firecracker. The police ran up the stairs while mother fainted, I stood frozen in time in the shadows.

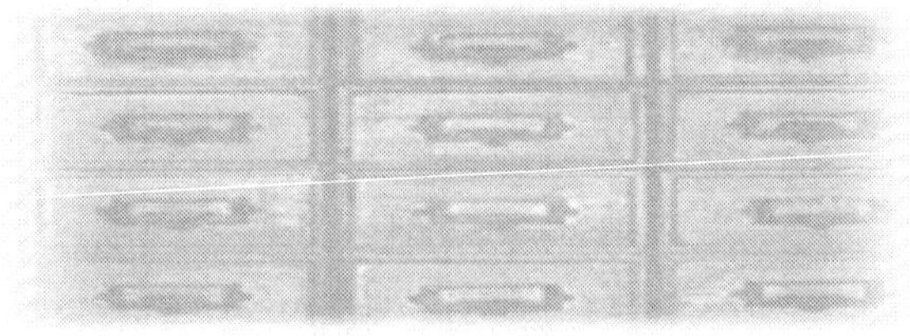

Chapter Ten

The shock of the noise sent me into almost a comatose state, in what seem like hours but was only minutes the house was filling with emergency personnel. More police arrived, an ambulance with EMS personnel. They took mother and me into the living room. Mother was still in a daze and not responding to any questions, people spoke to me, but I did not reply. I wanted to cry so badly, but the tears did not come. I could hear people gently talking to mother, coaching her to come around, then her quiet sobs, no gut-wrenching screams, which came later in the middle of the night when we were by ourselves.

"I am sorry Mrs. Kennedy, but your husband is dead", the female FBI agent said, "This is a hard question, but did you know your husband had a gun?"

My mother's blank stare, said it all and with a haunting statement mother said, "No I did not. I don't even know now if I ever truly knew my husband, he is a stranger to me. Our whole life was a lie."

The agents were kind to us, and just stopped asking anything. Mother and I sat side by side holding hands in silence. Mother was never very good at being a comforting individual, she always withdrew when things were difficult. We sat together in a deep silence while people did their jobs around us. Then I got up to go to the bathroom, they ask me where I was going, I said the washroom. As I was walking by the dining room, I overheard the FBI agents talking.

"This is a real disaster, we lose a prime suspect, a witness and our cases are going out the window." "This situation needs to be handled quickly and quietly, a tragic accident when the gentleman was cleaning his gun. That's the story we want out there, Mr. Kennedy was never part of an FBI investigation." "The family won't talk, so that should close the story on that end."

Another agent spoke, "are you sure about the family keeping quiet?"

"Absolutely, you only have to know about their background in Philadelphia, the wife will never want anyone to know about this event, to protect the daughter."

"Keep the local police out of the loop, they need to believe it was an accident, nothing more, the wife will probably move out of Boston, so the story dies here."

"Sir, we found his wallet with about five thousand dollars in it and a set of safety deposit box keys. No clue as to what banks."

"Write up the keys, but not the cash, the wife is going to need it, what a bloody mess," replied the lead officer.

With that I turned around and went to the washroom, they had not even seen me, it was like I was invisible.

Hours later after the body was removed, almost all of the police had left, except the original two FBI agents remained at the house. The head agent spoke to mom,
"Mrs. Kennedy, we found your husband's wallet, it had five thousand dollars in it, did he usually carry around that much cash?"

Mother seem confused, dad had told her that he only had two thousand dollars, but some inner sense of self-preservation came to her lips, "Yes Conrad, like to have lots of money on hand."
"Mrs. Kennedy, all your husband's and your assets will be frozen, but I will leave your husband's wallet with you." "I hope it helps."

With that they left us, to sit in a house that was as silent as a cemetery to deal with our grief.

That night mother cried so loud I thought my eardrums would break, but they didn't, I cried too, but softly to myself. The next day mother had us pack up our clothes to get ready to leave. Two days later Father was cremated, no service, no notices, nothing, my mother's love for father had turned to total hatred. That afternoon we left Boston for New York, a large city where we could become invisible.

Chapter Eleven

As I sit here remembering the past, the music from Pachelbel's Canon D Minor plays in my head nonstop. In one respect to remember the past with such great clarity causes incredible pain, but somehow by letting the music take over my senses, I feel like I am the narrator and not in the first person. I used this survival technique my whole life, and therefore no one ever really knew what I thought or what I was thinking. I fooled them all, it let me accomplish things and do things that would never come back to haunt me. The music let me disassociate myself from my human emotions and allowed me to do whatever was necessary to achieve my end objective. More memories flooded back about that disastrous time in our lives. The next few evenings I would go back to the past to remember and find my answers, somehow, I was only able to travel back in time during the late evening hours. So, each night of the week was absorbed by the past.

We arrived in New York on New Year's Eve; mother booked us into a small hotel in Brooklyn. She insisted that we wash up and get out. "Kathleen, I want to go to Time's Square to see the crystal ball drop to bring in the New Year, we need a fresh start, it will be interesting, I have only seen it on the television, it would be wonderful to see it live."

And with that we made our way to Manhattan and to Time's Square to ring in the New Year. Happy 1974, may this be year, that we put the past in the past.

It was hard for me personally, another year of new beginnings and in another strange city. I felt confused and apprehensive about everything, this was the beginning of my anxiety attacks, which would haunt for me for most of my life.

Did I really want to make new friends, what was the point? First, we had to find a place to live, mother wanted to make the money last, so she was looking for cheap accommodations. We started with a furnished bed sitting room, all that could be said was that it was clean and cheap. However, it was in an area where we could not go out at night. After a couple of weeks, mom spoke about me finishing school, but where was the question. During the day I would explore the area and be home by nightfall. One day mother left the flat at nine in the morning and returned in the late afternoon.

"Kathleen, I have found a school for you to finish your high school and graduate."

"Mother what are you talking about, I thought we were in hiding?"

"It will be fine, it's an all-girl school run by the nuns connected to the school where I was educated. They are willing to help out an alumnus, that's all you need to know, do your work, and keep quiet about the family."
"So, what happens if the other students ask me about my family?"
"You don't talk about the family, change the topic to something else. Become a listener and not a talker. An old trick, I used, was to make a vague statement and get the others discussing it and then I simply listened. In that way I never had to say more than was necessary."

So, this was what my life was to become living in the shadows, simply an invisible lump of grey matter, a faceless human in the sea of humanity. Thinking to herself, "why did Micky never come to see me in Boston?" Dad's death was surely listed in the local papers" "Micky when I needed you most, you deserted me, how cruel and thoughtless." "God, Micky I hated you!"

"The question was, do I still hate Micky, or as I have matured have those raw emotions changed and mellowed?" Continuing to speak to herself, "that's the problem I go between hatred and love, and seeing him now as he is, a priest, I am more conflicted than ever before." "When I was living in New York, I hated him completely, but as time passed so did my hatred." "It became indifference, one could not hold on to hate." "Even mother had stop hating dad."

Chapter Twelve

My first day back at high school was a cold and windy day in Brooklyn. When the winds came in from the northeast the chill cut through your clothing and you felt damp and cold. That was the problem with living on the east coast, the winter winds brought cold and dampness. I entered the office of St. Joseph High School in Brooklyn with my mother. After what seem like an eternity, we went into the office of the head mistress, a formidable woman by the name of Reverend Mother Sister Marie.

She chatted with my mother and then turn her attention to me.

"Kathleen, we are so pleased that you can join us here at St. Joseph's, you know of course that your mother is an alumnus from our sister school in Pennsylvania, Mount Saint Joseph Academy. We so look forward to having you as part of our student body. As I understand it from your mother you are willing to work after school in the library to help with your tuition, am I correct?"

Thinking to herself, "Thank you, mother," and then to the nun, "Of course Reverend Mother, that will be lovely, I really appreciate the chance to earn some money." Keep a straight face, a discrete smile would be in order, were Kathleen's thoughts.

Reverend Mother then gave us a tour of the school and I was given my schedules and introduced to my homeroom teacher, and the head librarian for whom I would be working. So, began the final year of my schooling.

Mother found a job close by in one of the local shops as a cashier, she never complained, but within a year, mother started to drink. Only a little at first, but by the end of her life she was a full-blown alcoholic.

School was fine, but most of the time I wanted to cry, the only thing that kept me from harming myself was my work in the library. When I was not in class, that was where you would find me, doing my job, reading, researching, in general keeping to myself, so that I did not need to discuss my family circumstances with anyone. I began to read the Psychology books, I wanted to understand what drove my father to kill himself. His life had become a total failure because of greed, and he must have gone into a deep depression, in the end he could only see death as a release.

Then I realized I was as depressed as was mother. I buried myself in my work and mother buried her depression in the bottle. Was I doomed like my parents, or would I find my way out of this maze of confusion? I fought my way out of the depression but would suffer from major anxiety attacks for the rest of my life.

Towards the end of the school year Reverend Mother called me to her office, thinking to herself, ‘please dear God don’t let me be in trouble’.

“Come in my child don’t look so worried, you are not in trouble, I have some good news for you.”

“That’s wonderful Reverend Mother.”

“Sit down girl and let me explain everything. I know your family has been through a difficult time, the details we do not need to be talk about, and all we need to discuss is how to help you have a better future.”

Kathleen replied, “Your kindness is overwhelming Reverend Mother.”

“Kathleen, we take care of our own here, not to worry. Let us get down to details, every year City University of New York, Brooklyn Campus gives a full four-year scholarship to the student we feel is in the most need and deserving. The opening is in the Bachelor of Arts program with the major being Information Systems. I know you loved working in the library so this will set you up for a job in the public library system. Also, I know the family finances are strained so I went ahead and got you a part-time job at the local library.

I hope you are pleased?”

“Reverend Mother, thank you so much, it’s been so long since anyone cared to help, I don’t know what to say?”

"Don't say anything Kathleen, just make us proud."
Finally, my life was turning around, I was going to have a future.

With those happy thoughts I went off to sleep, a quiet happy piece of music playing in my head, but I could not remember the name. Tomorrow is Saturday I should go and see Micky.

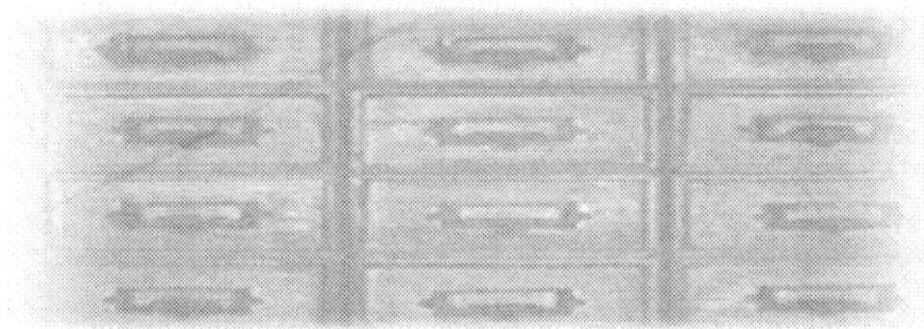

Chapter Thirteen

As I walked along the shoreline the wind blew through my hair, and as if the heavens could hear my thoughts it would sound like Chopin's Nocturne No 9. Here I was off to see my confessor, whom I secretly still loved, but alas he would never know my true feelings. Too dangerous to ever reveal to Micky who I was or how I felt. My own plans came first. I quietly walked into the church, it's so old and quaint, but peaceful. Looking around there was a couple of ladies near the confessional, I moved to the back of the church and into the shadows. There was no hurry, I wanted the time undisturbed to talk. Why had our churches in New York never felt this peaceful? Perhaps it was because in New York, nothing was ever peaceful.

Too much to worry about, too much to attend to, and no privacy at all. New York was just too crowded, to relax and think. Here the quiet sounds of nature filled the air, you could almost hear the trees and plants whispering to you, to breath deep and take in their incredible scents. As I sat there in quiet contemplation, I let myself completely relax to the beautiful music playing in my head. My mother use to play the piano and she loved to play Chopin. I was having my own personal concert in my head remembering those quiet afternoons in Devon, curled up on the couch while mother played, those were such happy times. I felt the overwhelming urge to cry at that moment, why had my life taken so many difficult turns and why was I now in such a dark place in my heart, mind and soul. However, I had travelled this place of my own accord and had no intentions of going back.

Oh, thank God, those women have left, now I can go into the confessional.

"Bless me Father for I have sinned."

"Hello Gwen, I am glad you have returned to work out your issues, confess your sins and move on with your life."

"Oh Micky, didn't your Bishop ever tell you that nothing in life is that simple?"

"Actually, yes, he did, but I thought you wanted to move on with solving your problems and making your life better?" "I know that you have had many difficulties, but with honesty, I am sure we can move you to a more moral outlook on life."

"Well Father, actually I do, but I believe you and I are working on different timelines, yes I want to confess, but there is so much history to cover, you know the why's and wherefores."

"I am confused, either you have sins to confess and want absolution or not." "Gwen the only way forward for you, is for you speak freely and openly." Father Micky spoke in a quiet tone, so as to keep Gwen relaxed. Thinking to himself that such a tactic might encourage her to speak more freely and honestly.

"Father that may be true for children and regular people, but I don't operate on the same timetable as the rest of the world, do you have a problem with that?"

"No, Gwen lets proceed at your pace" Still in his quiet and calm voice.

"Good, so Father, do you think that the sins an adult committed could be rooted in their childhood experiences, their traumas, their losses early in their lives?"

"Yes Gwen, it is possible that our childhood experiences affect how we deal with our adult experiences, but part of being an adult is taking responsibly for our actions and not blaming others. You do bring up a good point, in that our childhood experiences colour our thinking and we use those excuses to allow ourselves to do terrible things that are wrong. However, it doesn't lessen the severity of our actions and that they are completely against the teachings of Jesus."

"So, Father, you don't think a person should be able to use the excuse of their past hardships to justify their indiscretions as adults?"

"No, Gwen, I do not."

"Well Father, I guess that brings today's visit to an end."

"Visit?"

"Yes, Father it is a visit, I do so much like coming and talking to you. Actually, you are usually a peaceful person to be around, but alas not today. Well goodbye."

With that, Gwen got up and left, and speaking to herself, "you can sit and think about that Micky, a penitent walked out on you, how you will respond to that."

Walking out to where she had parked her car, Gwen was cursing Micky, "You self-righteous asshole, narrow minded prig, one day Micky you will find out what it's like to walk in someone else's shoes." "Bastard" With that off her chest, Gwen drove back to the resort.

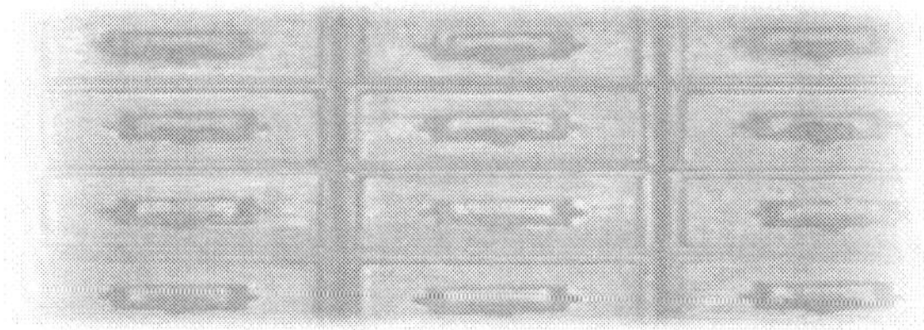

Chapter Fourteen

Sitting stunned in the confessional, Micky heard the sound of 'Silence' filled the air, or so it seemed, "I came to this Island to get away from the crazies and here I am hearing the confession of what is likely the craziest person I have ever encountered," Micky spoke out loud to an empty building.

'A visit, is she kidding me, is this idea of a Saturday afternoon social, should I be serving tea and cakes. Just what the hell is going on here? I feel like I am being played for a fool, a sounding board. I need to talk to someone about this problem, but who and about what, except that she rambles on about Philosophical questions, she has not mentioned any terrible crimes, sins, or indiscretions, which I could not speak about to anyone. What about her hypothetical questions, I could seek counsel on those. However, going to my bishop was not the solution, because the Bishop, would listen and ask me why I was letting this woman get under my skin, I could hear hours and hours of endless lectures without a resolution to the problem. The only thing to do is let her keep coming, eventually she will get to the issue, in the meantime Micky it's time for a long walk, dinner and an early bed.' 'I think Monday; I will go back to the library and do some more research on missing persons in the USA.

First, I need to think of a timeline, I wonder how old Gwen is, that should give me approximate years to look at for data.'

As I left the church for my walk, a terrible feeling came over me, the winds, smells and sounds of the island were completely absent, it was like I was in a vacuum. A sense of evil had taken over everything and for the first time in years I was afraid. With that thought I went back into to the presbytery. Speaking to himself, "Micky you are becoming fanciful." "You are letting the ramblings of a complete stranger get into your mind." "What is it about this individual, that they seem to be getting a complete control over your thinking." Then adding to his thoughts, "Kathleen was like that when I was with her, she had me completely under her spell. However, Kathleen was a kind and a relaxing person to be around." "The exact opposite of Gwen." However, Micky still locked the doors of the presbytery and then went to lay down.

Chapter Fifteen

'How dare Micky not think that the traumas of childhood would or should not affect our actions and could not be used as a justification for our actions? What a pompous ass! My anger is getting the best of me, I need a drink and to listen to some music to calm down. I will sit quietly in my suite listening to my music, a large glass of wine and the lights out. I will leave the curtains wide open so that I could look out at the night sky and lose myself in peaceful repose.' After a while Gwen slipped back into her own world, totally tuning everything else out.

'As I lay there quietly, my mind drifted back to the past, perhaps it was the sounds of Chopin or the sounds of the crashing waves coming through the windows that sent me down memory lane. Did I really need to remember everything that had happened in the last forty years? The answer was yes of course. In reliving those memories, I would truly understand the path of restitution and vengeance that I was planning. Those singular details would help me in building my plan and the execution of my final work, oh not, perhaps not my final work, but the final removal of my arch enemy Darcy.'

I quietly slipped off to sleep with those thoughts of revenge in my mind and heart. Suddenly I woke up, the music had stopped playing all that remain to be heard was the sound of the crashing waves and the sounds of the wind blowing through the trees. What a peaceful existence, if only my life had been that peaceful. As if on cue the memories came flooding back. Studying hard to get my undergrad degree, knowing that because my tuition fees had been a scholarship, the pressure was even greater to get top marks.

Then work at the local library to have spending money drove my anxiety level through the roof. I simple lived in fear that I would never meet peoples' expectations, this drove me only to work harder with little or no time for fun. It was all about the education and job that would open up doors for me in the future.

During this time Mother's drinking increased and she became not only an embarrassment, but a total narcissistic bitch. "What I cannot understand, she was so involved with the ladies' group at the church, why did she drink even more when she came home from meetings? Then when I tried to talk to her about things, anything, she turned the conversations to her problems. Problems at work, problems with money, and problems with her ladies' group, then when I told her to quit the group, she would fly into a rage. Everything was about her, nothing I did pleased her, it was to the point where I wanted to move out, but finances prevented me from taking that action.

Finally, I graduated at the top of my class. At my graduation I received a wonderful gift, I was given a full scholarship to do my Master's in Library Science/School Library Media Specialist at City University of New York, Queens College, Graduate School of Library and Information Services. This was to set me up for the rest of my life, I was so thrilled, my hard work had paid off, I finally was proud of myself. As was her usual behaviour, that night Mother, put such an incredible damper on things.

"So, Kathleen, instead of you getting out and getting a full-time job to support the house, what we have is two more years of schooling." "What is going to happen to me I will still need to work?" "Instead of enjoying my life by going out with friends socially."

"Really mother you have spent your whole life socializing, while I have tried to carve out a future for myself. After I finish and get my Masters' it will be my time to live the good life with no thanks to you or dad. Go ahead mother drink yourself to sleep, maybe someday it will be permanent."

Thinking back, I regretted those words, Mother's drinking became worse with time, and she died from alcoholic poisoning weeks before my graduation.

Somehow weeks after graduation, I began to change, that quiet person became outspoken, charming, and vivacious.

Chapter Sixteen

Two weeks had passed since my last visit from Gwen, and I must admit whenever I could go to the library I did. The librarian was very helpful, she showed me how to use different search engines to access different databases and newspaper articles going back fifty years. I spent hours going over articles and reports, but nothing stood out to give me any idea who my mystery lady was before coming here. In trying to figure out Gwen's age, I started to think that perhaps she was close to my age, which would make her a teenager in the early seventies. Certainly, any traumatic event that happen in your teen years could alter your perspective on life.

Days and hours poring over reports and articles from the seventies almost made me feel like I was going blind. Then yesterday I ran across an article about a man who was an independent businessperson had died just after Christmas 1973. There were very little details, but I felt it was implied that he had committed suicide. There was no information about whether he had a family or not, actually the only real information was his name 'Michael Kennedy'.

Christmas 1973, that was my last year at high school, strange that I didn't remember anything about this person, as the city of residence was Boston, my hometown.

However back in 1973, a death like this would receive as little press as possible, in order to respect the remaining family members. I doubt this information was of any use to me, I guess I will just have to keep looking. Odd though, that was the year Kathleen was gone after the Christmas break, could the two be related, no Micky, that's too far fetch.

Again, it was another beautiful day on the island, Saturday afternoon found me back in the confessional waiting for my faithful penitents. To be honest I think half of them came just to talk privately about family problems and a sympathetic ear. One or two parishioners came and went, then the church filled with only the sounds of the Caribbean waves and the scents of the tropical fauna filling the building. As I sat there quietly praying, my mind began to wonder, so many thoughts raced through my head, the past, the present and what my future would hold. I realized at some point I would be transferred back to the Archdiocese of New York, but I was hoping that it would be very far into the future. I like my life here, actually the weather agreed with me so much, I just wanted to stay here forever. Lost in my own thoughts, with a start I came back to the present when the subtle scent of a very expensive perfume filled the confessional, and I then in my head I heard "Silence".

"Hello, Father Mike, what a beautiful day, glad to see you are still at your guard post."

My guard posts. "Hello Gwen, still on the island?" "Yes, its Saturday afternoon, and I am hearing confessions. I don't get your reference of a guard post."

"Well, its quite simply really, you sit here in your wooden box, waiting for people to come and confess their sins, you listen, ask them if they repent and then you give them absolution."

"Then when they died, they get through the Gates of Heaven, but if they don't come to you and confess, that's not happening." "Thus, you are manning the guard house to the Gates of Heaven."

"I believe you have taken a rather simplistic view to entering heaven," was his reply.

Gwen's reply and attitude were really starting to get under my skin, it was like she was sparring for a fight. Well, she is not going to get one from me, I am here to help! These were Micky's thoughts.

"Simplistic or not, it is the reality of the teachings of the Church. You cannot go to Heaven if you do not confess and repent" She said.

"Yes, Gwen mortal sins, but I am sure very few people carry that burden." I replied.

“Really, what about murder?” she retorted in a direct and angry manner.

“I don’t understand where you are coming from, of course murder is the big one, but to my understanding most murderers repent in the end.” My patience with Gwen was beginning to wane and I felt my voice getting curter and louder. I need to control this now.

“Are you sure?” Now she was definitely sparring for a fight.

“The answer to that is no, I am not sure, but I put my faith in humanity, that every sinner will come to God looking for forgiveness.” I replied trying my best to remain calm, but I could feel my anger rising as this bazaar conversation continued. Thinking to himself, why does this woman make me so angry and confused, it’s so unlike my usual self?

Gwen’s next comment left me dumbfounded.

“Well Father I believe everyone is a killer, they just have different methods, some have the courage to come out and simply murder someone, others do it over time by driving people to their graves. Simply said they annoy a person to death, and before you say that is not possible, I believe it is and I believe every single person on earth has driven someone to their death.”

In my shock I ask, “Have you been drinking?”

"No Father I have not been drinking, however after this delightful chat, I think I will go out and get hammered." "Oh, and one last thing, what if the individual murders and feels no remorse, but still confesses, never mind we'll leave that for another day."

And with that incredible statement Gwen was gone, leaving me sitting there and wondering what had happened. Again, the sound of the "Silence" filled my head.

A dedication to the loss of Beethoven's hearing, but to me it represented my loss of sense of wellbeing.

Then Micky prayer silently to God, "Is there a flight, Gwen can be on today and get her off the island? Then, "sorry, I should be praying for her soul."

Chapter Seventeen

"What an arrogant asshole Micky has become, perhaps that collar has cut off the oxygen to his brain." I said to myself "He makes me so angry I could reach through that curtain and choke the life out of him, calm yourself Gwen, it's that temper that has you in your present predicament."

I went back to the resort had a quiet supper and retired to my room, poured myself a glass of wine, put on my music, turned off the lights and let myself slip into a quiet mediation. With the windows opened, the soft gentle breezes carrying the scents and sounds of the Island drifted into my room. Then as the music played, I let myself drift off into the past, I needed to exercise my demons, so that I could continue to carry out my plan. 1979 had been a difficult year for me and June had been a difficult month as well, weeks before my graduation, at the beginning of June my mother became very sick, by the time she would go to the doctor, she was past help, and mother died June 5th, 1979, the result of years of alcoholic abuse. As I was unsure of mother's finances the funeral was small and I had her cremated, the least expensive urn would do, and it had a place on the mantel in the living room. At first, I kept fresh flowers, but in time I went with very sturdy greenery. It was only after a complete year that I realized Mother had saved a small fortune, I could have done better by her, had a proper funeral, but then again, she could have done better by me and been a loving mom.

I graduated with honours in my program June 19th, 1979, and was fortunate enough to be headhunted almost immediately for a large research firm that specialized in studying companies and banks listed on the various stock exchanges. I did a variety of jobs in gathering information on companies that was then collated and sold to various government agencies and stockbroker firms. It was interesting work and certainly opened my eyes to the world of business. I began to appreciate more my father's world of business, not that I agreed with everything they did. Somehow, I thought the final reports left out important details regarding the financial stability of some of the banks and other companies we researched. Not only was I unhappy about the apparent and deliberate dishonestly of the company, but I spent every day taking the subway from Brooklyn Heights where mother and I had moved after a year of living in another area of Brooklyn. After a few months I met someone at work to share a motor car ride with but that only lasted for a few months. Then after two and half years of coming to work and never missing a day, we were all called on to the carpet because of problems that were happening with the Banks and the country as well. The world was moving towards a financial crisis. That deliberate act of deceit, lack of understanding and truthfulness lead to the financial crisis of 1982. By the end of 1982, I had no hope of a raise, because of the many things happening within the company. I left that September with the knowledge of finding another job would be hard.

It was during those years that I went through a complete personality change, I no longer worried about what people thought as long as they were thinking about me.
I enjoyed the company of many people, I wanted their attention, and I saw myself almost as a goddess like figure. And I could get people to do whatever I wanted. Looking back, I had mastered the art of manipulation. I was trained well by both of my parents as they were both masters of manipulation, Dad was overpowering in his technic, whereas Mother was subtle in her ways of getting what she wanted. Now it was my turn, 'Whatever Kathleen wanted, Kathleen gets, and that was my credo.

At work I was the centre of attraction with everyone around me, but when I got home, everything changed, I reverted to my anxious self and withdrew from humanity. It was like I was two different people, the public image of the vivacious redhead, who flirts with everyone with whom she comes in contact with and the very private individual who stays at home, goes to church, and keeps to herself. About the only thing both personalities had in common was that they would look someone in the eye and tell the most outrageous lies and people believed the lies and believed me.

As I laid there in quiet repose, the lingering thoughts of 1982 passed through my mind. Checking the paper every day for a job, as millions around the world were doing was exhausting. Mother's savings kept me off the street, but I had to be careful with every dollar. Christmas came, what a sad time, this was the first year I was ever going to be truly alone on Christmas Day. The first two Christmas Days after mom died were spent with friends from work, but not this year. One thing through all the turmoil in my life, I had continued to go to church regularly, it was my one place of respite.

About two weeks before Christmas, Father John came up to me after Mass, and said, "Miss O'Hare,
I understand that you are out of work right now and I was wondering if you would be able to help around the parish with the Christmas preparations."

I was taken back about how he knew I was out of a job, but remained polite in my answer," Yes Father, I am unemployed at this time, but I am looking." Then out of the

blue I said, "Father, just how can I help, I am not on any committees, and I don't want to cause waves."
"Don't worry about causing waves Miss O'Hare, I need an independent person to help me co-ordinate the different groups so that everything runs smoothly.
I was surprised by my answer, "Are they really that difficult to handle Father?"
"Well, Kathleen, I can call you Kathleen?"
"Yes, Father you may, and I believe I will call you Father John!" I replied, to which he replied, "We are on the same page." "And the answer is they are difficult because they all have wonderful ideas, and everyone wants to be first."

That two-week period gave me an incredible lesson in people skills; I became the master of manipulation, getting everyone to work together, keeping the peace. The fruits of my labours were realized on Christmas Eve, when the church decorations looked fantastic, the children's play depicting the Nativity ran so smoothly, and the choir knew their music. It was just wonderful, the best Christmas Eve I had ever experience in my whole life.

After midnight Mass, Father John came to me and said, "Kathleen you did great, what a wonderful organizer you arc, if you ever need a letter of reference, I will be proud to give you an excellent recommendation."

"Kathleen, where are you going to have Christmas dinner?" He asked. I replied to honesty, "I hadn't given it much thought."

His kindnesses overwhelmed me, "Well you will have dinner at the rectory, there will be about ten other people, you will enjoy yourself."

It turned out that one of the guests worked at the New York Public Library. Two weeks later I went for a job interview at the head office of the Library in Manhattan, the next day I got the job.

For the very first time in my life, I saw that good works did in fact pay off. With those happy thoughts I drifted off to sleep. I woke briefly, 'I must apologize to Micky; I really was a bitch today.'

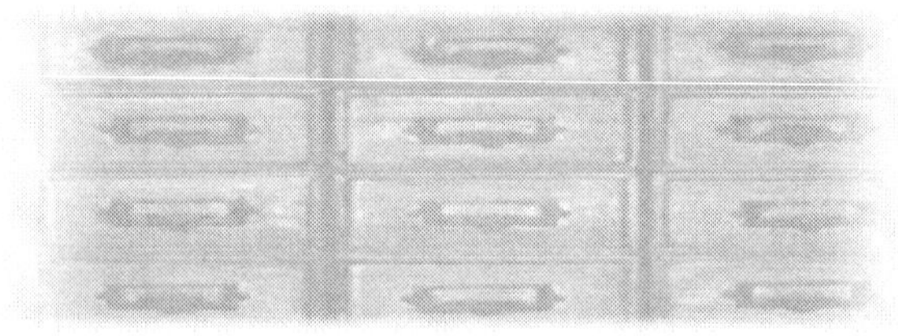

Chapter Eighteen

A few days had passed since my blow out with Micky, I had been hard on him, but if he would only see beyond the dogma and realize that humans suffered undeniable pain, and the church simply did not address their needs. I love the daytime, there are so many things to do to pass the time, yesterday I had a round of golf and today I was going on a deep-sea charter. I love the sea and especially the Caribbean, the aqua blue water, the feel of the sea spray against my skin as the boat cut through the waves. I never actually caught any fish, but I enjoyed hearing the chatter of the other tourists and seeing their delight when they caught a fish, it didn't need to be a marlin, they were still excited. God, I wished I could feel that excited about anything, all I did was go back into the past for good or bad, it drew me into the land of my demons. Alas those demons were making me into an unrepentant killer or at least leading me down to path to become one. Thankfully my good looks hide my inner self. All a stranger looking at me would see is a well-preserved middle-aged spinster, somebody's kindly aunt.

After the day of being on the open water I returned to my resort, had a quiet supper, and retreated to my suite. As always, my bottle of wine was there on the sideboard already chilled. I will need to leave a big tip when I finally return home.

After taking a long bath and putting on my comfortable clothes, I sat back in the darkness of the room, windows open, the sound and feel of the breezes passing through the trees and the sound of the night birds in the distance. I put on my music tapes, drank my wine, and slipped back into the past.

January 1983 opened up a new life for me, I now had a job worthy of my education. Here I was working in the acquisition's department of one of the largest public libraries in the world. I had managed to get a job at the New York Public Library, thanks to Father John. Yes, I knew my education sealed the deal, but he had put this all-in motion, starting with the dinner. My meeting with one of the head people at the library and I am sure he twisted a few arms to forward my career. I knew I was forever in his debt. I give thanks that Father John passed on before I began to go down the road of darkness, I was now on. It would have broken his heart too see what I have become. In a very strange way Father John was more of a father to me than my own dad. God does indeed protect his own shepherds and Father John was truly one of God's Sheppard's.

The pay at the library was more than what I had made before, but I was used to being careful with money. I took a flat in Williamsburg at three hundred and thirty dollars a month instead of moving to the East Village where a flat half the size would have cost six hundred dollars per-month. Actually, it worked out better as I could run along the East River almost every day for exercise and look across at Manhattan. I enjoyed my job and met lots of people; I even began dating a few fellows, but nothing serious. Between my natural good looks, glorious red hair, and a great figure, which I maintained with lots of running and lots of walking, I looked great. I took great care in picking my clothes nothing too trendy, more stylish, and sophisticated. I like being out with the crowd hitting the discos and all-night bars on Fridays and Saturdays, but I made sure never to go out with anyone from work and avoided the married men like the plague.

Some of the girls I worked with dated married men, and it always turned out badly for them. No surprise, I knew my dad cheated on my mother, but hell would have frozen over before he would divorce her. Men like that wanted to keep their status.

At work everyone praised me for my work and my work ethics, I would always be gracious and say thank you, but in my heart and my mind I knew I was far superior to them. Call me narcissistic if you like, but I was the best at everything I did.

My superiors and inferiors did my every bidding, a gentle smile, kind words; a gentle laugh at the most ridiculous jokes had everyone eating out of my hand. No matter what I asked of them, they complied with my wishes, I had become the master of manipulation, and after nine years with the same group, I needed a change. I needed a new challenge, more people to be my guinea pigs, my slaves. I discovered to both my delight and horror that I enjoyed power and having power over people.

After the music finished, the breezes continued into my room carrying the scents of the island's fauna. When I went to pour another glass of wine, I discovered the bottle empty. I crawled under the covers and began to drift off to sleep. "I must go see Micky soon" and with that final thought I was sound asleep.

Chapter Nineteen

Sitting quietly in the presbytery before going to the church, Father Sweeney was allowing his mind to wander again, speaking to himself the following ideas. "Another Saturday and another day of hearing confessions, I would have liked some time off to travel, to just do nothing. I could imagine what would happen, if I told that to the Bishop that I wanted a holiday, I could hear his speech now. "Father Sweeney are you crazy, except for daily Mass and your weekend duties, most other priest would say you are on a permanent vacation!" "I could understand if you wanted to visit family, but your parents are dead, and your siblings are scattered across the country. I am sure they would rather come here for a week, if nothing else to escape the snow." With those thoughts still in my head I headed over to the church from the presbytery ready for another Saturday of penitents. Halfway across the courtyard I felt the breezes stop as if the world had gone completely still, then I remembered Gwen. "Please dear God don't let her come today, I'm just not up to her insanity." As if God heard my prayer the breezes picked up and everything seemed to return to normal. I continued on my way into the church to get prepared for the afternoon.

As I sat back in the confessional, the beautiful sounds of Pachelbel's in the Garden filled my head, and I sat quietly in prayer.

Parked under the shade of a rather large old tree was a lone car with its occupant thinking about their own personal demons and failures. The lone occupant was Gwen preparing her thoughts for her next course of action. Speaking to herself in a muted voice, Gwen spoke, "Another Saturday has arrived, I needed to apologize to Micky, but how? Don't worry Gwen, I thought if nothing else you always know how to manipulate the scene to your advantage. As Shakespeare said. "All the world's a stage, and all the men and women merely players; they have their exits and their entrances, and one man in his time plays many parts, His acts being seven ages."

Well, I had indeed gone through almost all of the stages and I had played many parts; my next part would be my greatest performance. Just for a bit of fun I think I will drag Micky along for the ride. Fair punishment for deserting me in Boston. As they say time's passing, and I need to get to the church on time, 'Oh Kathleen you are on fire.' I giggled as I walked up to the church doors.

While Gwen was approaching the church Micky was already in the confessional thinking.

What a quiet Saturday, Micky was thinking, I've been here for an hour and not one person has come into the church. I guess I will have a quiet day after all, no need to complain to the Bishop. As if on cue, the breezes died down and, in his head, he heard "Silence". Micky actually felt a chill going through his body and yet it was in the mid-eighties outside. Then he smelt that distinctive perfume, and he knew Gwen was here and all the muscles in his body tensed. His breathing became laboured, and his heart was pounding. Speaking to himself, "Calm yourself Michael, slow deep breaths, don't let her set you up again." As he sat there waiting for Gwen to speak, he prayed and used all his energies to calm himself. Her first statement helped ease some of the dilemma he was feeling.

"Hi Micky, before you say anything, please let me apologize for the terrible way I spoke to you last time, I was having a bad day and I took it out on you. Please accept my apologies." Thinking to himself, 'I am floored, but have no choice but to be gracious and accept her apologies.'

"Thank you, Gwen, I do accept your apologies, everyone has bad days. Hopefully your days will improve." Thinking to himself and the next time you do have a bad day, find someone else to torture. 'Micky how un-Christian of you!'

Gwen's next statement made Micky tense up again, "I'm not here to confess to anything Father. I'm just lonely and wanted to talk without having to be face to face with anyone. That's why I like coming here to the confessional, our conversations are helpful but anonymous."

Then in her head, Gwen spoke to herself, 'I realize that I still love you Micky, and right now you are the only person keeping me from doing something evil. Your calmness and kindness are the only things keeping me from committing a terrible crime.'

To which Micky quickly replied, "I am glad I can help, but the purpose of the confessional is to be able to move on with one's life." "If you need to talk, you could always come to tea at the presbytery, and we could talk for hours." "Also, there may be others who are waiting to confess."

With Gwen's next statement he knew, she would lose it again, "Who are you kidding, I've been sitting outside the church for the last hour and not a single soul has come to the church. This is not the expressway to heaven more like the last stop, and people avoid it until it's really necessary."

"My apologies Gwen, I thought perhaps someone was waiting, as a rule I usually don't look out into the church to protect people's privacy, so let's talk." "You said you are lonely; don't you have friends down here on the island?" I asked.

"No Father, I have never had any friends, or I should say true friends. Most of my friends are more like acquaintances, not someone you would ever confine in, you know business friends." "Plus, I moved around a lot from my teen years and into my adulthood, so no I never had a close friend." Thinking to herself, 'except you Micky.'

Somehow in her voice Micky heard sorrow, perhaps his early judgement had been harsh. "I gather you never married."

A single word answer was all that came from her lips, "No."

"Did you want to discuss that?" Micky asked as gently as he could.

Again, the reply was negative "No, my parents' marriage ended in disaster, so I did not want to go through the same pain."

Again, all Micky could come up with was platitudes, "I would say I understand, but I would be lying, I guess I was one of the lucky ones, my parents' marriage was a long and happy one. Family was everything to my parents, we did not have much money, but we did have lots of love." "I don't want to make you feel bad, lots of people I have talked to over the years had difficult childhoods." "However, I don't understand how you never developed any close friendships."

Her reply saddened and perplexed Micky at the same time, "I guess my family's circumstances and that fact that we moved so much never allowed me to develop any close relationships. Also, that fact that my father was a criminal made me very secretive about who I was, it's not like I could say, Hi I'm Jimmy the murderer's daughter, now could I?" "Also, my career choice, had me doing research all the time, I actually have my Masters in Library Science. Much of my work is solitary, with very little interaction with others." Micky's next question made him feel like a complete idiot, "Are you not in the libraries working with the people coming into the branch, how is that solitary?"

Her reply was direct and to the point, "Actually, I worked in administration, acquisitions, behind the scenes, not in the public eye, so no, my contact with the general public was very limited. Thus, the only people I was in constant contact with was management, and you do not make friends with management."

Thinking back to his own chosen vocation, yes that was so true. Micky hardly would consider his working relationships with his bishops as friendships, more courteous survival tactics that were the highlight of his existence.

Yes, he had a few priest friends, but they all moved around on a regular basis, so keeping in daily contact was not realistic. While he was a parish priest in Boston, some of the parishioners did invite him to dinners, also some were family friends. So yes, he had people to talk to, but in his vocation, there were limitations as to what could be discussed. New York was totally different; those family interactions were less frequent and yes it was a much lonelier city in which to work.

Micky could not tell Gwen about the greatest friendship he lost. That was when Kathleen O'Hare had disappeared out of his life in 1973. They had become the best of friends sharing so many secrets, and yet there must have been one secret that Kathleen could not share. Otherwise, he would have known why she left Boston. All in the past, his past, this would not help Gwen in the least. So, he changed the topic.

"Gwen besides being a librarian extraordinaire what other interests' do you have?"

Her reply caught his interest, but at the same time made him wary, "Actually I am very much into Psychology and Psychiatry, you know the study of the human mind and how it works, how it can be used and manipulated to ones needs."

"What are your outside interests beyond Theology?"

"Well, my outside interests are Philosophy and History, you know the study of the human conditions and how history continues to repeat itself, you know the old saying 'those who do not learn history are doomed to repeat it' is one of my favourite lines."

"Sorry for the correction Micky, but the Philosopher, 'George Santayana's' original form of the statement was, 'Those who cannot remember the past are condemned to repeat it."

"Just my luck, I get caught up in semantics with a literary scholar," I replied.

"Oh, not to worry Micky, this can be our little secret, you like philosophical sayings, but have your own interpretations of them, anyways I am off, enjoy the rest of your day."

And with that she was gone again, still no answers, but his ego was bruised. Micky sat for about five more minutes and decided to close up the church. Then Micky went back to the presbytery, went to his room, laid down and fell into a deep sleep. Ghosts from the past came to him in his nightmares, he awoke about midnight, was hungry, exhausted, and confused. When was Gwen leaving the Island was his only thought.

Chapter Twenty

Oh! Kathleen, could you not let Micky have that one quote, did you always have to correct people? The answer was yes to both parts, I could have left him ignorant of the actual quote, and yes, I keep correcting people, it's pathological.

I made my way back to my resort, had a quiet supper and ordered two bottles of wine to be chilled in my room. Before retiring to my suite, I took my nightly walk around the compound. It both relaxed me and kept me grounded to nature. If I didn't do this every day, my mind would go off into all kinds of crazy directions. Taking solitary walks was my private way of staying sane.

However, I knew that in fact I was anything but sane, as defined by the shrinks, but I was sane, however on a different level. That was the problem with society, if you did something out of the ordinary, you were classified as insane. So far from the truth, killers were sane, but their sanity level was different, how else could they plan and commit their crimes. I had mastered the appearance of sanity, which was all that mattered. After walking around for about an hour, I retired to my suite, took a long hot shower, and slipped into my dressing gown. I went around the room and opened the windows, turned on my music, opened a bottle of wine, turned off the lights and sat on the chaise lounge nearest the windows. The night sky was beautiful and clear.

The full moon sent shimmers of light trailing across the Caribbean, which in turn set my imagination on fire. The wine relaxed me, by creating a fog in my mind, where only what I wanted to focus on came through to my senses. Within minutes I had travelled back in time to my father's death, I realized now from all my research into psychology and psychiatry that I had gone into deep depression after we moved to New York. No matter how I felt on the inside, I had to maintain outward appearances for mother's sake. Anxiety was part of my every waking moment, I was anxious about everything, my education, hiding secrets, trying to be invisible while trying to be successful. What a terrible burden I carried for so long.

Then mother died and I had to make my own way in the world. I was scared at first, but the Mother Superior from my old high school gave me the courage to continue. Landing my first job out of University also boosted my confidence. I was successful and began to enjoy the attention I was receiving for my good work and also my good looks. I loved the attention and continued to want more. At some point particularly after I landed the job at the New York Public Library, my ego began growing leaps and bounds, but at a terrible price to myself personally. The only person who kept me grounded was Father John from my parish in Brooklyn. What came to mind was one of Machiavelli's quotes "only a few know the real you," in my case only Father John saw who I really was, that frightened and lost girl from 1973, who made the best of things, but was scarred forever. As much as I trusted Father John, I never shared any information about my family life before New York. Somehow, he knew there was more to my story, but God Bless him, he never tried to pry it out of me. That was why I respected him, he accepted me at face value.

As I was approaching my thirty-sixth birthday, I wanted more out of my life, I wanted to be completely in charge at work, and that was never going to happen where I was working now. My ego had grown so large that I thought I knew what the best for everyone. Father John had passed away six months before; he was the only one who provided checks and balances in my life. I no longer had his influence in my life to keep me away from my ever-growing ego, I had become a complete narcissistic bitch. I needed a new city and a new job to ground me. Going through the library journals I received monthly; I saw a job posting for a library/media resource department head at one of the Philadelphia School Boards.

I applied, went for all of the interviews, impressed them with my knowledge and I had excellent letters of reference. After a two-month process that seem to take forever, I handed in my resignation at the library. There seem to be both sadness and a sense of relief at my departure. Had I really been that difficult? Yes, I had. At least I was honest with myself.

I started my new job August 1st, 1992, this would give me a month to review files and procedures before the beginning of the school year. What I lacked in diplomacy, I more than made up for in smarts, before the school year started, I already was reviewing their use of technology and databases for all aspects of running successful Media Learning Centres in all the schools. My hands would be full taking them into the twenty-first century, particularly as the budget for libraries had not increased for the last ten to fifteen years. After attending the first combination board and staff meeting, I realized that there was no use in asking for increases in the budget without a comprehensive game plan for expansion and improvement.

The next two years, my time was spent going to each of the over one hundred elementary schools and three high schools, to assess their structures, space allocation, library facilities, reference, and book collections, and whether they had viable computer resources to move forward. One startling observation was that schools in more affluent neighbourhoods had much larger collections and working computers, the same could not be said for the poorer areas of the Archdiocese.

My first presentation to the School Board for improvement would not require additional capital, but the re-allocation of excess resources from more affluent schools to needier schools. That was met with resistance, however I played the Catholic guilt syndrome to the max. That was the benefit of knowing you are always right and convincing others that you are indeed the brightest.

Let's just say I put some Christianity back into the Catholic School system, by manipulation of the hearts, minds, and souls of the board members. No one wanted to look un-Christian, I took such pleasure watching them squirm in their seats. The next eight years saw us improving the libraries across the board, I would ask for capital expenditures, when I had a definite plan in place. Although. I was respected for my efforts, I certainly was not loved, their lost not mine.

After 9/11, things began to change, slowly at first, but money was drying up. I accepted this, the country was at war, and we had moved ahead in the last ten years, so now I would be in a holding pattern, but I could make progress, just more slowly.

Whereas work had consumed my life since moving back to Philadelphia, I had reached my late forties and wanted to see more of the world, I started taking my holidays, I had accumulated almost six months over that last ten years. Plus, I had maintained a healthy lifestyle, and I must admit that I still could turn a few heads. I spent more time dating, nothing serious I had no desire to have a family, I just wanted companionship.

By the end of 2002, there had been significant changes at head office, particularly in human resources, or as everyone referred to them as the 'inhuman department'. Over the next few years, the changes in HR, spread out like a spider's web, so that their ideology of staffing models affected all members who had spent years in the education system. By the end of the 2010 school year, the libraries, finally took the hit, staffing models changed, much less staff and lots more work for everyone. Those who could retire, did, those who remained were now at the mercy of one miserable bitch: Darcy Marissa Mortimer, the Latin meanings for her names was 'The dark one who brings a sea of bitterness like a stagnant lake!'

Darcy lived up to her name and brought a sea of bitterness to everyone who had contact with her. It was like being stabbed with a needle of a noxious substance that eats through your body, except her toxins ate away at your heart, mind, and soul. I didn't think Satan had a sister until I met Darcy.

The sun was nearly coming up and I realized I had drunk both bottles of wine, yet there were no signs of tiredness in my eyes, those horrible memories would never let me sleep.

"Best I get breakfast and get out for the day," I thought, "I want to go sailing and feel the breeze on my skin."

And with that thought I went about my day, with no sleep, but ready to enjoy the offerings of the Island. I would spend the next five days sailing, come back to my suite, and drink myself into a quiet slumber, but every night memories of Darcy disturbed my sleep. I needed to talk to Micky; Saturday should be here shortly.

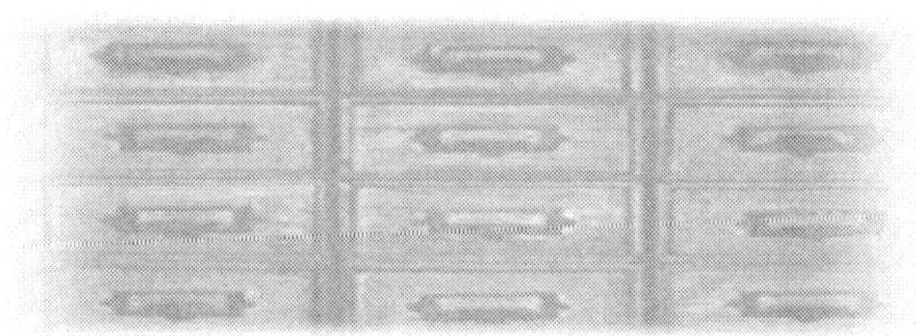

Chapter Twenty-One

At last Saturday had arrived, whereas Chopin was the calming voice in my head during the week, I looked forward to my conversations with Micky on Saturdays. I realized to protect myself and also him, our meetings must always be under the 'Seal of the Confession'. Such a shame but a necessity, in the confessional I could share all of my information and planning of the execution of my life's desire to terminate a problem, but in this box, Micky could never tell another living soul. My insurance policy against ever being brought to justice. I know he is not going to like the details, but it works for me, after all survival is the name of the game. I loved all of Machiavelli's quotes on life. I found that I appreciated Machiavelli's attitude towards life and how he felt things should be handled. In a way I felt a kindred spirit to him, in many ways I wanted to be him to handle life's circumstances with such clarity.

Actually, over my working life many of my colleagues had stated that I was very Machiavellian. One quote that seemed particularly appropriate to my current circumstances was "Never was anything great achieved without danger", and yes, I would be travelling down a very dangerous path, but with no regrets. I parked the car a couple of blocks away from the parish and made my way into the church. As always it was quiet with a gentle breeze coming through the open windows. Micky was lucky the parishioners took care of the church grounds and gardens. It was like a small piece of heaven transplanted for all of the souls who attended church here. A very beautiful gift indeed.

Sitting quietly in the confessional was Father Sweeney, thoughts drifting to the past and present, Father was speaking to himself in his head, “Hopefully I will have another quiet Saturday and I could go into town for dinner. Let’s hope Gwen is off someplace, scaring someone else.” No sooner did that thought cross his mind, but “Silence” sneaked into his brain, and it was the music piece of the day.

Micky sat quietly praying and thinking about survival, odd thought for a priest sitting in a confessional, but there it was, Gwen scarred him to death. Then speaking to himself, “Why did she scare me, simple under that calm voice, ran a thread of something insane and unpredictable?” “Perhaps because we were not face to face, my mind concentrated on the tone of her voice and on her words.” “I just know she needs help, but I am not sure how much.” “The fact that she is such an accomplished lair makes her dangerous.” “My father who was a police officer always said he would rather deal with a thief, than a lair.”

"Micky my son, you know what a thief is going to do and that is steal something, but a lair you have no idea what they will do and that makes them very unpredictable and dangerous."
As if on cue she spoke, "Hi, Father Michael, what's up doc?"
My response surprised even myself, "Hello Gwen, you do realize that we are not in a Saturday morning cartoon."

I quickly realized my humour was not appreciated with her statement, "No we are not in a cartoon, I was merely trying to be friendly, and do you have a problem with that?"
"No, no, not at all, I am sorry if I offended you." I used as my quick backtrack.
"Keep your shirt on Micky, I don't bite, just thought I would stop in and visit," was her reply.
Her next line of inquiry left me completed dumbfounded, "How did 9/11 affect your life?"
'How did 9/11 affect my life?' what a question to ask someone, but one question, I guess almost everyone I had encountered in the last fifteen years, had their own story. Thoughts swirled through my head of those last years from that morning of until now, I was still affected. I was lost in my own thoughts when Gwen spoke, "well Father tell me."

I replied, "I'm sorry Gwen, I don't think anyone has ever asked me that question, it's a long tale, I am sure you don't want to hear it."
"Yes, I do," she replied, "people think I am very self-centered and care for nothing but myself, that's not true, I do care, I just don't show it."
"Well, I guess I should start at the beginning," I said, "I was a parish priest at one of the churches in Manhattan, do you know I still remember every detail about that day."
"The sounds, the smells, the sense of disbelief." "Everything came at us so fast, the deaths, funerals, mourning relatives, a nation mourning really. Then the realization that we were a country at war, with an enemy that had no borders, no boundaries, no moral fibre just ruthless murderers whose ideology was beyond my comprehension."

Gwen's simply reply reached my heart, "I did not live in New York at that time, but I cried for days, I had lived in New York in my youth and knew all those landmarks, I had walked down those streets. I could hear in my head the sounds of Manhattan, even though I was hundreds of miles away."

The silence in the confessional stretched out for what seemed like an eternity. It was like we were both lost in our memories of that time. Then Gwen spoke up. “So, you were in a Manhattan parish at the time, how did you end up here?”

To which I replied, “do you want the long version or the short version?”

Her answer was kind; “Let’s go with the in-between version, that way I understand enough, but not too deep in details, that it brings you personally back to your trauma.”

“Thank you, Gwen, that is very kind of you, you are becoming a very complex person for me to understand and help out.”

“Yes, Father Micky, I am complex, but enough about me, I want to hear your story.”

With that encouragement, I set off into the monologue that was my story. “At first it was the funerals, then hospital visits, consoling families, which was the hardest. I could not really give the answer they needed, because even I did not understand.” “Those first few months, I doubt if I ever slept for more than three hours a night. I would go to bed exhausted, but the nightmares would wake me up and I simply could not go back to sleep.” For a moment I was quiet, lost in thought and memories, I could still see the smoke and the towers collapsing, I felt so cold.

“Father are you ok?” Gwen asked.

“Yes, Gwen, I just went off into myself, sorry.”

"No problem, just continue, we have lots of time."
"Well things just kept happening, The Afghan war, soldiers returning home, some dead, others badly wounded, families changed forever." "Then followed the Iraqi War, more ups and downs for my parishioners."

"Then in late September 2009, one of my most faithful parishioners' son was killed in Iraq, her only child, her heartbreak was more than I could take, the result was I had a massive heart attack." "As they say the straw that broke the camel's back."

"After months of rehab, the Archbishop decided I needed a complete change of scenery, he made a deal with the Bishop of this Diocese and did a swap. One of their priests went to New York and I came here." "I think I got the better deal." "I have been here ever since, actually I hope to retire here, I have decided I am fine with a green Christmas." As always Gwen's reply surprised me, "I hear you, my whole life has been either white or wet Christmases. I dig Mele Kalikmaka, this may not be Hawaii, but it's still tropical."

We both had a good laugh to my utter surprise at her response, it felt good to laugh, let's hope there is no one outside to hear.

What I thought was as good time as ever to ask her why she was on the island for so long, and I took it.
“And your reason for the tropical Christmas, Gwen, tired of shovelling snow?”

In good spirits she answered, “No my problem was a bigger narcissistic bitch, than myself” “Can you believe it, she won, and I am here.” “Anyways Father it’s complicated, and I don’t want to leave you in a dark space, so we will call it a day.”
With that very matter of fact statement she was gone, I was left with my mouth hanging open.

Walking away from the church Gwen was thinking, ‘Poor Micky, I should have been more discreet in my language, but it was the truth, a narcissistic bitch had beaten me at my own game, but she was in for a bigger surprise, that she would never see coming.’ To myself out loud I said, “Darcy must die, but the devil will be in the details, as to why and how?”
The answer for the revengeful act will be to those five editorial questions, who, what, where, when and why!”
“The ‘How’ is my decision.”
For the very first time in my life, I could remember the music of Mozart’s Requiem Mass, I’m good with that tune!

PART TWO

JUSTIFICATION

Chapter Twenty-Two

The long drive back to the resort from town had left Gwen, both tired and exhilarated, after a quiet supper, she retired to her suite to let her mind wander.

"Darcy must die!" That thought would consume my every waking hour, I began to dream it, breath it, it controlled my heartbeat. Whenever I ate, I could taste the satisfaction, which the idea brought to me. It was like sitting down to a sumptuous meal, where your every desire was fulfilled. Filet Mignon, medium rare, served with sautéed mushrooms with tiny garlic slivers. Mashed potatoes with small dices of onion and parsley throughout covered with a light gravy and a rosemary garnish, and last but not least steamed asparagus covered in hollandaise sauce.

The drink of choice, champagne, Dom Perion, then for dessert, Baked Alaska with a dark roasted coffee, black, followed by a warmed fine French cognac. What a feast, as would be Darcy's death.

As I sat in my room, in the dark, windows open, the sounds, the scents and the breezes of the Island filled my room. I had my usual bottle of wine cooling, Chopin on the machine, no not tonight, I had a recording of Mozart's Requiem Mass, which would set the mood for me to recall all the events that had led to this point in time.

As I laid back on my chaise lounge, my mind travelled back to the fateful day that change so many people's lives. Even the date would signify how bad it was going to get; Friday, September 13, 2002. All the senior staff had been called into a meeting with the school board, the upshot of the meeting was that there would need to be cuts made across the school board to deal with the reduced funding the schools would receive. As we sat there listening, I noticed that the heads of human resources were not present. The next announcement from the director answered that question. "We feel that it is only fair that we begin the trimming of personnel at the administration level first and one department, which has grown in the last decade beyond what is needed, is the Human Resources Department, I have accepted the head of the department's resignation along with most of his staff's resignations today. We will work with a pared down model going into the future. The first appointee is for the Superintendent of School Personnel, and that will be Ms. Darcy Mortimer. You will all meet Ms. Mortimer within the next week as she will be presenting her plans for the reduction of staff within the schools themselves."

"I will not be taking any questions at this time as this is an evolving plan, and I see no need to discuss items that may or may not be pertinent."

And with that announcement the meeting was adjourned, leaving everyone to speculate about their futures. "So, they have cleaned out a department that had been unusually thoughtful throughout the years to all staff and what have they replaced it with?" Was my question to myself? Nobody knew anything about this woman, where she came from, her work history only her name and some very unpleasant rumours. Well, I knew I could find out, but what about the others.

My heart went out that day to the lowest paid workers, their heads were always the first to roll. I will always wonder what Ms. Mortimer was thinking and feeling about that night at home, as she had been given carte blanche over determining the lives of one to two thousand people. Would she be kind? Or where the rumours correct that she was a descent of Machiavelli?

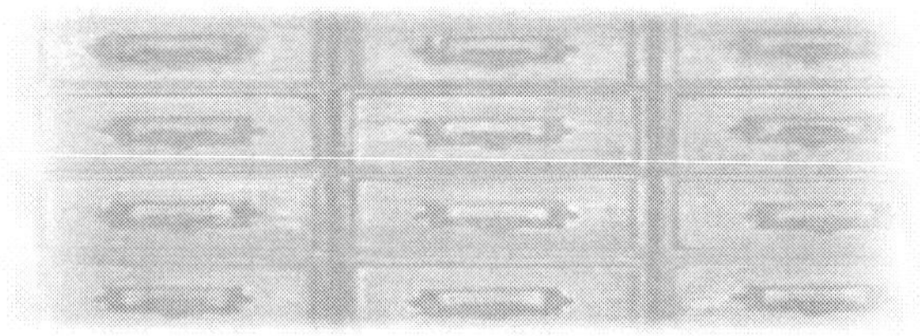

Chapter Twenty-Three

If Kathleen had been a fly on Darcy's condo walls that night, she would realize exactly what Darcy was about and what her plans were for the staff of the school board. 'Finally, I have the power, I have always desired' were Darcy's first thoughts as she returned home. Upon entering the room, Darcy put on the stereo and her favourite piece of music 'Edward Elgar's Enigma Variations', on a level no one understood, it spoke to her, perhaps because her whole life she had been an enigma to herself and others.

And then thinking to herself, it's a good thing I am using my maiden name, Mortimer, if the people knew I was engaged to Jonathan Shanahan, the son of one the board members, there would be whispers, but I will have started my work before that information gets out. The wedding is a year away.

I have heard whispers that people think I am a descent of Machiavelli, they only wish, in truth I admired everything about the man, and I knew I would follow the directions of one of his quotes "I'm not interested in preserving the status quo; I want to overthrow it."

And that is exactly what I plan to do. After all I have spent the last two years in a dead-end job as a literacy representative for the board. I have my BA in administration and my teacher's certificate, but I never planned to be in a classroom, very simply I hate children.

Hopefully when Jonathan and I get married, I can convince him that two children are enough, quite frankly I would prefer no children, no pets, simply no complications. Strange thing, Jonathan and his friends like to hit the bars so to speak to relax and unwind, on the other hand I wait until I am in the privacy of my home to relax. I still enjoy a little habit I acquired in university; I prefer to do a line or two of cocaine.

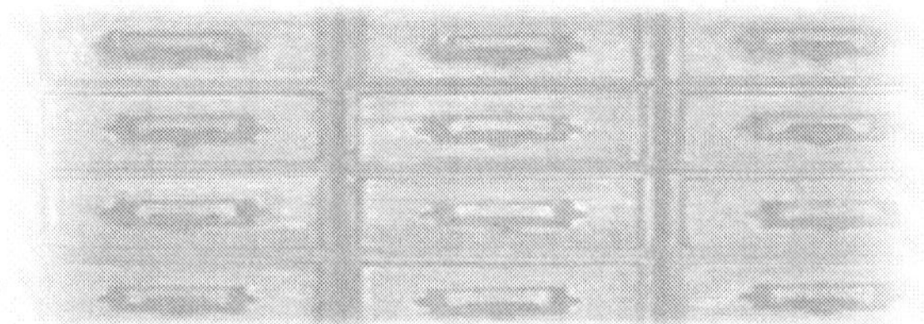

Chapter Twenty-Four

The clock showed that it was past midnight, but Gwen was still deep in a trance reliving the past, coached by her wine, the gentle Caribbean breezes, and her music tapes, she remembered every detail to its exact moment in time. Her thoughts continued onto what could only be described as a history lesson that was being reviewed for an exam.

As predicted shortly after January 2003, a new staffing model was presented to the board, and they accepted it completely without one question to Darcy.

The caretaking staff would be cut by thirty percent at the end of the current school year, those who were close to retirement would be offered a package, new fellows were gone, and the staff that were left were in their forties and fifties to carry the burden. In my mind, I thought how many of them will live to retire either alive or in good health?

My job brought me into close contact with many of the caretaking personnel, as I visited all of the school's and had to deal with concerns about space allocation, redesigns of school libraries and just general problems regarding the libraries. Over the next few months, I heard how the cuts would affect the cleaning of schools and how this would be prioritized. I could tell from these discussions, that the libraries and media centres would be at the bottom of the pole in every aspect. It just meant the librarians would be on their own it they wanted to make physical changes to their work areas. I advised my library staff to make their decisions now and get it completed before the end of June, or it would never happen. My key phrase to them was 'minimise, get rid of clutter, open up space and get rid of old and badly damage materials and furniture.' "Get rid of all unnecessary stuff before the end of June as you will have no one to help you in the fall." And were my words ever accurate.

I had also become the confidential informant to all, actually in reverse, everyone told me any little tale about Darcy that they heard or saw. One of the caretakers told me how she was visiting one of the married principals after work if you get my meaning. That was strange as her engagement was announced in February, that she was marrying Jonathan Shanahan in July 2003.

To my mind perhaps Darcy has a few more paramours. It was at that point I decided to keep a journal of all the tidbits of information that came my way about our beloved Darcy.

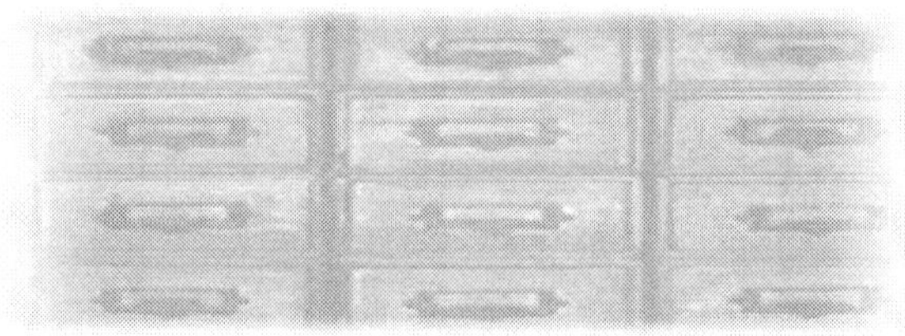

Chapter Twenty-Five

Darcy consumption of cocaine had increased since taking control of staffing models for the board, it was affecting her reasoning at times, that was leading her to bad choices, little did she know that others were watching, taking notes on her activities, which would eventually lead to her downfall.

She had begun to visit Melvin at his elementary school on a regular basis. Melvin had a large office, lots of privacy, a good size couch and a willingness to please her every desire. The staff avoided Melvin like the plague because he was such an asshole, so no one seem to pay that much attention to their coming and goings. However, whereas they avoided both Melvin and Darcy, everyone was well aware of their indiscretions, and gossiped about it whenever the opportunity present itself.

In Darcy's arrogance, she felt completely safe in the knowledge no one would cross her or cause her grief in regard to her actions. But in fact, three people in that school had it out for Melvin and by extension Darcy, each with their own reason and game plan.

The information I gleamed about Darcy from this one particular school was golden. The staff hated the principal so much it was unbelievable. Everything was about Melvin, no one had anything good to say about him, only bad stuff. If Melvin had been truly scrutinised by upper management, even the school community, he would have been on the unemployment line. His affair with Darcy was saving his ass, to the detriment of all, his was safe for now.

In equal parts the secretary Livia and the caretaker Mark totally, despised Melvin. Livia because he treated her like she was an idiot, and Mark, because Melvin simply hated any man that made him look weak. The third person surprised me, Rebecca, a teacher's assistant had a secret that could end her career in the Catholic Schools, which was that Rebecca was a closet lesbian. Melvin knew and held it over her head, he gave her the most difficult assignments with no help and bullied her mercilessly. How Darcy ever found out I don't know, probably from Melvin, but she did, and she cultivated the relationship to the point where she had a brief affair with Rebecca.

This was dynamite information on Darcy, a bi-sexual, but to try and bring it out would be a career destroyer. Three damaged people because of one couple, who could never be touched. If this was one school how many more damage individuals were being bullied by Darcy for their secrets and personal problems. To my utter surprise a fourth gem came to my attention in mid-April, and that was that a teacher who had been at the school in previous years had been intimated with Melvin in order to receive excellent references for advancement in the board.

The highly aggressive Emily had moved through the ranks, with what appeared to be great ease, however when confronted with any problems, she was completely useless. Anyone who came in contact with her, questioned how she could have been given such rave reviews. Then she completely screwed up at a school, where she was principal, the information was given over to Human Resources to confirm her credentials. Darcy was asked to investigate the problem, however when she found out the truth about how Emily had been given promotions, rather than remove her from the school board, she merely transferred her and hushed up the whole affair. Darcy reasoning was very base, being bi-sexual, she wanted to pursue an affair with Emily. Emily would definitely be on the spot when Darcy came calling! And she would!

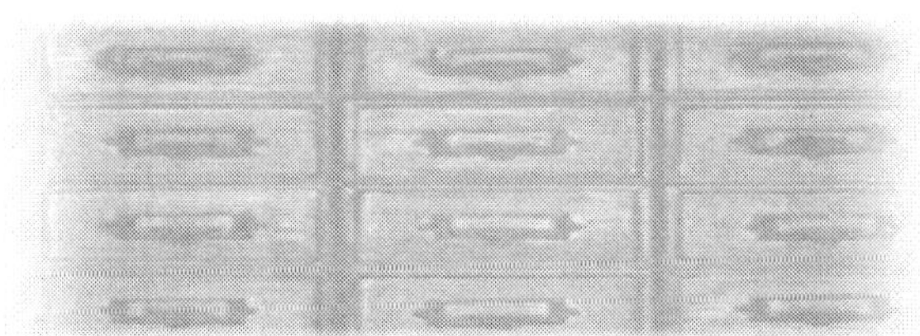

Chapter Twenty-Six

Gwen had fallen into a deep sleep on her couch, so that when the sun rose, she had forgotten momentarily where she was and then it came back to her a hundred-fold. Here she was in exile on a small island in the Caribbean, because of Darcy. The anger and resentment were building, and no amount of her trying to reason internally with herself, could slow the progress of Gwen's plans for Darcy. After a long shower, Gwen had breakfast and then went out for a day of sailing.

Returning after dark, she went back to her room, played her music, and went back into the past to relive every detail. As she reminded herself frequently the success of any project is in the details, and she definitely needed to remember every detail, so as to protect herself and lay the blame for her climatic act on others.

To herself, "I need to remember every detail in my monologue to Micky, the dress rehearsal must be flawless, what is to be in the future, must be stated as if in the past and every detail must be consistent."

By the year 2005, Darcy's actions had begun to cause problems for the school board with the unions and with the communities' affected by her decisions. The School Board decided to expand the Human Resources Department to include other people making the tough financial decisions regarding staffing models. The class sizes were to increase and there would be a reduction in the number of support staff in the classrooms. The two new people added to the HR department were Heath, a teacher who had come up through the ranks and understood the classroom dynamitic and the second person was Mr. Howell, an accountant and a businessman through and through.

Poor Darcy, these men got along well and discussed items with clarity and respect for each position. This made things difficult for Darcy, as it was almost always two against one in any battle. Darcy turned every discussion into a battle as a delaying tactic.

Darcy had an agenda, although it seemed like hers alone, actually it was the agenda of the Shanahan's. The family had headed up the board for close to fifty years and there were financial discrepancies in many of the board's financial transactions throughout the Shanahan's grasp of power. Darcy was their secret weapon to remove anyone who could connect the dots. Although the family secretly hated her and the thought of her marriage to their beloved Jonathan made them sick, it was a necessary evil in order to protect the family.

In them finding Darcy for Jonathan, it solved two problems, the board, and the fact that Jonathan was a totally useless idiot.

The matriarch of the family was well aware of Darcy's failings, the drug abuse, affairs with members of both sexes, plus and assortment of other problems.

Through all of that Grandmother Shanahan saw Darcy's usefulness and protected the girl as much as she could. She often said to her son, "as long as we keep Darcy's muzzle on when she is with family and take it off when she is at work, what better pit bull could we ask for?"

This information had come to Gwen secretly and she vowed take it to her grave. But as Gwen sat in her room alone and slightly drunk, she wished she had never taken that vow, and had instead blown the story wide open. Alumni associates can be good for finding jobs, but the secrets they ask you to keep can destroy your life, Gwen understood that all too well!

Chapter Twenty-Seven

Darcy's next target was Kathleen. For five years she had made the changes necessary to bring the finances into order to cover up the family messes, but Kathleen had been a thorn in her side always questioning her decisions. She did not know how Kathleen did it but everyone like her, Kathleen was the confidant of almost all of Darcy's adversaries. In her mind Darcy spoke to herself, "how do I get the bitch out of my life, I cannot control her, and my senses tell me she probably knows everything about me.
I hate the bitch, but how to get rid of her?"

Darcy had decided that the best way to dispose of Kathleen was to build her own army of friends, not easy as Darcy's personality seem to scare people away not invite them in, but she did recognize people's weaknesses and she would exploit them to her advantage.

One personality quirk that she picked up on was people who had unusual sexual appetites and their preferences. And this she used to her complete advantage, Darcy was like a homing pigeon, when it came to people's vulnerabilities, Darcy found them and used them to her own satisfaction and advantage.

Perhaps Darcy's abilities to sense out people's uniqueness's were the fact that her father was a career criminal and her mother had been an escort. Strange family dynamics, but well hidden from the world, she made sure no one connected her to her family's past, after all they had ensured that she was given a good education. So according to them she could have a better life. Home base had been Las Vegas, but she had gone away to school on the east coast from high school on to university. Family visits were rare, and she never took anyone home to Vegas. Both of her parents died in her last year of university, she told no one, explanations would be a drag. Their death set her free from her familial past and allowed her to move forward to a much brighter future.

Mr. Howell proved to be such a straight lace gentleman, that she could not manipulate him, but Heath was a totally different story, by the second year, he was agreeing to her outrageous suggestions. It was like Heath had crossed the rubicund of philosophy, that's how good Darcy was at manipulation. Over the years she had recruited others to her side, not that they were happy about it, but once she had her hold on them, it was like being in the crushing grip of a python. It was either take it or die!

However, Kathleen did not succumb to Darcy's charms, if fact she was repulsed. This made Darcy very uneasy, because she knew from her sources that Kathleen was building a dossier on her and not knowing what she knew and didn't know was driving her crazy, so much so that she went to her husband's grandmother for advice.

After laying out all her concerns to Grandmother Shanahan her answer to Darcy was both clear and direct. "Don't worry about Kathleen O'Hare; I know more about her than anyone. I will have a talk to her, alumni to alumni. She will see my point and I can guarantee she will do my bidding. Also, Miss Bright One, I would also suggest you take over leadership of the Literacy and Library Division, you will be able to make changes that drive her crazy." "One year should do it, and then I will insist that the Board makes you head of Human Resources." "You should be able to dispose of Kathleen after that, after all you seem to be very good a destroying everything you come in contact with, my dear!"

As she got into the car that afternoon, the sun seemed brighter, the sky clearer, her path ahead was straight and would be cleared away of debris. Darcy felt at that moment in time happiness, not an emotion of which she had any real understanding.

In her blindness of her own importance, Darcy would never see the enemy coming. Self-absorbed people seldom do!

Chapter Twenty-Eight

After a day of sailing, Gwen retreated to her suite both tired and exhilarated. “I find that when I go sailing, I become intoxicated with energy, it’s like being reborn, everything is fresh, and I feel focused.” With these positive thoughts Gwen returned to her suite after a solitary dinner to relax and go back into the past. A hot bath, comfortable clothes and her faithful bottle of chilled wine set the scene for the replay of history. Tonight, was overcast as a storm was coming towards the island. Gwen turned on one of the small lamps that gave a subtle soft glow that did not take away from the relaxing music that she had chosen.

Tonight, Vivaldi’s Four Seasons, it musically described her life of changes, it helps Gwen remain claim and in control of her hatred and her violent nature.

To the outside world and those who encounter Gwen every day, they would never think that they were in the presence of a murderous mind. Quietly thinking to herself about the storm, Gwen said quietly into the still and silent room. “Tonight, was just overcast, the winds a little more forceful, but tomorrow night will be the worse, which was when the tropical storm would hit, it’s supposed to have winds up to somewhere between 39 to 73 miles per hour, but anything could change in twenty-four hours.”

"God was that such a prophetic statement for what the past and future was to hold for me forever."

The school year ended in June 2010, Darcy waited to the very last day to inform the library staff, that most positions would be cut. In twenty-four hours, Darcy had changed the lives of over one hundred people, and they were powerless to stop her. Each librarian was to manage at least two school libraries. All staff that were library assistants were simply let go, some received packages, most found themselves after years of dedicated service on the unemployment lines, when unemployment was at all time high because of the recession of 2008-2009. The cuts were both cruel and inhumane, there was no warning, no time for people to plan their finances, to get their houses in order.

By the end of July, five of the sixty personnel let go, had committed suicide. By the stroke of her pen Darcy had by extension murdered them, but she would never be brought to justice. Her crime was masked by the verdict of suicide, but to Gwen and others it was murder, pure and simple.

Many of the remaining library personnel, took a retirement package, they were the lucky ones. Those who remain, their lives were about to go down a dark deep cavern, some would simply die long before retirement was a possibility.

The reduction of staff meant the school libraries would only be open one or two days a week at most. To people who had dedicated their lives to the pursuit of knowledge and had encouraged generations of students to seek out knowledge using many formats, it was a tremendous psychological blow. But Darcy had no soul, it was all about money, certainly not the children. In fact, she was at odds with the Boards motto, which was put the welfare of the students first.

What was it, oh, yes, "We are here to encourage the spiritual, physical and mental wellbeing of all of God's children through thoughtful and consistent education practices." What a pile of bullshit, it was money and nothing but money, in fact I would swear on the bible that Darcy's god was the dollar bill.

Filled with anger and hostility Gwen threw her wine glass across the room, it crashed against the windowsill and shattered into hundreds of small pieces, too tired and exhausted to clean it up Gwen went to bed, and tried to sleep, it didn't come easy at first but eventually the wine took control of her mind and body and Gwen drifted off into a restless sleep.

Going into and out of her nightmares, Gwen saw the faces of so many friends whose lives had been destroyed by Darcy's actions. She saw the faces of the living and the faces of the deceased. It's like they were reaching out to her to be their prosecutor, judge, jury, and executioner. All they wanted was justice for what they felt was a great injustice towards themselves.

Speaking to herself in her unconscious state, "am I strong enough to complete the task or will my sense of morality prevent me from going forward with the unthinkable."

And then, "only time will tell."

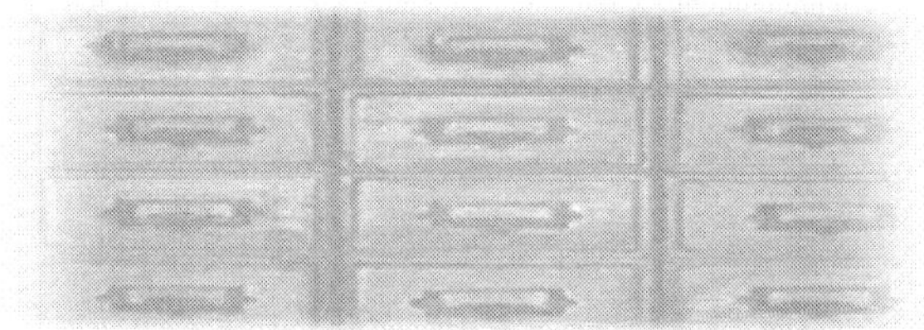

Chapter Twenty-Nine

The next morning Gwen woke up with a terrible headache, not only was it the effects of alcohol but the barometric pressure was very low ahead of the approaching storm. Speaking to herself, Gwen said, "They have given it a name, Bonnie, how appropriate, Bonnie from Bonnie and Clyde." Gwen always suffered severe headaches before storms, somehow once the rain started the headache lessened, but the storm was a good eight hours out.

Gwen got up and walked to the window, only to step on the broken glass, "shit, when did this happen," and then she remembered. "An extra tip for my maid, but it's worth it. Thank God I always wear slippers" "A throw back to when mom kept the thermostat at sixty-eight degrees to save money on heating."

Gwen called down for breakfast, apologized to her maid and spent the day in her room. Gwen didn't leave her room all day. This was the first time in the months since she had been down here on the island. Today, everything would come from room service.

When the waiter brought Gwen, her supper, he told her that all the windows and shutters needed to be closed and fastened. Her reply was tense and to the point, "I need fresh air, I cannot stand being in a room with no windows open."

His reply was kind but nevertheless, direct, "I am sorry Miss, but those are the safety rules, everyone must obey them." Sensing Gwen's mounting anger and frustration he relented, "Miss, I will leave the small window in your bathroom open, it will allow fresh air in, and we should have little or no water damage." "We may lose power, often we do, but it is usually back on in two to three hours, the staff will check on the visitors in their rooms, but we may ask everyone to come to the main building if the storm intensifies, do you understand?"

"Yes, yes, I understand, it's just that I feel so sick, I just want to be quiet and by myself." Was her reply.

"I understand Miss, we will check on you, the storm will only last a few hours, and apparently it is moving fast as the winds are very high." Was his kind reply.

"Does that mean it's more than a tropical storm, is it a hurricane?"

"No, Miss they are saying it will stay as a tropical storm, but with winds at about 117 kilometers per hour, almost the wind speed of a category one hurricane. We are hoping that it only brushes pass the island, we pray for that anyways."

"Then Juan, I will pray for that too!?

"Thank you, Miss, you are kind."

Thinking quietly to herself, am I kind, well sometimes yes, other times a big no!

As the evening approached the first droplets of rain began to fall, gentle at first then increasing in both density and speed. The winds howled, the noise was deafening and as the power of the tropical storm enveloped the island, but what could be described as the hurricane of memories that flooded Gwen's mind were as equally intense.

"How twenty-four hours can change a lifetime," well starting in September 2010, Gwen suffered many twenty-four-hour changes and not even one was good. The Tuesday after Labour Day, Gwen came into her office at Head Office to find her staff gone.

She had taken the month of August off to travel through Europe, "It was time I saw the world," she said to herself. The room was empty, desks with their pens, paper, telephones, and computers sitting there, waiting for their masters, as if everyone had simply gone for lunch. The emptiness was devastating, a land devoid of human life, the only stuff that remained were items a person would find in any office. Gone were the personal things that made it a room fit for humans, plants, knick-knacks, and family photos.

The absolute bareness of the room final hit Gwen hard, she broke into tears, quietly crying to herself, the tears followed down her checks and cascaded onto to the floor.

The rain outside reminded her how hard she had cried that day. Her perfect world was gone, left was the emptiness she had felt when both of her parents had died. This had become her life and some monster had destroyed it. As the tropical storm intensified outside, the lights went out, but the light in Gwen's mind came on with the images of Darcy in the doorway and her cruel and absolute humiliating tone to Gwen.

"Kathleen, I see you are back from Europe, how was it?" "As you can see, I have made changes in the last few weeks." "Since the number of school library staff has significantly decreased, I saw no reason to keep this rather large department going." "All head office library staff have been laid off; I hope you understand."

Pulling herself together Gwen had only one question. "Why?"

Her reply was both cruel and to the point. "Let's just say it's my way or the highway." "You still have your job, because there are people who are on the board, who like you and remember when you were hired, but when they retire, your time will be up." "Oh, as a small courtesy, you may pick an office assistant from some of the surpluses I will be doing next week."

The next comment cut the worse, it denigrated everything Library Services had stood for the last sixty years. "Also start downsizing what is stored in this room, I will be asking building maintenance to locate an office in the basement where your department will be housed, and we need this room for more important board departments."

As the winds roared outside with such powerful intensity, the storm that was taking place in Gwen's head was of equal intensity. The blinding rage matched the blinding rain that was falling against the roof and soaking everything.

In her mind and speaking to herself, yes, twenty-four hours had changed my whole life, but as the storm was passing so is my blinding headache, hopefully the next twenty-four would help me finalize my plans.

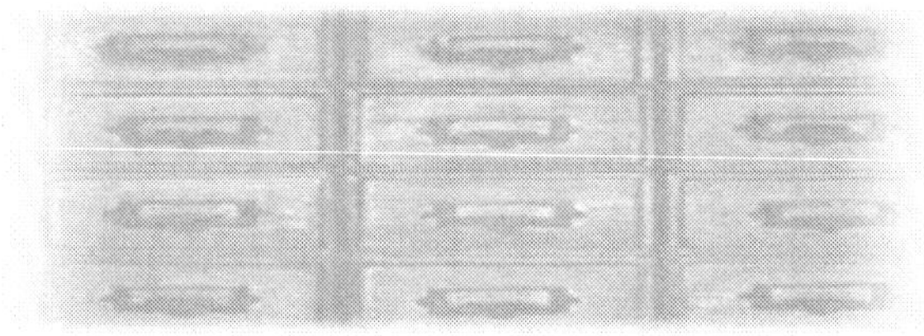

Chapter Thirty

The next morning, the sun came up, the skies were clear and the freshness of the air that occurs after a rainfall was powerful, for Gwen it was the next stage of remembering the past and deciding on how to reconcile it to the present. Every detail had to be exact in her head, or it would trip her up with her future plans. Gwen realized that she was very compulsive, in everything she did. She would plan, review, and review her plans multiply times, so that when she made the move to do something, it was a direct and complete act. No second guessing, she had the road map all laid out. All contingencies taking into consideration, no follies.

The sea was still too rough for sailing, but Gwen decided to sit by the pool for the afternoon, most people were off to town or busy with other things. Nobody took particular notice of the lady by the pool, who was listening to music with her headphones. She was simply left to her peace.

Gwen had found the YouTube piece that was a continuous playing Chopin's – Nocturne Op9 -No2, she had this piece playing on her computer for months while she prepared for the movement to the basement. It was her way of preparing for continuous darkness, as the office area they would be moving to, had no windows. It was to Gwen a prison and Darcy was her warden. Sitting here quietly by the pool, she slipped back into the past and remembered every detail of those four months of preparation for the big move. Left alone by herself for the almost a month, to begin the weeding and sorting of materials and records in the office, the music was her only company. Darcy made sure no one had time to stop and chat with Gwen. To Gwen it was as if she was being shunned, a cruel practice by some to punish an individual who went against the norm or others' philosophical beliefs. It made no sense, Gwen had always played by the rules, done her job, gone out of her way to help others, if anything Gwen was becoming more human than she had been most of her life. Thinking to herself, "that's why I cried that day, for one of few times in my life I felt undeniable grief, the loss of friends and the total destruction of everything I had tried to build." "Was it envy that drove Darcy or just pure evil?"

At that point I remember a bible passage: 'Wisdom 2:24: But by the envy of the devil, death came into the world.' And that's just what it was death by degree of an organization at the devil's hands. Could the devil be a woman, man, or sub-human, what?

Others in literature had references about envy and the devil, one that easy came to mind was the works of Sir John Malcom, a man of incredible life experiences and an incredible understanding of the human mind and soul.

Evil would continue to invade my life in the form of Darcy. After the first of October, I was given a list of people I could choose from to be my assistant, I decided on Cecilia, like me she was a spinster, that's what they call ladies of our age. Cecilia was like the violin in the orchestra that was always a note behind the rest, but she always gave it her best. Not particularly attractive, but her passive aggressive personality made her an excellent companion to work with and in time we became good friends. Like myself she was shunned by Human Resources but unlike me she was also shunned by most of the administration personnel in the Board. For whatever reason, she was moved from school to another school every year, and yet most who worked with her could not understand how this continued to happen.

Two weeks before Christmas 2010, Cecilia and I made our move into the bowels of hell, I could hear Darcy cheering in my head, "enjoy the dungeon!" Well, we made the best of it and decorated it for Christmas, two days before Christmas break, we hosted an unannounced Christmas party, many of the building staff snuck down for a drink and refreshments, we had Christmas music playing that day, and close to five o'clock, a group of us, sang 'White Christmas'. Darcy never knew about the party she had left early with her husband for the Bahamas.

As if being woken out of a dream, a slight tap on the arm brought Gwen to the here and now, "Excuse me Miss, but you did say to call you at five o'clock for dinner." Was what the pool boy said.

"Oh, thank you, yes I did say call me at five, thank you, I guess I was a million miles away," was my reply.

"Thank you, Miss."

Thinking to herself, Gwen wondered how long she had been time-travelling. What seem like only minutes had in fact been three hours. "You do lose track of time here, I must go and get ready for dinner, after I should be able to take a long walk around the compound."

"Tonight's thoughts will come in time no need to rush them, I want to enjoy the daylight as much as possible, remembering the basement office brings back feelings of claustrophobia and the aggression of being confined against my will."

Chapter Thirty-One

Nighttime fell, and Gwen returned to her room, to attend to her usual routine. But her music of choice was the same as the afternoon, Chopin's Nocturne Op 9, it was now the piece of music that brought every detail of those remaining years of work to the forefront of her mind. It was a long and lonely nightmare that was persistent, and she knew in order to succeed in her quest, she needed to exercise the demons in her mind from that time period, so that they did not hamper her actions in any way possible.

The sky was clear tonight, the windows open for the breezes to blow through her room freely, carrying the many scents of the tropical fauna and the smell of the sea. To complete the scene soft music, wine, and memories.

Gwen got herself comfortable on her chaise lounge by the window, glass in hand, allowed her mind to drift into the past that came too easy.

"Have I ever spent a full night in my bed, since coming here, no I don't think so, only after complete exhaustion do I fall into bed."

Christmas 2010 was a lonely time for Gwen, she had been asked to dine at an old relations house for Christmas dinner, but apart from that one event, she never left her condo except for food and church. If she had known what was coming in the New Year, she may have gone out and party more and hard. But the last four months had taken much of Gwen's energies away. Her grit was depleted, she had almost lost the will to live. New Year's Eve, she watched on the television the celebrations from Times Square. Watching the crystal ball fall, brought back that first year her mother and her had been in New York and had gone to Times Square. That night Gwen cried for hours until she fell into a deep sleep.

The next day for Gwen was peaceful, but the evening continued as her therapy sessions. At times these sessions were difficult, gut wrenching and turbulent for Gwen to relive, but oh so necessary to reach her end game. Drifting in and out of the past and now, Gwen suffered as she had never imagined, the last six years had been the worse to live through, they actual beat out her father's suicide for reaching low points in her existence, and everything could be laid at the feet of one monster, 'Darcy'! Again, Gwen felt the turbulence of the twenty-four-hour syndrome. After the Christmas break,

January 1st, 2012, was supposed to bring relief to the beleaguer library staff, but another day that will live forever in Gwen's mind, January 15th, 2012, was the beginning of an atomic war between her and Darcy.

Gwen was called into a board meeting and informed that Darcy would also now be part of the library staff team as the literacy co-ordinator for the school board. To add insult to injury she would remain in her offices on the executive level, while Gwen and Cecilia remained the basement.

As Darcy had done in a general way of hiring practices in Human Resources, she was now pushing for cultural diversity, to be in tune with what was happening in the whole country, political pressure to push diversity in every government department.

Darcy had changed the hiring practises to meet quotas over quality, her statement to Gwen was strait and to the point. “I would like all our school libraries to be staffed with personnel that would represent the cultural diversity of the community, do you understand?”

In a cold and detached manner Gwen’s reply was straight and to the point, “I am sorry, but my staffing model has always been to ensure the libraries are staffed with knowledgeable and qualified individuals regardless of their ethnic background. I believe children learn best from qualified staff.”

Darcy’s reply cut to the core of Gwen’s believes, “frankly I don’t care about that dribble, my interest lies in whatever is in the now, that's my ticket to my future promotions." And with that she dismissed Gwen, turned her attention to her computer screen and picked up her phone, it was the non-verbal cue for Gwen to leave her office.

Upon returning to her office Gwen took the first available object hurdled it across the room at the wall, it was only after it smashed into hundreds of pieces, that Gwen realized that it was a cherished trophy she had been presented with at her five-year anniversary at the board. The blinding rage Darcy had set her in; had blinded her to everything around herself.

It was like she had become two very different people; the calm and polite Kathleen one moment and a raving sociopath the next. The change between responses frighten Gwen, she was becoming more and more dis-oriented as the days passed.

Gwen began leaving the building almost every day around ten o'clock with the excuse she wanted to check up on all the schools in regard to their libraries, but in fact she was out on a fact-finding mission of her own. Quiet visits with library staff and other staff gave her and in-depth understanding of how the personnel cuts were affecting the quality of education across the school board. Somehow in those quiet chats, with kind and sympathetic words, she was able to elicit an incredible amount of information about Darcy, and none of it was good.

Systemically, Gwen began building a dossier on Darcy, hopefully to use in the future. But unknown to Gwen, Darcy had her spies, and she was able to keep one step ahead.

Things were beginning to improve slightly in the economy, but not in areas of high unemployment. In those areas, crime was increasing, homicides, rapes, robberies, all sorts of crime were increasing. In Philadelphia in 2012 the murder rate soared, and the ten deadliest neighbourhoods saw many young men gunned down. By June 2012 many of the staff at the schools in these neighbourhoods wanted out. They simply were tried of going to funerals, plus they feared for their own lives.

Darcy's time as literacy co-ordinator came to an end early in June 2012 as she now needed to turn her full attention to the staffing problems she was facing. People were taking early retirement over placement in high crime areas, and she need to act fast to stem the tide.

As crime continued to rise in these neighbourhoods, families moved and enrolment in the district schools fell. The board was now faced with amalgamation of schools as well as closing the oldest buildings. This process would take a couple of years, which left the remaining staff time to figure out their futures. The school year ended on a quiet note for Gwen and Cecilia, with Darcy's departure from their daily lives, the atmosphere was quieter, but the basement was still a basement.

Gwen went to pour herself another glass of wine, but the bottle was empty, with that realization and the fact that she felt so tired, Gwen turned off the music and the lights and fell into bed and drifted off into a deep but restless sleep.

The gentle breezes carrying the island's scent through her windows, offered to Gwen a calming influence against her memories.

Memories that kept coming back, childhood memories, young adult memories and current memories, they never left Gwen. Those memories were neatly placed in her memory bank, like books shelved in a library. They were catalogue by category, ready to bring out and review when the time was right.

All the memories in vivid detail, no detail forgotten, how Gwen wished that she could block them out and eraser some of those memories. But try as hard as she could, that never happened.

The rest of the night she spent drifting in and out of sleep and reviewing her memories, never truly relaxing.

Chapter Thirty-Two

Another day in paradise or forced exile as Gwen referred to it was taking its toll on her mental faculties, the more she was remembering and going into the past, the more she was becoming disconnected to her surroundings, it had been weeks since she had been to see Micky.

Her logic to herself, "I am not ready to confess, and my game plan is not complete." With that thought in mind, Gwen went for a day of sailing, she always came back feeling exhilarated, ready to face any challenge that came her way, which gave her one positive thought about her exile; "I love sailing, the feel of freedom, it's like all my cares are washed away and I can look forward to the future."

With that positive attitude Gwen had a quiet dinner, her long nightly walk and then retired to her suite to prepare for her evening of remembrance and reflection. Gwen prepared in her usual way for what had become her self-styled theory session, low lights, starlight skies, quiet contemplative music and wine. After a glass of two of wine, Gwen returned to the past and continue with her therapy.

September 2012, saw Darcy back in Human Resources, by November the school board made her head of department. Mr. Howell had retired over the summer, which would allow for the restructuring of the department, there would now be one head of the department, with two assistant heads. Finally, Darcy had the ultimate control she desired. She made sure Heath was one of the assistants, and she would hire from outside the board, so that the person was beholding to her and to her alone.

The decision to close schools came quicker than people had anticipated, with six schools closed across the board over the summer, September was a difficult month re-organizing staffing models and what students would attend what schools. Plus, the federal government was pushing for students from poorer areas to be bused into more affluent neighbourhoods. What a quandary for the board!

The pressures of dealing with all these staff changes was playing hard on Darcy, her behaviour was becoming more erratic, with only a few knowing the real reason, her drug habit. Standing in her office Darcy yelled to the empty room "that bitch needs to go, she sees through me, it's like her eyes have x-ray vision and she sees into my soul, and she knows it's hollow."

Of course, Darcy was referencing Gwen, but only she knew that was the person in question.

Sitting at her desk and writing emails to annoy Gwen with unrealistic demands, Darcy heard 'Beethoven's Sonata

Claro de Luna' in her head. To Darcy it represented peace and tranquillity, relaxing sounds of reassurance.

Little did she know that as Gwen was opening these emails, and controlling a severe urge to come up to her office and simply terminate her? She was also hearing the same piece of music, but to Gwen it offered the exact opposite, there was no tranquillity in her life only darkness and despair. Neither woman realized that their souls were travelling into the same place of darkness and one piece of haunting music united them, without a spoken word.

The tipping point came just before Thanksgiving 2012, Darcy had sent out an email to both Gwen and Cecilia, on the Wednesday night at five o'clock just before the holiday, that the six elementary schools that were closed needed to have all their library stock packed up for distribution to the remaining schools.

If this was not big an enough challenge, the icing on the cake was she expected the ladies to do it themselves and she wanted it completed it before Christmas.

The problem for both Gwen and Cecilia was they had already left the building, so this disturbing news was the first thing Gwen saw on the Monday morning.

When the intensity of emotions hit Gwen, she snapped, and with incredible strength and force she took the only weapon she had in the office, a trophy baseball bat and smashed her computer into hundreds of small pieces, the result was that the electrical surge caused the lights to flicker and that brought maintenance personnel to her office.

The rest of the day was spent with Gwen being taken to the hospital, after a psychiatric evaluation, it was determined that she had had a nervous breakdown and that she would need time off, with that Gwen found herself on administrative leave on company disability benefits.

That night in Philadelphia two women of totally different moral backgrounds, but simpatico in personal desires, each wanting the other out of their lives.

Darcy enjoying her victory over her nemesis, celebrating. Gwen in her darkened condo, in complete defeat. Both intertwined in goals, both wanting the complete destruction of the other, both hearing the same piece of music 'Sonata Claro de Luna', the depths of sadness, elation, and a dark place that only they would travel together.

As Gwen laid on her chaise lounge, wine glass and bottle empty, she had reached her pinnacle of justification for all her actions past, present, and future. Quietly getting up she moved over to her bed and collapsed into a troubled sleep, with the gentle Caribbean breezes blowing across her body, like a soothing hand to calm her soul.

Chapter Thirty-Three

The morning found Gwen, well rested, but still travelling in the past in her head. Her response to everyone she met around the resort was automatic, delivered with a pleasant smile and almost sounded sincere, but to a few of the staff, they knew something was not right with the kind lady.

It was agreed amongst some of them to keep a quiet eye on her, her drinking was known by her maid and the room service personal. Also, management knew about her excessive alcohol consumption, but all her cheques were good, so who were they to question her lifestyle. However, her room maid was very concerned and mention to her manager that Ms. Wahl had never slept under the covers yet, in all the months she had been in residence. Management was very direct with the staff, mind your own business, the lady will be fine. However, Isabel her maid was afraid that one morning she would find Gwen dead.

Disconnected to her surroundings, Gwen was now almost constantly in the past and remembering. The School Board, Management and Human Resources had insisted that she see the company psychiatrist weekly. This was so that they could continue maintaining her position without filling it with another individual.

Plus, it was a requirement to continue to receive company benefits, it amounted to her getting almost a full paycheck and never having to go to work. Thus, seeing what she called the company shrink once a week, who was driving her crazy, but a necessary evil. The person kept asking her what was troubling her, but Gwen never gave a direct answer. She did know what was bothering her, it was Darcy, but Gwen trusted no one, so this shrink was getting nothing out of her.

Months of therapy and no advancement in her recovery, actual Gwen knew she could go back to work any time, but the thought of being in the same building as Darcy was sending her backwards. So, let's play the game, were her thoughts, I can do this as long as I am getting paid. As the months dragged on, Gwen spent her time jogging, going to the shrink and known only to herself, creating on paper the orchestra of disenchantment, made up of Darcy's greatest victims to carry out Gwen's' final act of revenge. Gwen targeted twelve people to be her string orchestra of revenge, her twelve disciples so to speak. She knew she had to befriend them and manipulate them into her emotional depraved world in order to complete her mission. It would take time to get them to see that her way was the only way to deal with their hatred of Darcy.

Along the way Gwen would need DNA samples from each of them. Thinking to herself, "I might be crazy, but I will not take the fall for this action, O, my God, I have become my father." It was at that moment in time that Gwen realized she was her father's daughter. That shocking revelation upset her, but then in her dissociative mind, Gwen could see the value of being her father's daughter, a man who was morally bankrupt, self-centered and who would do anything to place the blame on others.

Speaking quietly to herself, "I hope I am better at covering my tracks, than dear old dad, suicide is so permanent, and I just can't see inflicting pain on myself, even if it is only for a brief second in time."

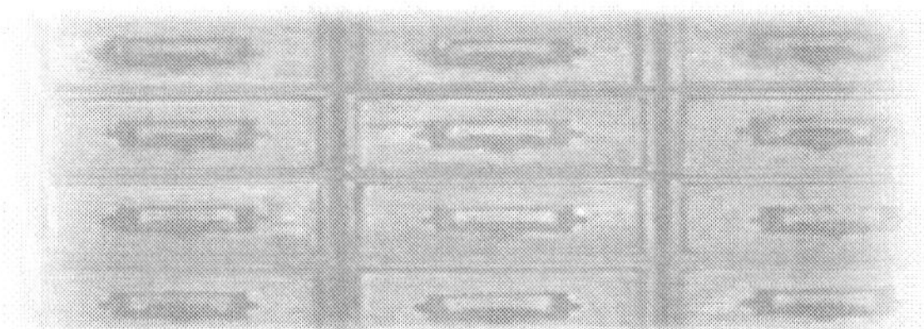

Chapter Thirty-Four

The past continued to play in Gwen's head, it was the recording machine that simply never stopped. So, her journey into her past continued, not into the distant past but now closer to today and her quest to set in motion her act of revenge. Remembrance continued, the next eighteen months saw Gwen once a week at the shrink's and the remaining days solidify her relationships with her disciples, and what a crew they were, the damaged ones.

By the end of 2015, Gwen had assembled her orchestra, it would be a string orchestra and their concert piece would be Chopin's Nocturne N20 in C sharp.

To Gwen, the music spoke of a fragile mind and soul, which was filled with great sadness, like every one of her musicians. At some points in the music, it reaches a period of coldness, acceptance and with it a solemn tranquility, such nuances that only the truly sensitive damaged heart could feel.

The orchestra was comprised of Mark, the caretaker who was very bi-polar and who had no qualms puncturing a hole in the Freon line to disable the central air conditioning in the part of the school that housed the classrooms of the teachers, he hated the most. This man was easy to manipulate, the depth of his hatred was perfect match to the deep sounds of the double bass. The next two instruments, cellos, sad and loss; yes, and human, were Melvin, the principal, who was a classic narcissist bastard, who displayed histrionic personality disorder as well.

When Darcy had finished with him and found him no longer useful, he was banished to the worse school in the board. His hatred of Darcy was ripe for the picking.

The other cello was Livia, the secretary from Melvin's old school. She had gotten a position in human resources as the department secretary, but only so Darcy could control whom she spoke with, as Livia was a constant danger to Darcy because she was too observant.

However, Livia's passive-aggressive behaviour was a very real concern to Darcy, as she never knew when Livia would rebel and let out all the dirty secrets.

The next four individuals were to be assigned the Voila, an instrument that produced a deeper and mellower sound over the violin. These individuals were support staff in the schools, their jobs were to deal with the difficult children, whether it was behaviour, academic skills, or physical limitations. Everett was a charming fellow who was very kind and helpful, but Everett suffered from paranoia, he was a closet gay, whom Darcy found out about and had abused him often and made him one of her many spies.

Darcy knew how to sniff out the problems, Rebecca was a lesbian, with whom Darcy had an affair with to get her to be her spy. The problem in that regards, was that Rebecca was the classic anti-social personality, so she was of little use to Darcy, because of Rebecca's social shortcomings, Darcy persecuted her whenever possible.

The next two ladies proved to be even more interesting, not because they stood out in a crowd, but their personalities made them perfect targets for Darcy and for me perfect instruments in my plans. Claudia was always off sick, and simply was the eternal victim of circumstance.

It was like she had a target on her forehead, which said shoot me and Darcy did that at every possible moment, not with bullets, but with hurtful and cruel words that were just as damaging.

My fourth voila was Giselle, like Darcy a married woman, but also like Darcy, bi-sexual. To put it mildly Giselle personified the term paranoia personality disorder. These individuals were classic for my orchestra.

What string orchestra would not be complete without its violins, and I had five teachers who over the last twelve years had run up against Darcy and lost. Their stories suited the haunting sounds of the violin when it was being played to a dramatic piece of music.

Emily of course had slept her way to the top, but was an absolute disaster, her aggressive personality style, annoyed Darcy to no end, plus she had slept with Melvin, a really bad call on her part. Cecilia my partner in library services was also on Darcy's hit list, she was simply backlisted for being a passive-aggressive who was simply too kind. Cecilia was a hugger, who sometimes did not use good judgement, hugging students was a no-no, which Cecilia had ignored too many times. I found that out, buried deep in her personnel file, which explained why she never got a permeant position in any school. Not that Cecilia had any malice, only that she did not understand boundaries.

My next teacher was from one of the high schools, a tough nut to crack, but when I did, I found out that his abrasive-aggressive behaviour had caused the school board no end of threatened lawsuits. Carson was simply a negative person, saw everyone in a negative light and treated them accordingly. In his later years Carson had developed Type II diabetes and he was paranoid people would find out, if his treatment of students was ruff before, after the diagnosis, it only got worse. Carson was on Darcy's hit list to get rid of, she was merely waiting for the right circumstance to come along.

And then there was Dolores, who had suffered so many injustices in her life, she was the eternal victim as well, with all the trappings of the victim personality disorder. Dolores liked medications; she had begun seeing different doctors to get as many pills as possible. It was like Darcy was a bloodhound who could sniff out the weak and vulnerable.

My classic conquest was Heath, Darcy's partner in crime in HR. As Heath began to realize that he was only an end to the means, his hatred towards Darcy slowly began to grow. Heath had another personality problem that he shared with many on the orchestra, he also had a victim mentality, which lead him to being a closet alcoholic. Heath would be my first violin, fitting as he was one of the most damaged individuals at Darcy's hands. It was the orchestra of the dammed, the men castrated and neutered, the women sterilized by Darcy's actions and words.

This was my orchestra of the disenchanted, depressed and with my subtle manipulation of their hearts, minds, and souls, they would become my orchestra of revenge.

With these reassuring thoughts in her head, Gwen went to bed and thought to herself, "tonight I shall finality sleep under the covers and relax, and the plan is coming together."

Months of wining and dining each individual, giving them her undivided attention, Gwen had worked her way into their hearts and minds. Each and every one of the orchestras of the damn, viewed Gwen as their closest friend and confidant. Little did they know that they were only pons in Gwen's game of chess against Darcy.

However, thinking like a librarian, Gwen thought of these individuals as titles in a catalogue. Each and every one of them had been made redundant. Just like old books being tossed aside, no longer need, because they no longer represented current information. Outdate books and materials in an ever-changing world. The cruelty of receiving an email to say that you were redundant to the Board. Being tossed out like yesterday's garbage, inhuman, animals would be treated better.

That's what my orchestra of the disenchanted was, ***'A Catalogue of Redundancy'*** to Darcy.

Chapter Thirty-Five

This had been another quiet week for Father Sweeney, it had been weeks since the tropical storm Bonnie had passed through, thank God, there had been very little damage to the island. A few downed trees, a few tiles off of roofs, but compared to other storms, the island had come out ahead. The church and the presbytery had lost a few roof tiles, but that was all, his parishioners had done the repairs, so there was no need to contact the insurance company.

The premiums were high enough, a claim would kill the church's bank account. The gardens had been cleaned up of the debris, and everything looked picture perfect.

The contrast of colours on the church grounds would have made an excellent picture for a travel brochure. Set in a sea of green trees, lush green lawns, flowering shrubs, roses, and hibiscus, sat the church building with a stucco exterior painted a soft pink with dark blue trim, and the presbytery a deep blue with the same dark trim. Classic Caribbean!

With this sense of calmness, Father Sweeney crossed from one building to the next contemplating his good fortune to live in such natural splendor. Looking up at the sky, a small cloud passed overhead and for the brief moment he thought of Gwen and said to himself, "I wonder if Gwen has left the island, it has been over a month since I last heard her speak in the confessional, perhaps the experience of a tropical storm scared her off, not likely, but I can hope. "Micky that's not nice, you know better," speaking to himself.

Still in high spirits, Father crossed into the church and did his preparations for Saturday confessions, sitting in the confessional, Father went off into his personal space of tranquility. That tranquility was only interrupted a few times with penitents in the first hour, then everything went quiet, completely quiet, it felt like Father Sweeney had been transported into a vacuum and then he heard it, "Silence" and his heart almost stop. "It can't be, I thought she was gone, stop it man, she is an individual who needs your kindness and understanding." "Remember you are one of Our Lord's disciples;" he called out to no one in particular.

A moment later everything returned to normal, the breezes, the sounds of the birds and the distance sounds of humanity. Speaking to himself, "Micky, you need to get control of this situation, you keep going off into darkness, when there is no need."

Trying to relax himself, Father Sweeney, let himself travel back to the mental place of tranquillity, so much so he did not notice someone enter the other side of the confessional, a slight hint of perfume lingered in his mind, but he was still in his happy place, when he heard the following. Gwen's opening statement was," "So, Micky, that was quite the storm, do you get them often down here?"

Father Sweeney nearly jump out of the confessional box, such was the shock he received upon hearing Gwen's voice, but he calmed himself and replied, "Yes, it was quite the storm, but we have had worse, actually we are now into hurricane season, so expect a few more in the coming months."

"Really, yes, I am aware of hurricane season, you do remember I am a librarian?" Gwen replied.

In his embarrassment Father replied, "Yes, sorry, I forgot for the moment, are you spending the summer down here?"

To which Gwen stated rather quickly, Oh, no, my family has a lakefront property in the 'Pocono's, it was my mother's family property, that came to me. Oddly the only thing I inherited from my parents; the government took the rest."

Father Sweeney replied, "Did the government take everything, because of your father?"

Gwen replied, "Yes, they took everything, they could, the house, all worldly possessions, I did not even get one piece of my mother's china, they took it all. The one good thing my father did was leave the cottage in my mother's maiden name, they did not know about it, so they could not take it too." "Another good thing was that my mother's parents disliked my dad, so they left their money in trust for my mother, she got a yearly amount, so that she was able to keep the cottage." "Odd you know she would not let go of it, even in hard times. I guess she wanted something from her past to remain intact."

Father Sweeney asked, "Did your grandparents not name you in the trust?"

She simply replied, "No they died before I was born, so mom was their only heir." "However, mom did transfer ownership to me while she was alive, so there were no death taxes on the property." "It's a nice piece of property, I enjoy my quiet times there, but it's terrible in the winter. I am not a snow person."

"So, you will spend the summer there?" was his question.

"Yes, I will, it's not a weekend getaway, it's across the country from my current home."

Thinking to herself, Gwen realized she had to change the topic and create the sense of distance by misdirection from that property in Micky's mind and her own reality.

"These are painful memories for me Father, do you mind if we change the topic?" "Actually Father, I know this is a lot to ask, but could we continue this confession after Mass tomorrow, say two o'clock after you have had a chance to have some lunch."

"Gwen, I usually don't do confessions on a Sunday, but I would make this one exception, if you promised to get us closer to solving your problems."

She replied, "I agree it is time to address the issues, see you tomorrow."

And with that she was gone, though the scent of her perfume lingered, Father Sweeney, continued to sit in the confessional for another half hour, afraid, but afraid of what, and of whom. He did not even know who he was dealing with and that left the lingering question. "What the hell is this all about?"

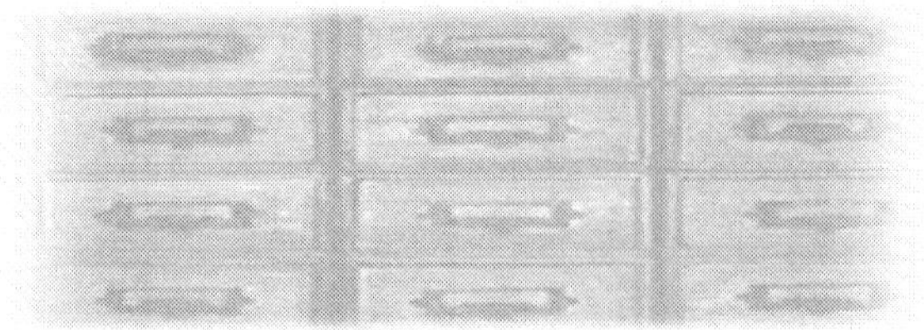

Chapter Thirty-Six

That night Father Sweeney tossed and turned in his sleep, haunted by nightmares of death and destruction, the burning towers were aglow in his head, and the continuous playing of "Silence". The music never cessed to play but continued until daybreak. After a night of restless sleep, he got up at five o'clock to get ready for the early morning Mass, it was too early for Isabel, so he made his own coffee. Sitting quietly at the kitchen table, he gave Isabel quite a start when she came in, "Father, what are you doing up so early?"

"I thought you liked to wake up to the smell of my coffee, you always tell me it's your alarm clock."

He simply replied, "well today my nightmares where my alarm clock, please sit down and join me, I have ten minutes to spare, what is up in your life."

Her reply was one of a confused individual "pardon me Father, I do not understand 'what's up', and is it American slang?"

"Yes, Isabel, it is American slang, what it means, what is new in your life." Micky said with laughter in his voice.

To that she lightly replied, "Father, you need to get out and about the town, you would be surprised at the things you would learn about the world." "Let me tell you, I have one lady I take care of at the resort, she's a heavy drinker, getting worse, and she even broke items in the last two weeks. Staff very worried about her, but management don't care, she got lots of money, pays cash for everything. That makes them happy."

Father Sweeney responded in kind, "Yes, you are right I do need to get out and about more, so this lady has she been at the resort long?"

"She came in January, very sweet, older lady, I would say about your age father, but since the storm, she has stayed away from everyone. Most of the time she goes sailing, what you would call a loner." "Oh, Father you need to go to the church, I will have your breakfast ready for you when you get back, then I need to get to work."

Micky took his last sip of coffee and headed off to the church, but thinking and speaking quietly to himself, "Could Isabel's lady and my Gwen be one and the same, strange, maybe I can find out more this afternoon?" All of a sudden, Micky realized that he had refer to Gwen as his. "Get yourself together man, Gwen is a winter parishioner not a possession." Correcting those thoughts in his mind he continued to the church along the path that was bordered by rose bushes.

The scents of the different varieties were enough to help anyone forget their problems or anxieties.

After the early Mass, Micky came back and had his breakfast and then he went back for the noon Mass. He had time for another cup of coffee before two o'clock, putting off lunch. He had decided to have a late lunch after Gwen had left, he could calm himself with a solid meal. So that was how Micky's morning went, coffee, Mass, breakfast, Mass and final a strong cup of coffee to see him through the drama, oh yes it would no doubt be dramatic. Two o'clock came and Father Sweeney had himself in place to finally hear Gwen's confession, thinking to himself, "If she is Isabel's lady, this should be very intriguing."

Intriguing would have been one way of putting it, but for Micky it would go beyond intriguing to an outright horror story and encounter.

The sound of "Silence" filled not only Micky's head, but it seemed to remove all the natural sounds that one would hear sitting quietly in the church. Again, so preoccupied by his thoughts, he had not heard anyone enter the confessional, he was brought out of his nightmare, by what would turn out to be his living nightmare.

"Hi Father, thanks for agreeing to hear my confession this afternoon." Was Gwen's opening statement. She seemed almost business like in her tone. Should I be worried were Micky's thoughts. 'No, Gwen just needs a friend to talk to, strange to think that she is so different from how I remember my Kathleen, who was such a bright and cheery person.'

"Well let's begin, shall we?" Micky wanted to get this over with as quick as possible, but to his shock and horror Gwen did not.

"Well, no Father, it's not that easy, shouldn't we begin with the usual pleasantries?"

"Of course, Gwen, beautiful day, did you have a nice lunch, where would you like to begin?"

The silence was deafening in the confessional, it was almost eerie, but then she broke the silence.

"Ok to the point, I want to murder my greatest enemy and to feel no remorse." She stated with such a calm voice that shivers went up and down Micky's spine.

Micky replied in the calmest voice he could muster, "You don't mean that, do you?" "You plan on breaking the fifth commandment, 'Thou shalt not kill.'

Gwen's reply was also calm, "Yes, I do! Problem?"

"I think we need to go back to the beginning, of your relationship with the person, to understand your apparent hatred of this individual and the actions you wish to take against her."

"Fine you want the beginning, well you know how 9/11 affected your career, well it also affected a lot of people, particularity those in government agencies.

Whereas the military had an increase in their budgets, those that were considered lower on the pole of importance saw a drastic cut in their funding and budgets. My industry saw many cuts and layoffs over that time period. But what made if more unbearable was the introduction of a blood sucking vampire, who spent the next twelve years sucking the life out the organization by destroying the health and mental wellbeing of its employees. She weaponized her department to kill the careers of the employees, in some cases, she shattered their lives and those of their families. She reduced the staffing models of every department, leaving people with unrealistic workloads that literally did kill some of my colleagues. The harm she has inflicted will take another ten years to repair, quite simply she needs to be stopped."

Controlling his tone Father stated, "Gwen you alone cannot make these decisions about human life." "You need to talk to others, who are in authority, express your concerns."

Gwen's voice was beginning to rise to almost a screaming voice, "Yes, Father, I can do it, I am judge, jury and executioner, I will complete my task and I will be proud of my work."

"Do you not feel any guilt or remorse for such thoughts?"

"No, I will do away with a parasite of humanity, actually I am elated at the thought."

"Gwen there is no forgiveness from God, if you do not repent and offer remorse for your actions." "Gwen, you need professional help, I beg you to get that help and not do something that will destroy the rest of your life."

"I don't need God's forgiveness; I am not doing this for God. I will do this for the poor souls that he did not come to the rescue, from the vampire's teeth." "Quite honestly, you can take your remorse and forgiveness, put in your pipe, smoke it and deliver to your Holy Father, I don't need anyone's forgiveness, and do you understand." "Goodbye"

With that incredible outburst she was gone, Micky sat for another hour in the confession, frozen by shock and yes, terror. Here he had spent months talking to what he could only assume was a deranged monster, and yet somewhere deep inside he felt there was so much more to her story.

It was like reading a novel only to discover the last chapter torn out. Quietly and slowly, he got up and made his way to the presbytery, feeling like he was ten years older in one afternoon. The day was beautiful, but in Micky's heart he carried a dark spot, put there by a person who had not wanted to make a true confession, who felt no regrets about their intended actions, he felt like he had failed as a priest. "For me this is the first penitent who will never be sorry." Then quietly praying to himself, "Please dear God, don't let this insane person be Isabel's lady."

Storming out of the confessional was Gwen, moving at the speed of light down the two blocks to her car. Her movements could be described as fast and furious, anyone who would have seen her would definitely get out of her way.

"The arrogant asshole, how dare he tell me right from wrong, well guess what Micky, the worse is yet to come, you will become my unwitting accomplish, you cannot save my enemy."

Chapter Thirty-Seven

After an hour, Father Micky got up and left the confessional, prayed at the altar, and went back to the presbytery, feeling exhausted, confused and completely worn out. Speaking to himself, he said,

"How could anyone become that angry about another living soul that they could be so filled with hatred and be willing to lose everything as a result of their actions?" "I did not help Gwen today. What could I have said better to get her to realize that she needed to feel remorse for her intended actions and seek professional help?"

Too tired to eat, Father Micky made himself some toast and a cup of tea, took it out to the front porch, sat down on one of the chairs and ate. The soft breezes, the subtle fragrances from the flowers in the garden relaxed Micky, in the distance, the sound of birds and the crashing of waves against the shoreline calmed Micky and took him back to thinking about his training in the seminary.

What had they been taught about confessions, if you feel you cannot reach the person's conscious about their actions refer them to someone higher up the chain. In a large city you would have a monsignor to refer the individual to, but here on this island, my only recourse was to refer Gwen to the Bishop on the main island.

She would never do that, it was up to me to get through to her about the seriousness of the actions, she is considering taking. What else had we learned, not to take it personally, it's not my crime or sin, it belongs to her. We were trained to listen, to give advice, but not to carry other's sins on our conscious; it's their problem, not the problem of their confessor.

Excellent advice and training, a rule I had always lived by, but for some reason I could not explain, Gwen's problems seem to have permeated my conscious and, on some level that I could not explain, my sub-conscious.

Quite beyond explanation I had broken the rules of my training and had let the sins of the penitent prey on my own conscious. Why? Had the months of Gwen's visits quietly and secretly drawn me into her personal drama. Perhaps it was my own quest to look up information and investigate about her history, I had allowed myself to fall into this terrible situation that I now found myself.

I was haunted by Gwen's intended crime, but I know nothing of the details, only that it is to be a murder. Speaking out loud to himself, "I cannot warn anyone about Gwen's intended actions, my only hope is to convince her that murdering her enemy is not the answer, I only prayer God, I am successful."

Sleep did not come to Father Micky that night, by Tuesday he was having chest pains again and needed to visit his doctor. After a complete examination, the doctor told him it was an anxiety attack. Although the doctor did prescribe a sleep medicine, he also suggested that Micky find other methods to relax.

Alas, Father Micky was lucky, his doctor believed in not only modern medicine, but also the use of holistic medicine. He recommended tapes of music that helped someone to gently go off into a relaxing sleep.

“Michael, do you have internet at the church?” the doctor asked.

Micky’s reply to his unusual question, “Yes, we do, why?”

“I have been doing some research on relaxation techniques, can I get you to become one of my guinea pigs?” the doctor asked.

“Guinea pig are you kidding me?” was Micky’s reply.

“Why not, if it helps you to relax, get a good night’s sleep and avoid anxiety attacks, what have you got to lose?” was the doctor’s question.

Micky quickly replied, “Your right, I am willing to try anything to feel better, but no needles or pins.”

“No Michael, no needles or pins, just using your ears to listen to beautiful music and delta wave beats.” Was his reply, and with that he gave Micky his assignment to try for a week.
“I want you to try this routine for the next week; we will see how it works and then take it from there.” First no caffeine after six o’clock, have herbal tea with your supper if you must.” “I want you to check out YouTube on the internet, one particular piece is called ‘Deep sleep music for stress relief with healing delta binaural beats’, it is eight hours long.” We will see how you are next Tuesday.”

With this new-found knowledge Micky headed back to the church and made a conscious note to himself to follow the doctor’s advice.

After arriving back at the presbytery, Micky thought back to all the times he had used the computer at the public library to try and research about Gwen, why had he not used his own computer? Very Simple! Distrust!

Somewhere in the back of Micky’s mind, he believed that everything he did on the Church’s computer was monitored, and he wanted to remain anonymous in his search of her history and not have it show up on the search history of his computer. Another post 9/11 anxiety, distrust!

That night Father Micky had supper and with-it herbal tea, not particularly to his liking but he was willing to give it a chance. After searching the internet and YouTube, he found the doctor's site and saved it to his favorites.

"Tonight, I will follow, the doctor's advice, but I am going to take the sleeping medicine," Micky said to himself. "We will see what tomorrow brings."

The next day, Micky woke up feeling refreshed and willing to take on the world, what had Isabel said, get out and see the island, get in touch with the island and its people. What was to be a first for Micky was that he would go out in public without his clerical collar. Since from the time he was ordained, he always wore his collar in public, it was only around the house that he did not wear it all the time.

This was a big leap of faith for Micky; he would be meeting and talking to people without his suit of armour. Halfway down the driveway, Micky froze, another panic attack, this time he wondered how to react to others, almost tempted to go back and put his collar on, he shrugged off the idea and spoke quietly to himself, "don't be nervous, treat this like a scientific experiment, how do people speak and treat an individual who is just your average person and not a clergyman." "Interesting concept, perhaps I can add to my knowledge of humanity, do people treat individuals by their clothing, and by extension do we use our uniforms to receive advantages not afforded to others." "Yes, Micky, this is to be a day of discovery."

With this new-found sense of adventure, Micky set off to discover his village and island in a whole new light. Micky did own a car, but he decided to use his bicycle to get around today, yes it would be a slower pace, but the details he would see would compensate his curiosity.

Speaking to himself; "I don't need to see the entire island in one day, I think today I will head down to the docks and look at the boats." "There are multiple piers, some for private boats, and others for commercial boats and the remaining piers for the commercial fishermen." "I think I will check out the pier where they rent out boats for the day and have day cruises for the tourists." "Maybe I will get a better understanding about the tourists that rent boats by the day and those who rent a boat with a full crew."
"Somehow I think the deciding factor is the almighty dollar."

Micky left his bike, chained to one of the posts at the opening gate to the piers. He continued on foot to the piers where the sailboats were docked and could only admire them. There were so many different sizes, some small enough for one person to manage, but definitely not long distances. Then there were magnificent sailboats, which would require a crew. Some so beautiful that Micky knew he could only admire, as he would never experience sailing on one of these incredible vessels.

Sitting there on the docks and off in his own private world, he did not notice the person coming up beside him, until they spoke. "Father Michael is that you? I did not recognize you without your collar." Turning around Micky look straight into the face of one of his parishioner's, Captain Joe.

"Oh, hello Captain Joe, yes I was out looking around the island, someone told me I needed to broaden my horizons and learn more about the daily happenings, and yes, more than what I hear in the confessional."

"Ha, Ha, well Father, you do have a sense of humour, I tell you what, I got two groups going out on my beautiful ship here, why not join us?"

"Are you sure?" Micky replied.

Captain Joe said, "of course I am sure, just pretend you are part of the crew, the guests won't know the difference, just stay out of harm's way." "Have you ever been out on a sailboat this large Father?"

"No, actually, I have never been on a sailboat."

"Well then Father you are in for the treat of your life."

So, this was my first big adventure, I would enjoy every moment. As Captain Joe had asked, I stayed out of everyone's way. Most of the guest were eating, drinking, or sitting on deck chairs sunning themselves. You could tell which group was which as there very little interactions between the two groups. Except for the polite courtesies, each group stayed together. I quietly watched them for about the first hour, after that I turned my attention to the sea.

I found a place near the bow of the boat, sat in a chair, and closed my eyes. I decided to let my other senses do the work. I could feel the spray of the salt water on my face and arms, and the smells of the open air. The wind against my skin, felt like something brushing the skin and relaxing all my nerves. The sounds were a mixture of the people's voices, the sounds of the wind, waves crashing against the haul of the ship and the calls of the seagulls who followed along at a distance.

Six hours later we returned to the docks, I waited to all of the passengers had left before I spoke to the captain.

"Captain Joe, thank you so much I had an incredible adventure today, thank you for your kindness."

"Not to worry Father, the next time you need a day off, come on down, I can always have you come along as a crew member, hey, I got it you are our chaplain."

"Thanks Joe, I'll remember that, and it would be a privilege to be your chaplain."

With those parting remarks, I headed back to my bicycle and back to the church, speaking to myself, “I think I will have a good night’s sleep tonight, the combination of fresh air, sleep music and medicine, should do the trick. With those upbeat thoughts in his head Father Micky headed back to his church.

Chapter Thirty-Eight

While Father Michael was exploring the island, Gwen was back at the resort reviewing all her plans. Playing Pachelbel's Canon in D major, while she sat and contemplated her next moves, she remembered back to the days when Cecilia and she played this music in their dungeon of an office, in order to pretend they were part of nature and the real world. How Darcy hated this particular piece of music, she complained that we were always playing elevator music in the library office and suggested we find another type of music to play. What had she said one day, oh yes, "Why not play some heavy rock, after all you feel like you are wearing balls and chains, I do believe are the accessories for that type of music." What a hateful woman.

Sitting now all alone in her suite, she continued to think about what life would have been like if Darcy had never existed. Could she erase the last twelve years? What if she could rewrite history about the school board without the existence of Darcy? It would be so in keeping with today's politically correct society, if they don't like the storyline, they simple rewrite it to suit themselves. What was it; they removed all reference to something, to pretend it never happened?

Could I erase the memory of Darcy, as if she never existed? Why not, others have, surely, I can find a way to erase Darcy? With these thoughts of finality in her head, Gwen continued with her thought process of analyzing everything to fact check every detail of her plans.

After almost four years of being on medical leave, Gwen had a lot of time on her hands. She had been using it wisely, she had convinced her orchestra of the disenchanted to follow her lead, and however she had never told them the whole plan. Perhaps because she had not totally formulated it, but she needed to get them primed and ready to go when she was sure of the pathway.

During those years of what some would say was an idol wasteland, Gwen had started watching different television programs, which she had never had time to watch before. Two completely different genres of television programs of which she found of interest were history programs that were fact based, one of her favorites being 'Forensic Files' and the other what can only be described as murder mystery, actually quite gory for her taste was the series 'Dexter'.

Although she was not thrilled by the graphic images, she was completely impressed with Dexter's methodology. What she found so impressive was his ability to function in the real world, but to have such a dark past time, but she understood his reasoning, that of bringing someone to justice when the justice system had failed. This played into Gwen narrative, as she wanted to bring justice for so many of her fellow staff members who had been damaged by Darcy. Continuing on that thought, she could justify killing and disposing of Darcy, because Darcy would never face justice for what Gwen classified as crimes against humanity.

By watching both programs, Gwen learned how DNA evidence was gathered, how people were caught, because of small details that they had overlooked. Dexter's kill room covered in plastic was defiantly the answer to the execution of Darcy, but there would be a lot of preparation and secrecy around what she would need to do, in order to prepare everything.

Space for the kill room was not a problem, she would use the cottage in the Poconos, getting the materials required would be a little more difficult. She did not want Darcy to bleed out quickly, so that each of her twelve members of the orchestra of the disenchanted could be part of the execution, speaking to herself, "Just like the scene out of Agatha Christie's, Murder on the Orient Express." Then thinking aloud to herself "My God, Gwen how many books have you read, and still remember details, yes definitely in the thousands."

Just like Micky, Gwen had used the public library for all her research. She did not want the history on her personal computer to show her research topics, what was that, cover your tracts and don't get caught.

She had decided that she would terminate Darcy through exsanguination, however she would not cut any main arteries, those cuts would create to quick an exit for Darcy, and she needed to prolong Darcy's discomfort. That would require what? She would need the following: Saline solution through an IV line; drugs to prevent clotting, another drug to render her immobile, but alert. Talking to herself; "no need for pictures of her victims, I want to only have her hear each of her victim's impact statement, and yes her mouth will be taped shut." "In no way Darcy are you going to defend your actions." "Disposal of the body will be easy, encase each part in concrete, and take the boat out into the middle of the lake, and goodbye Darcy, sleep with the fishes." "The blood can be leached into the soil, gone eventually forever."

I needed to return to the States and find someone who can help me acquire everything I need; also, I need to work on my orchestra of the disenchanted to come on board with my plan.

As Niccolo Machiavelli stated, "The end justifies the means." With that closing thought Gwen packed and headed to the airport.

Once back in Philadelphia, Gwen spent her days with her orchestra of the disenchanted, working on their mental weaknesses. Spending time with them, getting close, dinners, the show, the theatre, sporting events any activity that allowed for casual conversations. Always working into those conversations, their experiences with Darcy and bringing up painful memories.

It was when they were at the most vulnerable, that she would bring up the subject of how appropriate it would be if Darcy simply disappeared from the earth. Gwen never talked about specifics only the hypnotical. She was breaking down their inhibitions slowly, so that when the time came to act, they would follow her into hell.

Chapter Thirty-Nine

The summer's months were passing quietly for Father Micky, after the first round of storms at the beginning of June, the tourist population dropped, the snowbirds had returned to their northern latitudes, and everything slowed down on the island. Thinking to himself Micky stated, "We really are on Caribbean time now, no rushing, enjoying the days, the sun, all of nature's beauty and a sense of tranquility that the winter months did not afford." "Usually starting by the beginning of November the tourists were returning and the snowbirds were flying south to avoid the snow."
"Then life gets hectic for the natives, more work, more demands on their time and usually the tourist want everything done by the clock." "Well, that's months down the road, enjoy your days Micky, see the entire island, and yes, take advantage of the free sailing trips offered."

June had hurricanes and tropical storms that were threating at the beginning, then everything settled down for July, the best summer month in years, no major storms to worry about, and then speaking to himself, "absolute peace and thank God no Gwen."

Continuing to speak to himself, Father Micky stated, "Captain Joe had me come on board almost three times a week, he always introduced me as the ship's chaplain, not sure why, but I did end up doing some therapy sessions at the bow of the boat, it had become my chapel on the waves." "Who was I to complain, some of the people were so impressed with me, that I had received some significant donations for the church." "Another bonus was that Captain Joe had introduced me to other boat captains, who asked me to bless their vessels, and I was getting so many offers of free fishing, who could resist." Then thinking to himself; one day proved to be the highlight of the season, I caught the largest sea bass I could have ever imagined, the boys on the boat were amazed and, the captain said they would pack it in ice for me. "Father Michael, your lady Isabel is one of the best cooks on the island, she will make you an incredible meal, tell her we say hello."

I gladly took the fish packed in ice home and put it in the freezer. The next morning, I presented it to Isabel. "Good morning, Isabel, I hear you are one of the best cooks on the island, and I have a surprise for you." With that I took the bag out of the freezer and showed it to Isabel.

She exclaimed: "Father Michael did you catch this, it's wonderful."

I replied with great pride, "Yes I did, and I am told you can turn it into a feast."

"It will have to defrost first, but yes, I will prepare you a feast." She replied, but continued speaking, "I must say since you have started visiting the different areas of the island and becoming more involved with people, your health is improving."

Again, thinking quietly to himself, listening to Isabel speaking about my getting out and about and my health improving, I had to agree with her that I did feel much better, I had even stopped taking the anxiety medicine to sleep, most nights, I just drifted off and slept a sound and peaceful sleep.

"Isabel, my doctor is great, but your advice did the trick, yes I feel my health is improving, thank you from the bottom of my heart." "I have an idea Isabel, the day you prepare the fish, please have your family joins us for dinner, it would make me so happy, you know I miss the big family dinners of my childhood." "Where there was lots of chatter, good food, and fun."

"Alright Father, it's a deal," she replied.

Two nights later the whole family was there, fifteen in total, including Isabel and myself, and like the miracle of the loaves and fishes, there was lots of food for everyone.

The scale of hurricane occurrences changed in August, whereas July had been quiet, August went the other way, starting around the first of August, we got hit by Hurricane Earl, a category one, but it packed a punch, then came Fiona, a lovely Irish name, but she was no lovely colleen.

Towards the end of the month, we were preparing for Hurricane Gaston, he was looking to form into a category three; this would send whatever tourist left on the island packing. The church volunteers were already putting the shutters up on all the windows in the church and the presbytery. It felt so gloomy walking around both buildings, but I understood it was a necessity.

I will always remember the morning of August 25th, Isabel came into make my breakfast and do her chores around the presbytery, that day she brought shocking news.
"You wouldn't believe it Father, she's back, and with this major storm coming."
"Who is back?" I asked.
"You know the lady I told you about in the spring, the older lady, that I took care of at the resort, she's back." "It's crazy there are no other tourist, but her, management are making arrangements to keep her comfortable."

My mind was racing, my heart pounding, I was no longer listening to Isabel, instead the only thing I was hearing in my head was the music 'Silence'.

"Was I to be driven mad, not from losing my hearing, but because my hearing was too good!"

Speaking to myself in my head, I said, "Dear God no, not Gwen." "Save your servant from the devil, no Gwen was not the devil, but she could be his sister." "That's crazy talk Micky, one mention of her name and you going down this road of insane paranoia." "Get control man, she is just a very sad person who needs, your guidance to bring her back to God and away from personal destruction."

With those comforting thoughts, Micky continued with his day.

Chapter Forty

When Isabel had told Father Michael that Gwen had returned to the island and the resort on August 24th in fact, she was not quite accurate. Gwen in fact had returned on August 15th and had stayed at another resort on the other side of the island. Keeping to herself as was her normal way, Gwen went fishing and sailing almost every day. She was keeping an eye on the weather forecast as she wanted her final visit with Micky to be at the height of an incoming hurricane, she wanted to have such an impact on him, that he would never be the same going into the future. Quite simple she wanted him to be haunted by the past as she was haunted by hers'. "A long-ago love turned to hatred, so sad, but my reality." She spoke to herself, and then continuing in her thoughts, my love for you turned to hatred, why, 1973, why Micky did you not come to comfort me. The most horrible time in my life and my one true love never came to my rescue.

No reassuring hugs, no kind words, just emptiness. Surely you saw the news, say the papers, it's like you pretended I did not exist. Was I that much of an embarrassment to you. They say that time heals everything, that's not true, the feeling of being deserted never goes away.

When she was not pursuing, outdoor activities, Gwen spent her time on the complimentary computer in the visitor's lounge. First, she had researched what materials she would need and where they could be purchased. The rolls of plastic, bags of cement, shovels, twelve folding chairs and plastic bags would be easy, she could purchase them at any hardware outlet, but with cash only.

The medical supplies would be much harder to acquire, they had to be purchased with medical licences from a medical practice or medical clinic and or a hospital. Well, that left her out of the purchasing loop. However, over the years working at the school board, she had spent many days at the schools and had made many contacts with the students. She had overheard them talking about buying stuff over what was called the Dark Web. You could purchase anything, for the right price.

This seemed like the only answer to her dilemma. One student came to mind, which she might try to locate was Jerome Smith, super bright, but with a real criminal bent, too bad, he could have been very successful in anything he tried, but he always wanted the easy way to get what he wanted. So sad for him, but for Gwen it was an incredible advantage. After all she had removed his internet search history from his student account that would have gotten him expelled.

What had Jerome said, oh yes, "I owe you Miss O'Hare, anytime you need help call on me." Well guess what Jerome, I will come calling, were Gwen's thoughts.

"The problem is if I give him cash, he may not come through, I will need to give him an incentive, but what; I will need to find out what he desperately needs, agree to help him and then give him, his assignment;" were Gwen's words to herself. Then continuing her thoughts, I know Jerome was terribly devoted to his mother, regardless of all his shortcomings. That was why I had prevented him from getting expelled, I remember that day, when Mr. Carson had found out what he was doing, he was pushing for expulsion. I was at the high school that day, heard everything that was going on in the principal's office. When no one was observing my actions, I went into the system, using Darcy's override and cancelled out all of Jerome's search history.

With the lack of evidence, the school board could not go ahead with his expulsion. Later in the library, I called Jerome aside, and told him what I did, "Jerome, I erased your search history on your student account, I did not do this for you, I did it for your mother, hopefully you will graduate and one day turn your life around." Humbled Jerome replied, "I will try Miss O'Hare for you and my mom, thank you, thank you. And Miss if you ever need help, I owe you, my life."

In this small way I felt I had paid back for all the kindness that had been shown to me at my New York high school. That was the past, I now needed to concentrate on the present, and Jerome will be my shopper.

I think the best way is to buy multiple prepaid VISA cards, perhaps two thousand dollars. I will give my list to Jerome and tell him whatever is left after all purchases have been done, he can have the remaining cards, plus a five-thousand-dollar bonus in cash. That should keep him quiet, until I finally deal with him, no lose ends, but that is in the future, were Gwen's closing thoughts.

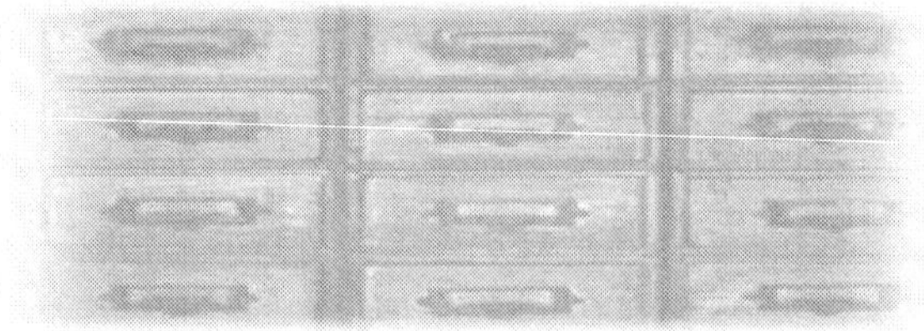

Chapter Forty-One

The day had come for Gwen to make her presence known on the island, so on August 24th, she moved back to her old resort. They were in shock to see her, they explained that most people had already left the island because of the incoming hurricane, they call it 'Gaston', they told her it was projected to be a category three storm. They would make her comfortable, but they needed her to stay in the main building. Gwen was ever so nice, not a problem, she was just happy to be back, whatever they needed her to do, she was perfectly fine with and would meet all their request.

Gwen was delighted to see her maid Isabel again, not just because she liked her, but she also knew that she was the part-time housekeeper for Micky, and would no doubt tell him in the morning that the lady had returned to the island. Speaking quietly to herself, "run and get your anxiety medicine Micky, you are going to need them." How did she know Micky was taking anxiety medicine? She had tailed him around the island. She had watch him visit the doctor multiple times, watched him go out on the fishing vessels. She could see him evolving into a more whole person. Sometimes she was excited, other times sadden, for she felt he was moving away from her and her grasp on his psyche. If she lost that grasp, then she could not bring him done mentally, which she desperately wanted to do, payback for his desertion in 1973. No, she could never let that go!

After supper, Gwen did her usual walk around the compound, it was so different, when it was completely deserted, eerie, but in some way known only to Gwen, it was her garden of paradise.

That night she settled down for a good night's sleep, the breezes blowing through her windows and the sounds of Chopin in her head. Tomorrow, she would set the scene for her alibi with the staff.

The morning came, the sun was still shining, but the winds had definitely picked up, after breakfast Gwen sat down with a few of the staff, to ask them how their summer had been. Gwen was good at that when she wanted to be, she could get everyone at ease, have them talking almost as if they were all family and not employer/employee. It had work over the last four years getting her allies ready to do her bidding, now she needed these people to remember where she was going and to place her as far away for the United States as possible.

Gwen explained that she was staying for about ten days, then she was flying onto Dallas and from there to Puerto Vallarta, Mexico to board a cruise ship, from there she was travelling to Hawaii, changing ships, and continuing on her world tour by ship. Telling the staff, "I have decided to take a world tour, and what better way than to do it by cruise ship." "I hope to travel to as many ports of call as possible, to see the world." "I am just so excited, I will get to see Australia, the Far East, sail around the coast of Africa, then into the Mediterranean to see a lot of Europe, maybe even a river cruise through France or Germany. Then onto the Baltic Sea, back to the North Sea and then around the coast of the British Isles and then sailing back to New York from Southampton." "A lifetime of adventure for me, I call it my retirement gift to myself."

The staff were so caught up in her story telling, that Gwen knew that when the shit hit the fan in the next six months, they would remember her being as far away as possible from the crime scene. While she was talking, the manager of the resort asked her about her luggage, "Ms. Wahl, you have only brought one small suitcase, how will you manage for a whole year?" To his query, Gwen had her answer down to perfection, "Oh yes, well I sent one case onto the cruise line offices in Mexico and the rest of my luggage I have sent on to Hawaii to the cruise line offices there. They will keep them in storage until I arrive to board the ship." "Do you know it was cheaper to do that, than to pay for extra luggage on each flight?" After a couple of hours of chatting, Gwen said, she was going to lay down, and that she would be happy to have lunch at one o'clock.

After she had retired to her room, they staff spoke amongst themselves that retirement was definitely agreeing with Ms. Wahl, she was so different from before, open, friendly and they were sure she was no longer drinking.

That night after dinner, Gwen made mental notes of everything she would need Jerome to purchase, rolls of plastic, garbage bags, cement, duct tape, twelve folding card chairs, and shovels from a hardware outlet. The other stuff would be more difficult, IV-lines with all the parts, needles, saline solution, probably four bags.

Then for the drugs, Ketamine to knock her out at the start, then Heparin to prevent clotting and to ensure that she continues to bleed out and finally to immobilize her, but to keep her conscious Pavulon. Darcy will be paralyzed unable to fight us, but she will be conscious to hear and feel everything. I will have to rely on Jerome to get this stuff through the Dark Web. "Why mental notes", Gwen asked herself, to which she answered, "you cannot take to chance of leaving anything that could incriminate you".

Only three days to my dress rehearsal with Micky, I need to rest now and walk through it all tomorrow and then plan how to set up the stage for my performance.

Thinking to herself, just like any Broadway play, you need to rehearse and rehearse, until you do your dress rehearsal, the only difference is that Micky is the dress rehearsal.

It will include everything, except the corpse, I cannot carry that around, now, can I?

With those macabre thoughts she continued on her way, thinking and planning.

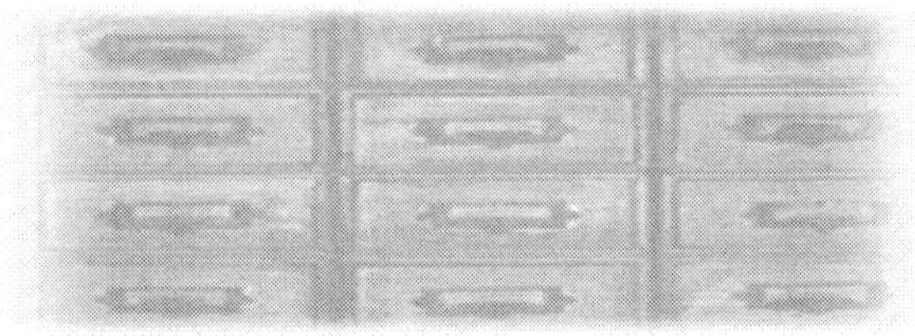

Chapter Forty-Two

The next day Gwen spent the day walking around the compound and went into town for a change of scenery. The whole time she was reviewing everything she would say to Father Michael when she went to the church on Saturday for confession. As the western part of the storm was approaching the island, Gwen could feel that the winds had intensified as she was walking about, tomorrow will be even stronger, which means Sunday will see the storm at its most intense.

Knowing she had a problem with bad migraines, Gwen had started taking medicine ahead of time, to lessen the impact from the drop in the barometric pressure. Speaking to herself; "I just need Micky tomorrow to agree to do my confession on Sunday afternoon."

"Hearing my story at the height of a hurricane should leave a lasting impression with him."

While Gwen was mapping out her strategies for the weekend, Father Michael was also making decisions; he had decided to move the weekend Masses to Saturday afternoon following confessions. That way he felt he was ensuring the safety of his parishioners. Father Michael started with calling all the resorts that his parish served and told them of the time changed and asked them to share the information with their visitors and staff.

He made calls to local business, that he knew and asked them to spread the word. Finally, he made up notices to place in front of the church, and then he drove to different areas that had poster boards and placed the notices regarding the changes. He also spoke to as many people as possible and asked them to spread the word. The forecast was for the height of the storm to hit the island around noon on Sunday, and Micky wanted to protect his flock, after all he was their Shepherd.

As Gwen sat at one of the bistros having her afternoon coffee, she saw Father Michael, going about and talking to everyone and then she saw him post a notice on the bulletin board across the street. After he was out of eyesight, Gwen walked across to read the notice. Her first words were a mirror of her thoughts, "Shit, are you kidding me, this puts all my plans in jeopardy, never mind Gwen, you will come up with a solution." "I will still go and see him tomorrow and see if I can come later that evening or early on the Sunday." With those thoughts in her mind Gwen headed back to her resort as Father Michael was heading back to the church. It was so strange that their two paths never crossed. Well actually they had, but Father Michael just never realized that indeed their paths had crossed.

Saturday came and Gwen headed to the church, she wanted to be the first in the building, so that she could set in motion her plans for later, after speaking to Micky in the confessional, she could set up the time he would agree to and then she could get away before anyone recognized her.

At two o'clock, Father Michael came into the church, knelt down and said his prayers and continued onto the confessional box. What he did not know was that Gwen was already on the other side waiting for him. Out of the blue, he heard.

"Bless me Father for I have sinned" After a momentary shock, Father Michael collected his wits about himself and state, "Gwen when did you get here, I mean, I did not see anyone in the church."

"No, Father, I was already sitting here waiting for you." "I hope you are fine with that?"

"Yes, Gwen, it's okay!" "Have you come back to talk about what you confessed before?"

"Yes Father, I have, and I also realized I was very rude to you last time, actually when I said I had intentions to murder someone, I miss spoke, what I meant to say was I wanted desperately to murder them." "I needed you to talk me out of it, but I did not give you the chance, for that I am truly sorry."

Father Michael was so taken back by her sincerity, he did not realize that she was in fact setting him up, and his reply showed how naïve he was, "Gwen I am sorry, I did not take the time to listen more, perhaps we can pick up where you left off, you said you did not kill the person, thank God."

Then Gwen replied, "I still need your guidance Father, but I know you will be getting ready for Mass shortly, can I come later to see you?"

To which he replied, "Why not stay on, and then after Mass we can talk?"

"No, Father I don't want to drive back in the dark, maybe I could come tomorrow morning say about nine o'clock, then I will be gone before the worst of the storm is going to hit the island."

"Gwen, I am not sure that is a good idea, the timelines they give are not definite, and the height of the storm could come over night."

"I'll tell you what Father, if it's not bad in the morning, I will be here at nine, if it is, I will come Tuesday."

"Ok, Gwen I will agree to that, but let's try to get your problems resolved this time."

"Agreed, goodbye Father, see you either tomorrow or Tuesday."

Then she was gone, as quietly as she had entered the church, Gwen had left, no one else was in the building and the silence was deafening. Since no one else was coming for confession Father Michael began to prepare for Mass, half an hour later the church began to fill, thinking to himself, "Nothing like a good storm, to get everyone praying." Then watching as the pews filled, Father Michael recognized many of his sailing parishioners, and there was Captain Joe.

"I can see they are taking this storm seriously, nothing like really bad weather to put the fear of the Lord into even the bravest of humanity." "What had someone said to him once, oh yeah! "There are no atheists on the high seas, especially during a storm."

Feeling confident that Micky would be there at nine in the morning, Gwen went back to the resort. On the drive back, the wind was blowing hard, and the tree branches were swaying back and forth, leaves were flying off and littering the road and the windshield of Gwen's car. But as fast as they landed, the winds blew them off, tomorrow will be harder in the rain were Gwen's thoughts.

Then she began thinking about the evening, "What I need is a good night's sleep, so I am completely accurate tomorrow in my tale, remember, no slip ups Gwen."

Later that evening Gwen justified her actions with one of Machiavelli's quotes: "It is better to act and repent, than not to act and repent."

She was going to act and yes repent, after all that's what Micky expects!

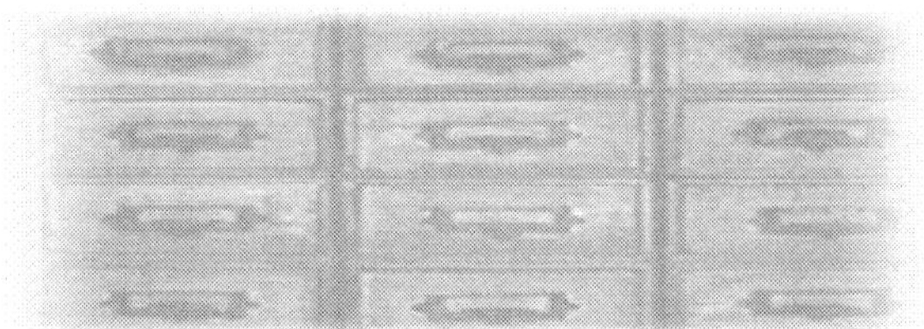

Chapter Forty-Three

Saturday night had past, and the storm had stalled, the island was still on the western side of the eye, so the winds and rains had not reached their peak yet. Father Michael had got up at six o'clock and had prepared his breakfast, Sunday was Isabel's day off, also he had told her last night after Mass, to stay home and be safe. Alas he was to be by himself today, but that was okay, Micky had learned a long time ago to take care of himself, his mother had taught all of her children to be self-sufficient.

Micky put on his coffee maker, decided to fry up some bacon and eggs, saying to himself; "it's going to be a very long day, I think I will do some home fries and some fried tomatoes and mushrooms." Continuing to speak out loud to himself, "A typical English breakfast for a typical American; what a paradox." "Oh Micky, times have changed, gone are the days of cereal and orange juice, now it's a full breakfast, which usually takes me to the afternoon, light lunch, later supper and sometimes afternoon tea.
It is amazing how some of the English traditions continue on these islands, and how quickly one adapts to them."

By eight o'clock Micky was all prepared to face the day, the winds were picking up and the rain was coming down harder, thinking aloud to himself, "I wonder if Gwen will make it today?" "Probably yes, that woman seems to be able to cope with anything, nothing stops her, and I really wonder if even the good Lord could?" With those abstract thoughts Micky decided to put on his mackintosh to get over to the church, it wasn't a far distance maybe fifty yards, but an umbrella would collapse in this wind. Keeping his head down, moving as quickly as possible, he could hear the sound of thunder in the distance, and both the wind and rain were picking up their intensity. After getting over to the church, he unlocked the main doors, thinking to himself, "just in case someone needs sanctuary."

As the winds and rain increased the electric lights began to flicker, Micky decided he better get out the candles and start lighting some, by eight-thirty the hydro was out and Micky lite as many candles as he could. "That's one thing about Catholic Churches, they are never in short supply of candles!" he thought, "and here on the islands it was doubly true."

Sitting quietly near the front of the church and saying his prayers, Micky could hear and feel the storm's intensity increasing, the winds were beginning to sound like howling animals, their cries of fear carrying over the distances. The air carried a very subtle but distinct smell of the sea, perhaps it was because the storms formed over the open waters of the ocean, and the raindrops carried that smell, it wasn't powerful, but it did exist, when you took the time to concentrate your senses.

At ten minutes to nine, Micky moved into the confessional, his instinct told him, come hell or high-water Gwen would be there and he wanted to preserve the anonymity of the confessional as best he could. Sitting in the quiet confessional with a candle on either side of the dividing wall, Micky could hear the front door open, and the approaching steps across the tiled floor. "Nine o'clock, right on time, typical type 'A' personality." The footsteps stopped abruptly about ten feet from the confessional, and then nothing, seeping into his sub-conscious was the musical piece 'Silence', at first the sounds of the storm were more powerful but as the moments dragged on the sounds of the storm diminished and the sound of the music increased in his head.

Speaking to himself, Micky stated, "I think instead of calling this storm 'Hurricane Gaston, I will call it Hurricane Gwendolyn' funny Micky old boy, but terrifying just the same."

Chapter Forty-Four

The music died down in his head and was replaced with the sounds of the howling winds and the driving rain hitting the roof and in the distance the sound of the thunder was increasing in not only volume but frequency. Quietly waiting for something to happen, he heard the following.

"Bless me father for I have sinned." When did she walk into the confessional, had I been so lost in my own thoughts, that I did not hear her approach?

"Hello Gwen, I wasn't sure you would get here." "The roads must be bad, and I am sure it was hard to see through the rain."

"Yes Father, it was a difficult drive, but I took my time, so here we are."

"Yes, we are Gwen, I am ready when you are," was his reply.

"Are you telling me to get on with it, Father?" Gwen snapped back.

Panic crept into Micky's heart and mind, but his reply was both gentle, but forceful in one, "Actually Gwen, I was thinking that we should begin so that you are able to reach a conclusion and see you safely back to your hotel." "Also, we have no hydro, and I do need to keep an eye on the candles." "Plus, I have left the church doors unlocked, in case some poor souls need to get in out of the storm." "We

often have people come into the building during severe storms, they feel safer here than in their small houses." "I would not like to have your confession interrupted."
"Good save Father, I am impressed, and you are a survivor too." "Yes, you are right we should begin." "And so, I shall!"

Chapter Forty-Five

"Where to begin, well I guess I need to begin at a time when everything went wrong, that was about sixteen years ago," was Gwen's statement.

"That long ago?" Father Michael asked, thinking to himself, this storm will be over, and the next hurricane will be knocking at our door, if she going to go on at the speed, she has been travelling this year.

As if to read my mind, Gwen said "Oh, I don't need to cover every detail, just a quick synopsis, so you get the idea of what brought my friends and I to this point."

"Your friends, I don't understand?" was Micky's question.

Again, as if she had a crystal ball, she gave a direct answer to my query, "yes, my friends, you don't believe I could accomplish what needed to be done on my own do you?'

"No, no, whatever you say, I think the best is for me to listen, I will try not to interrupt too much."

"Good idea Father, this will in fact will go much quicker, if you remain silent and just listen."

Feeling intimated by her forthright manner, Micky kept his thoughts to himself and allowed her to proceed in her tale.

"It all goes back to 2002, there were changes in our organization, and the Board of Directors started making budget cuts; every organization was doing that, but to make matters worse, they hired what could only be described as a hit person, whose job was to cut the staff in half." "Everyone called her the blood sucking vampire or the Dark One." "And she was evil."

"In short order she began the process of dismantling the staffing models, which had been in place for maybe fifty years." "Those who were lucky enough to retire or who were fired, were the lucky ones, those who were left were in for a terrible time, hell on earth." "You have to understand Father, most of these people I knew for close to twenty years, we were like family, perhaps dysfunctional at times, but still family."

"We cared about each other and shoulder each other's joys and sorrows." "That's what a family does." "But this monster attacked each person, attacked their integrity, ate away at their souls and for some she left them broken." "And what was the most humiliating for everyone was that she was given the job, not because of her credentials, but because she was married to the son of one of the board of directors." "That family had been stealing from the organization for years, which was why there were so many budget shortfalls."

"They needed her there to do their dirty work and silence those who knew what had happened over the years in regard to all financial transactions."

As I listen to Gwen the howling winds and thunder seem to increase in intensity almost as if nature was adding the soundtrack for her story. More cracks of thunder, louder and louder as Gwen continued on into her narrative.

The smells inside the church were changing, not the usual scent of the island fauna, because everything was boarder up. No, the smells were of damp wood, plaster that had been wet and then dried, the smell was definitely moldy. Thinking to himself in practical terms, we need to treat this problem and soon.

After that momentary thought into the real world, Micky transported his brain back to his here and now.
But yes, the building smelled moldy.

"Four years ago, Father, I had a mental breakdown, and was forced onto disability, like a sports person being sidelined, unable to participate in the game, but still there watching every move in the game." "My close friends kept me informed about everything that was happening at the organization and I watched as they themselves began their own personal descents into hell."

"That was when I formed my orchestra of the disenchanted, we came together to decide how to remove the Dark One from existence."

At that point, there was a terrible loud crack of thunder, the storm had picked up speed, and seem that it was now intensifying. Thinking to himself: "Are we moving into the eye wall before the eye of the storm, was that why is seem to be so much more forceful and powerful." "So, Gwen had a mental breakdown, so brave of her to mention it, but the sounds of the storm just became stronger outside and now the storm was seeping into my brain." Continuing on that course of thinking and speaking to himself; Father Michael said, "I am trapped in this building with a mad woman, and nobody knows."

Then he asked Gwen, "I don't understand your reference to the orchestra of the disenchanted?" "What is that?"

Her reply was as calm as her voice, "Not literally an orchestra, Father, but figuratively, you see each of my twelve musicians or disciples if you like, are like various instruments in a string orchestra." "You have your double bass, your cellos, and violas and of course what string orchestra would not be complete, they need their violins."

"Together they come together and create the piece of music that is the final act in the Dark One's life."

Thinking to himself; Father could only compare the noises from outside that seem to envelope the church as a terrifying experience, equal only to the fear he was feeling in the enclosed space of the confessional. It felt like the walls were closing in on him, even though they were not.

The crashing thunder, the rain beating against the roof and walls of the church and the wind howling, the noise was increasing with each passing moment, was this Gwen's idea of music for the end of a person's life. Please dear God no!

Chapter Forty-Six

The sounds of this storm, and the story that I was being told came back to me eight months later as I lay on a stretcher in the presbytery, the medical personnel working desperately to revive me. It was like an out of body experience, I could see them doing compressions on my chest and using the breathing resuscitator apparatus to force air into my lungs. Then I heard them shouting and trying to coach me back to life, "Father Michael stay with us."
There was Isabel sobbing uncontrollably, and there was Captain Joe, trying to calm her and yelling at me,
"Father Michael, we need you, don't leave us." It was then, that I travelled back in time to this day.

I was sitting in the confessional listening to Gwen, but totally absorbed by the sounds and forces of nature that was Hurricane Gaston, my private joke was that I called it Hurricane Gwendolyn.

The storm had intensified over the last twenty-four hours, and I felt like it was moving faster than they had predicted. After Gwen had arrived, the storm seemed to intensify even more, did her presents add to its power.
The thunder was closer, and you could hear loud bangs and the sounds of things cracking, which I had to assume were lightning strikes and the objects in their wake.

The force of the wind and its howling was at times so loud, I could hardly hear Gwen speak, but I was getting enough of her words to realize, that in fact she had gone ahead and murdered her enemy. Why did I not stop her that day months ago, perhaps I could have talked her out of it, but I had failed?

The storm for me was increasing, but Gwen's voice remained calm, was she the eye of the storm, or was she so focused on her tale, that nothing outside of her own sphere of her mind matter or affected her. It was like we were in two separate places in the storm, Gwen the eye that was churning up the winds and the water, and I, who was feeling the full blast of the storm, and yet we were only about two feet apart, with only a wood trellis screen between us.

Then without warning, a powerful silence envelope the whole church, was the eye now passing over us? If the sounds of the storm had been terrifying, the silence that now surrounded us was in fact more frightening, because once it passed, we would be in the eastern half of the storm, speaking to himself, Father Michael said, "and that eye wall could destroy the building we are in!" As I tried to listen to Gwen, I found my hearing was still not right, had the strong noises I had encountered so far have affected my eardrums, everything I heard Gwen say was as if she was talking over a bad phone connection.

What bits and pieces I was hearing made no sense, she was talking about some orchestra and how they had come together, to share their grief and sorrow. At that point I knew I needed to stay completely focus on her, so that I did not say the wrong thing, I wanted desperately to get out of this building alive. I gave all my focus to Gwen and then she continued with what could only be describe as a prologue to her true confession.

"During those four years of being on medical leave Father, I met with a lot of the staff for coffee, dinners, the occasional day outings," "However for some of us, we formed a bond that was so close, we knew each other's pain and the depths of each sorrow." "I jokingly called us the orchestra of the disenchanted, they quickly and innocently followed my lead." "After much coaching, I was able to get them to agree to my plan to remove the 'Dark One', some were queasy at first, some of the others had more drastic ideas, than I did on her disposal."

"When the full plan, came together we sat and thought about the setting, how would we proceed, who was responsible for what?" "All questions that needed to be answer, I took the lead and became the conductor of the orchestra, I selected the music that would be played based on the personal trauma and temperament of each one of my musical instruments, sorry, I mean disciples."

"Of course, the first piece of music the 'Dark One' heard was my favourite, Pachelbel's Canon in D major." "The perfect piece of music as it was the one, she hated the most."

"The other three pieces of music I picked were 'Albinoni Adagio in G minor; Chopin's nocturne in C sharp minor and Barber Adagio for strings' each piece suited to my musicians." 'Three of my disciples were driven by Albinoni's adagio, four of them much more suited to the chosen Chopin piece and the remaining five disciples were answering the call of Barber's adagio."

As Gwen continued to ramble on about music and personality types, the storm outside was changing, the winds were picking up, the sounds of thunder were increasing as was their frequency. Then the rain began slow at first then it increased so much that between the sounds of the wind, thunder, and rain, I could no longer hear a word Gwen was saying, I had moved into the more powerful eye wall of the storm in both reality and in my head. What was so strange was that Gwen seem to be frozen in time, she was still in the eye of the storm, wait a minute she is the eye of my storm.

My storm circulating in my head, the pounding of the rain on the roof, was amplified in my brain.

It was like being at a rock concert, where they would have the volume so high that you could not hear the person beside you speaking. My brain was hurting, and I could feel a headache coming on, but there was no release from my suffering.

Adding to my misery was the sound of the wind, blowing, at times it sounded like a huge truck driving by, or the sounds a train makes when it is traveling fast through a tunnel. Sitting on the other side of the screen was Gwen, she was totally unaffected by the noises, it was like she existed in her own vacuum. Gwen was the eye of this storm in the confessional and the eye of the storm raging in my brain.

How could she continue on speaking when so much was happening around us? At times the winds were so strong I was sure that the roof wound be ripped off, or that the walls would crumble. We had beautiful palm trees on the property, but if one was taken out by lightening, it would come through the roof and then what would happen to the both of us?

Gwen, however, was travelling in her own time zone, talking away, telling her story, assuming that she was the centre of attention. Well, she was the centre of attention, but only in her mind. My centre of attention was survival.

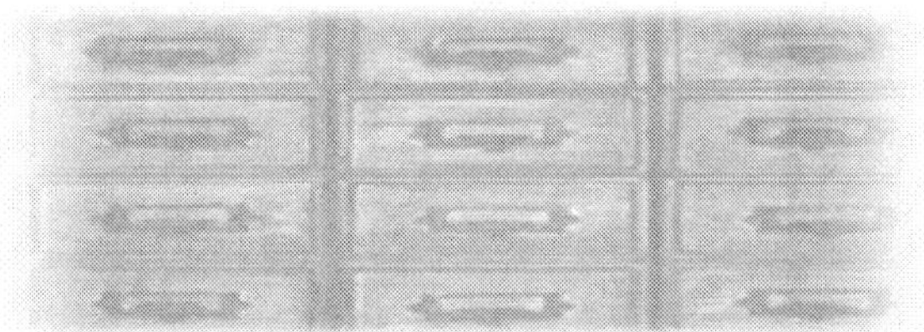

Chapter Forty-Seven

While I continued to be in the eye wall of the storm, Gwen remained lost in her own dimension as the eye. The humidity was building, and I felt I like was suffocating in the confessional box, all I could do now was open up the door on my side and let the breezes flow through. When I did this, there was some relief, but perhaps the relief was more from not feeling like I was in a box, a coffin. Was this how I was truly feeling that I was in a coffin?

As the storm rage, and lightning strikes were taking place, I noticed that on the far wall, flickers of light when there was lightning, the shutters on one of the windows on the wall behind me must have been blown off, why else would there be those flickers. My focus was moving away from Gwen and her continuous prattling to the images that were dancing on the wall whenever there was lightning. There seem to be swaying branches, dancing in the wind, at some points the wind must have been so strong, that they were bending sideways. I used this pantomime on the wall to calm me, as Gwen continued with her story. Somehow a visual distraction reduced the hold on my mind from the sounds of the storm. It did not reduce my fear of my circumstances but created a diversion.

While my mind had wander, Gwen had continued non-stop, she never missed a heartbeat. My standard words to get through this ordeal where, “Really, unbelievable, No, what you are saying can’t be true,” I felt like those words, kept me alive, not from the hurricane outside, but from storm that was taking place here in the church.

Gwen continued on talking about a student, whom she had helped, so when she needed supplies bought that required a criminal activity, he owed her, and she collected. I think she said his name was Jerome something, I did not catch the last name and I was not about to ask her a second time. One word, FEAR!

Gwen spoke about everything they created, both a court room and the execution room, but the way she was speaking it sounded like everything was in one room. Then she mentioned something about them using a deserted cabin in the Pocono’s. Speaking quietly to himself again Father Michael said, “If I ever get out of this alive, I will be researching about unusual deaths and disappearance in Pennsylvania.” “Not that I can bring justice, but I need to know the truth.”

That one failing of mine, needing to know the truth about everything, would eventual be my downfall.

"You know Father the concept on how to set up the room, came to me when I was watching the TV series Dexter, did you ever watch it? Was both her statement of fact and question in one?

I simply replied, "No Gwen, I am not a fan of murder stories, to tell you the truth I still enjoy watching reruns of Gilligan's Island, that is more my speed in television programs, I simply like comedy."

"Oh Father, there are so many types of programs you could be watching, dramas, documentaries, comedies, the list is endless." Was her reply.

In my head, I am thinking, is she that nuts, there is a storm so strong out there, between the crashing of thunder, the driving rain, and the sheer force of the wind, that I am expecting the roof to be torn off at any minute, and she wants to discuss genres of television programs. I got to get her back on track, even if the storm or she kills me.

"Gwen's let's get back to your story, shall we?"

"Oh Father, I think we are going to be stuck in this building for a few hours, no need to rush is there?"

With that comment, my heart sank, and my thoughts were Micky you are never leaving this building alive.

"Anyways Father, back to my confession, shall we?"

"Yes, I think that's the best idea."

How can she be so calm? Were Micky's thoughts.

"Shall I continue?" she asked. "Please do," was my reply.

"As I was saying before, I got the idea on how to set up room, with plastic, proper lighting, shall I say etcetera from Dexter!" "Jerome had purchased all of the medical supplies and drugs I needed on the Dark Web, then I had him purchase all of the other supplies, one good thing is that Jerome's fingerprints are on everything and it's his face that will show up on security cameras when the time comes."

"Enough of that, I guess you want to know how we got the 'Dark One' to the cabin, that was easy, I just did what Dexter did, I pulled my vehicle up beside hers in the underground garage, came up behind her, needle in the neck with Ketamine, and she was out like a light." "Did you know no one pays attention to a grey van, it's like they are invisible?" "Also, like Dexter, we dressed in mono chromatic colours, I found I prefer materials that were the colour raw umber." "Two hours later, we were at the cabin and ready to prepare her for trial and execution."

"The best thing about taking her that way is she was leaving for a trip, so no one would be surprised that she left her car in the underground garage of her workplace." "And quite honesty, since no one like her, no one would pay the least attention to the fact that she was gone, well at least for a few weeks." "It must be nice to be so loved, that no one cares where you are, no I mean hated."

Gwen was still in her eye of the storm moment, totally unaware that she was telling the story of a monster, and she was the monster. At that moment, there was a flash of lightning, followed by an extremely loud crack and a huge bang and then the ground shook as a large palm tree in the garden lit the ground. Here I was in the ring with a monster, while a monster of a storm was destroying everything around me.

Speaking to himself, Micky said "please dear God, spare my life today and I promised to be a better Sheppard of your flock."

Micky realized that he had begun to bargain with God, the one thing he had always warned people not to do, "Well Micky old boy, when the shoe is on the other foot, you sure can change your tune."

Chapter Forty-Eight

The storm was so powerful outside, that I now felt like it had permeated the building, and that the storm was inside, but no it was not in the building, it was now part of my brain, my whole body was experiencing the storm, it had seeped into my blood stream and was now coursing through my veins reaching every part of my body. How long before it claimed my soul. While I was going through my own personal hell, Gwen continue in her position as the eye and continued on as if nothing was taking place beyond her personal story. What an egotistical bitch!

Calmly she described how they had set up the room, completely cover it in plastic, then they had set up twelve chairs for the jury. Whom from my understanding were also the victims of Darcy's callousness. They had given their impact statements to their 'Dark One'. Gwen described how she was the judge and that she had her bench all set up, in fact from the sounds of it, Gwen never touched the individual in question. She had everyone else carry out her wishes. A cunning conniving bitch, she took damaged souls and used them to carry out her vendetta.

I wanted to ask her questions about what she was saying, but then I realized that she had even forgotten that I was there, it was like she was going at the speed of light to tell all the details to the universe, but not expecting a reply.

She described how they had stripped the woman and put hospital gowns on her, they had strung her up on a wooden cross, with her feet dangling into in a large basin. Gwen explained that the basin was for collecting the blood as it seeped from her body, drop by drop. Micky's only thought, 'she is completely insane!'

"It was done very systematically Father, after arriving at the cabin, we brought our tormentor in, stripped her of her street clothes and dressed her in hospital gowns, even though we were going to kill her, we still wanted to preserve her modesty."

"That's a laugh, that woman slept with anything that came into her crosshairs." "But I digress." 'Then we put two IV lines into her arms, one on the left the other on the right." "One IV-line would carry Heparin into her blood stream to prevent clotting.

In Micky's mind he was thinking, "Why the hell do you need to prevent clotting." As her story was to progress, he would get the answer to that question, and it would almost make him physically sick.

Then Gwen continued on about what would be in the second IV-line, "this line sent Pavulon into her blood stream, so that she was paralyzed, but conscious to hear everything that was said to her." "Also, it would lessen the pain from her punishment, but not completely eliminate it."

"Nothing is pain free in this life Father, but we can lessen the agony."

All I could think at this point was "Dear God, how did they execute her?"

As the storm continued to play havoc with my brain, Gwen continue along in her own world, totally devoid of the knowledge of the emotional impact her story was having on me. Then to my complete shock, she asked the following question, "I hope I have not frightened you too much Micky?"

Frightened me, I feel like a caged animal being readied for the slaughterhouse. However, I said nothing.

"Micky you realize that what I am telling you about, had to happen, we had no choice, you must understand that it was for mankind."

I wanted to scream at her and tell her that those decisions were not up to her, and her orchestra of the disenchanted. If it was a legal matter, it was up to the courts, if not it was up to God when the individual in question died. But my fear of Gwen was too great for me to speak my mind.

I let the storm and Gwen control everything from that point and focused inwardly on my prayers for my own salvation.

Then a some point my salvation seemed to no longer matter, I had to speak.

"What you did was monstrous, you need to repent, you need to go to the police." "You came to tell me this so that you could clear your conscious, knowing I would be powerless to have you brought to justice."

"Gwen you may not receive justice on earth, but someday you will be judge."

"Yes, Father all of this is true, but I need you to listen and not interrupt again." "Understand!"

His reply was simple, "perfectly".

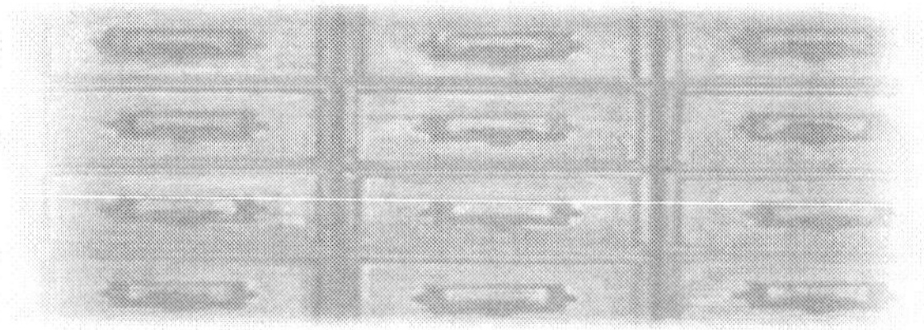

Chapter Forty-Nine

All the elements of the storm continued as did Gwen, it was like the two were in complete simpatico, feeding off of the other's energy, to make everything seem larger than life.

I could only imagine what the cabin was like, probably rustic, a place away from the hectic life of the city, but comfortable. I was sure that in its day before it was used for evil, it had been a getaway, of warmth and peace.

A fireplace with wood logs burning, the fire creating shadows on the walls, and the quiet. Sleeping under warm quilts and reading books. I bet her family never had a television, it would have been bedtime stories around the roaring fire, hot chocolate, treats and then bedtime. What would Gwen's family say if they knew she had turned it into a slaughterhouse, all the goodness removed by a single act? But from what Gwen had said about her family, they were all dead and unable to pass judgement.

She continued with the story of the trial, "I called the court into session and then asked each one of witnesses to give testimony." "Each of the twelve witnesses, spoke about how the 'Dark One' had affected their lives, she had destroyed some careers, other's she had led them down the path of sexual desire, then only thrown them over when she no longer needed them." "They cried Father, when they spoke of their sorrows, at times, the court room would be silent." "Those times gave us, time to gather our thoughts." "After listing her crimes against humanity, I allowed each of the witnesses to give their impact statement." "Father, the evil she had inflicted, left them emotional scarred for life."

"Then we took a vote of the jury, and she was found guilty unanimously."

"Father, everyone sat quiet for about half an hour, not a noise could be heard." "Then I summarized all the testimonies and impact statements, so that the 'Dark One', understood why this was happening to her." "That seem only fair, don't you think?"

What, she is asking me a question? Then thinking quickly, Father Michael said quietly in his head, "careful how you answer Micky, you could be next." Then speaking to Gwen, "yes, Gwen it was good of you to let the person understand why they were in their predicament." "Was she allowed to explain herself?"

"Oh no Father, her mouth was duck taped, so we did not have to hear her lies anymore," was the reply.

To himself, Father Michael thought, I can only imagine the terror this individual felt, double that with the inability to defend, was a nightmare he hoped never happened to him. He had to ask another question, "did the individual see who her accusers were?'

The answer was direct and to the point, "no she was blindfolded, no one wanted to look into her lying eyes."

Again, in his head, but not voiced was the thought, perhaps had they looked into her eyes, they may have seen remorse, and she could still have been alive today.

Don't bring that point up to Gwen, Micky, it could be a trigger.

Again, silence filled the confessional, except for the sounds of the storm, you would have thought the church was empty, then out of the blue Gwen stated. "As judge it was my job to pass the judgement and state the punishment, and I did." "I must admit Father, that deep down inside me that day, I felt sadness, I had never pictured my life coming to this point, and I never thought I would orchestra the taking of another's life, but I guess none of us knows where our lives will lead us."

In his head, Micky was thinking no, we never do truly know what life has in store for us, but hopefully the majority do not kill and have that as their legacy. Then he heard Gwen continuing in her story, speaking as if she was back in the cabin.

"The judgement of this court in its verdict, is that the defendant is found guilty by a jury of her peers and is sentenced to death." "The execution will begin immediately, each of the victims will be allowed to cut the defendant with knives." "When each victim has had their time, the defendant will hang until she has bled out."

Gwen continued on with her monologue, now in the present talking about the past, "What seemed to take hours, was actually only about forty minutes, each victim had their piece of music played while they stated their disdain for the 'Dark One'." "At first the ladies' cuts were shallow and I was thinking at this rate this process could take days, but when the men started, they went more for the major veins, the hospital gowns were completely red from her blood and the pail she was standing in was filling nicely, that would make disposal of the blood more efficient."

"Fifty minutes later the 'Dark One' drew her last breath, it was done, and it was over." "In silent procession the gathering left the room and left to go back to their homes and lives." "I stayed behind to ensure that the final disposal went as plan." "That's all Father."

A cold sweat covered Micky's body, he felt nauseated, fear was gripping every nerve ending and he felt like passing out, but a tiny voice inside his head don't, you will never wake up from this nightmare.

Thinking inwardly, Micky was trying to calm himself. He knew she would be expecting him to question her and try to reach some sort of reasoning about her actions.

Micky sat motionless and concentrated on his breathing, trying to control his heart rate, if felt like it was about to explode out of his chest. He needed to breath, fresh air, not the stagnant air that was filling the confessional.
It was like the stench of death had found its way to this island and encompass his church.

"That's not possible Micky, you are letting your imagination run wild." "Control your thoughts Micky, be practical, you will survive."

With these thoughts now racing through his mind he turned his attention back to Gwen.

Chapter Fifty

"Well Father, that's what happened, it was a day similar to today, heavy rains and winds, the scary sounds of nature." "Thunder cracking and rolling in the distance and moving closer as the storm approaches." "I fine storms both terrifying and exuberating at the same time." "The fear will I be injured by a lightning strike, will it hit a tree, will that tree crush me?" "Will the rains be so heavy, that the river will flood, will the bridge I am driving over be swept away in a torrent of flood waters, could I drown, what would be that experience?" "Then I switch to being invigorated by the storm, the electrical charges in the lightning, making you feel that you have come to life, the blood rushing through your veins, your heart beating to the sound of the raindrops, I become one with nature and I feel all powerful."
These were Gwen's wild statements.

"How do storms affect you, Father?" was her surprising question.

I quickly responded, "I don't think of storms in those terms, more like a fact of life and figuring out the best way to stay safe." "But I understand the need for rain, it refreshes the air and nourishes the earth, but I do hate strong storms that alter peoples' lives." "I guess, I see things differently than you, but that's fine, it certainly would be a boring world if everyone thought the same way." Then to himself, "Safe out Micky."

I wanted to move this conversation along, I knew the storm was still very dangerous, but I also knew that if Gwen got bored, she would leave regardless of the dangers outside.

"You have not asked about the body, Father, why is that?" she asked.

My answer was simple, "I knew you would tell me if you wanted me to know, but I believe you do not."

"Quite right, I do believe for everyone involved, somethings need to be a secret." "You understand, don't you?"

"Yes, I do," was my quick reply.

Then Micky continued, "Gwen at some point you will need to make your way back to the resort, so perhaps we should move this along, no offence."

"None taken, but yes I do want to drive well there is still some daylight," was her reply.

"The next question is obvious Gwen, why are you telling me this now?" Micky asked.

"I want forgiveness Father, and I need to repent, it was only after I saw her life slipping away that I understood the magnitude of our actions. I need God's forgiveness; I will need to spend the rest of my life making restitution for my actions."

"I am glad you want to make it right, but what about the other souls that you took along for the ride, how do you the make their lives right?" "What about their souls, Gwen, how can that be made right?"

"I don't know Father, but I do believe that's their duty to make peace with their God."

"That's it, Father, I think, we are done now." She said as if she was completing an interview.

"Do you still want absolution?" I asked. "You need to make things right." "For everyone you involved in your actions."

"Yes, I am sorry for what I did, and I will spend the rest of my life trying to make it right?"

"Will you go the police?" I asked, worried about what her reply would be, but I was not surprised by her reply.

"No!" That one-word answer.

"Understood" to which I replied in kind.

With those short statements, I heard the door of the church open, it was caught by the wind, slammed against the wall, and I got out of the box and saw that I was by myself, the door was forced open by the wind, and I was unable to close it, which can be done tomorrow.

Chapter Fifty-One

The main doors of the church had been forced open by the winds, and the rain spray was coming in and making the ceramic floors slippery, Father went carefully over and tried to close them, but the wind was just too strong and dealing with Gwen had sapped all of his physical energies.

Sitting on a pew in the middle of the church away from the walls, Father Michael sat quietly reviewing everything he had been told over the last two hours, he felt weak and drained.

How anyone could become that unhappy in their life that they would go to such extreme measures to eliminate their enemy, were his thoughts. Gwen certainly had proved to be an unusual person; he knew he had not truly reached her conscious. She had said all the rights things, but in his heart, Father knew that she felt no remorse at all. Those other souls she had encouraged to commit the greatest mortal sin, and she felt no remorse at all, what had she said, oh yeah,
"I don't know Father, but I do believe that's their duty to make peace with their God."

The coldness of the remark, said it all, she felt absolutely no contrition, no regret, no sorrow and most certainly no self-reproach. One could best describe her with the following words, remorseless, relentless, and ruthless and yes, savage. Then speaking to himself in his head, afraid to speak out loud, I feel numb with the knowledge that for the better part of a year, I sat not two feet away from this woman, and no idea what she was like and capable of doing. I had actually felt sorry for her at times when she spoke about her family, her youth, and her career ups and downs.

Was all of it fantasy, or just a way to get me to believe her? God, did she take me in, Micky you fool, at your age to be taken in by such a con-artist. Looking back to my years of training at the seminary, I don't believe we ever discussed such a personality type, mores the pity. How many other Gwen's are there out in the world committing unspeakable crimes? Do you really want to know Micky? No, I do not.

Sitting quietly listening to the raging storm outside, the eye was gone, but the power of the storm was still playing in his head and was reaching his sub-conscious. Micky turn his body and was looking out the church doors when he heard the sound of a lightning strike, the roaring thunder right on top of the cracking sounds. And there before his eyes he saw one of the larger palm trees begin to sway and then it began its fall to the ground, missing everything, but the ground shook like an earthquake had hit.

Witnessing that power of nature and moving like the speed of light, Micky grabbed his mackintosh and raced across the fifty yards to the presbytery. He was like a running back trying for a touchdown, and his touchdown was getting through the doors unharmed.

To weary to even think of food, Micky grabbed some water and double his anxiety medicine dosage, took it, and then went and laid down. As the medicine kicked in Micky began to fall asleep, but as he was slipping into a deeper sleep, he was dreaming of seeing raindrops falling on the courtyard, but they were the colour of blood. Micky woke up briefly from that dream and whispered the prayer, "Please God allow me to wake up in the morning."

Part Three

“SELF AWARENESS

&

ELIMINATION

Chapter Fifty-Two

After Gwen left the church, she made her way back to the resort, what was usually about a twenty-minute drive, took her over three hours. As always Gwen made it to her desired destination, nothing ever stopped her, and she just went very slowly when required. Gwen was not a fast driver, so nothing ever came up on her quickly, quite the opposite, she was always looking as far ahead as possible. If the visibility was bad, she simply drove slower. What worked out to her advantage was there were no other cars on the road at that time.

The staff were shocked that she had gone out in the storm, but she assured them, that she had not gone far, she explained that she started out, realized it was too dangerous and had pulled the car into an old garage, until she felt it was safe to drive back. Telling them, “it was a stupid thing for me to do, I was never so scared in my life.” “I will never do anything that stupid again.” Gwen returned to her room to dry off and pack.

Tuesday, August 30, the airport reopened and as she had stated Gwendolyn Wahl left the island for Dallas.
Two days later a Kathleen Kennedy arrive in Philadelphia and disappeared in the crowds. No one was on the flight to Puerto Vallarta.

Back in Philadelphia, the retired librarian from the board spent the next few weeks with her apprentice, sending him on her errands. One thing she had done was to buy burner phones, she had never given Jerome her phone number, she had always called him from a pay phone. Telling him from now on they would only communicate using these phones.

Being involved with the criminal elements of society, Jerome realized what a good idea it was for both of them. The strange lady referred to her time as the prelude to the completion of her task.

Her patience paid off at the end of September, a major hurricane was forming in the Atlantic and was tracking towards the eastern seaboard of the United States. Everything had been prepared at the cabin, Jerome had been extremely helpful, and she explained away all the plastic, with a story of major renovations. Three items, she had not asked him to set up were the jury's chairs, her bench or the prisoner's box. That she could handle on her own. Jerome did not ask for details, if he thought the drug and medical purchases strange, he never mentioned it to her. He did wonder why she wanted a container of hydrochloric acid, but he knew she did a lot of scientific experiments, so he let it pass without explanation. Jerome was used to dealing with strange people and strange circumstances, but Ms. O'Hare was different, she had come to his rescue so many times during his school years and even after. He knew for a fact that she was almost completely supporting his mother.

That one day when she was bringing bags of groceries for his mother, they had argued. Ms. O'Hare wanted him to turn his life around, get a job any job, but to stop hanging out with the criminals. The stress was killing his mother. That was in the past, now he was doing Ms. O'Hare's errands, strange as they seemed. Ms. O'Hare would never hurt a fly; I just know she has a good reason for getting these items.

With those thoughts he continued with the shopping lists. The additional items he purchased from the hardware store outlet, were probably for next spring after everything was done, speaking to himself Jerome said, "I bet 'Miss O' has a big party planned for next year, what a great lady, always thinking ahead." Gwen was hoping Jerome had not mention it to anyone else, all of his errands and purchases, and his handy man work. Shortly that would not be a problem, what was the old saying leave no witnesses.

She had requested that Jerome meet her at the cabin on October 5th, just to check everything, plus she wanted to pay him, his bonus. It needed to be that day, she told him as she was leaving for France the next day and had to leave the keys with the contractor.

Gwen walked into the cabin with Jerome and told him how impress she was that he had done everything as per her instructions, "this will make is so much easier for the contractor, thanks Jerome you are the best." "Here's the money I promised you, please do something nice for your mother."

"Also, here is a packet of your favourite, just be careful, someday Jerome you need to quit this stuff, then things will get better." Jerome mumbled his thanks and left the cabin. Just as Gwen had suspected he would not drive far, actual he had driven farther into the woods, she knew what he was about to do. "I just need to wait this out, then this problem will be eliminated."

Gwen knew that the heroin she had given Jerome was laced with fentanyl, after all she had added it from a street purchase, powerful and uncut. Gwen waited for about an hour, then she walked to the parked car it was still running, but its driver was slumped over to the side, sticking out of his arm was the needle, he was already turning cold. His eyes were opened, and the pupils dilated, yes, he was gone, problem solved. Gwen reached into the car and turned it off, and then she reached into his pockets and retrieved the five thousand dollars, and the remaining prepaid credit cards. “How odd, he still has over a thousand dollars left, you were going to get a nice bonus Jerome, well not quite,” were the words she spoke over Jerome’s corpse. Gently she returned his wallet to his pocket, drop his cellphone on the ground beside the car so that it would be affected by the elements of the weather. She also took the burner phone that they had used to communicate with and slipped it in her pocket. She then closed up the car and locked it up, using the automated locks. Gwen was always prepared; she just loved her leather gloves.

Switching to heavy duty work gloves, she covered the car with branches, so that it was invisible from the road, speaking to herself, “its October, it will be spring before it is found.”

As Gwen stood and took one last look at the car, that was, but was not, then she remembered that St. Jerome was the patron saint of librarians. Well, her Jerome was no saint, but he did serve her purpose and came to her aid. Speak about the irony, she thought to herself.

Before leaving for the city, she went back to the cabin shed were there was the container of hydrochloric acid that Jerome had acquired, and she placed both of their burner phones in the acid to destroy them.

"Now it's time to get on with my project, sorry Micky you were just the dress rehearsal, now it will in fact be the real thing." As she was speaking these thoughts to herself, she knew she had absolutely no remorse in her heart, mind, and soul.

Chapter Fifty-Three

Friday, October 7th, Darcy was leaving for her trip to the Bahamas, as was her custom; she was leaving her car in the underground garage at the board offices. Sitting in the grey van beside Darcy's car on the car's drivers' side, was Gwen. Speaking to herself, "it's now or never Gwen, stay strong." These were Gwen's thoughts and words as she sat in the underground waiting patiently.

Keeping to her established habits, at two o'clock, Darcy exited the elevator and walked to her car, to get her suitcase. Her failing, she never paid attention to anything that did not interest her if she had she would have wondered why the van was parked beside her car. As always, she was too busy with her own thoughts to take in anything, as she reached her car, she felt a stabbing in her neck and then just darkness.

Gwen tossed Darcy into the side door of the van, closed it up and drove out of the garage, no one bothered with her. Just another delivery van in their boring day. Gwen's luck was with her, the only cameras for the underground were at the exit doors, and the elevator doors at the garage level. The cameras did not cover every inch of the actual underground, thinking to herself, 'that will probably change in the future. But today everything was good for Gwen.

It took over three hours to reach the cabin, because of the rain, not a heavy downpour, but the roads were slippery. It was also slower because Gwen was not using the main roads but instead the seldom used county roads. Reason being that there were no traffic cameras. Knowing that the rain would increase in a day, because of Hurricane Matthew making landfall off the Carolinas in the next twelve hours, Gwen's timing was to recreate the sense she felt during the hurricane on the island. Matthew would be a huge storm, at its height a category five.

Lots of rain for the next few days. There will be rain at the cabin, perhaps not to the intensity during her confession to Father Michael, but rain on the roof no less. Also, the bad weather should keep most people away from the cottages and certainly off the lake. "I cannot be seen dropping body parts into the lake, while other boaters are out and about." "Everything is working in your favour Gwen, enjoy."

Chapter Fifty-Four

At first, Darcy woke up and felt nauseated, still in a fog, she had no idea where she was, or what was happening to her. The last thing she remembered was going into the parking garage, after that nothing. What was happening, she could not see, someone had blindfolded her, was this a prank, not funny? This was so Jonathan and his buddie's idea of a joke; the last twelve years being married to the imbecile had been dreadful. The only reason she stayed with him was to ensure she kept her job, her beautiful home and of course the wealth and all the privileges it brought. The Shanahan's knew her well, they knew she would put up with anything for prestige.

At least Jonathan didn't keep track of her, so she was free to pursue her own past times. The rule was always to be discrete. Feeling the heat of the room, Darcy was beginning to sweat and feel even worse as time went by, she could hear nothing, it was like being in a vacuum, and all she could hear was her own breathing and heartbeat.

Both of her arms had a tingling sensation, it felt like needles stuck into her arms, by why both. Her skin had the feeling of being covered by a piece of material, but she felt she had no undergarments on, what the hell was happening?

Thinking to herself, “I don’t feel like I am laying down, I feel like I am upright. I cannot move a single muscle, yet I am feeling the pain of my arms outstretched and tied to something. My feet are in something that is either steel or ceramic, it is so cold, and my feet feel frozen.” “Oh my God, I feel like I am being crucified.

As fear was entering Darcy head, she could hear music being played, did she recognize that piece, and yes, she had heard it many times when passing the library office. How she hated their choice of music, but what was the name, she had asked Cecilia what it was once, what had she said, yes, now she remembered Pachelbel’s Canon in D major. Why did libraries always play classical music?

In what seemed like an eternity, the music just kept playing on, it was as if the person had put the recording on a loop, it would reach the end and then start all over again. The confusion was building in her head, and she tried moving her body, but it was like a dead weight, she could feel her skin crawling, but nothing moved. The heat of the room was causing her to perspire, the water was running down over her skin, in a way it was cooling her, but then the heat on her skin returned and the misery was even harder to endure.

Slowly the volume of the music was lowered and then a voice from her past spoke, and every fibre of her being knew this was no joke, but probably the end of her life.

"Well hello Darcy, so surprise to see you so casually dressed, dungeon green hardly suits you." "And Darcy, I can just imagine what you are saying now in your head, "Kathleen are you insane?" "And of course, the answer is no, I am just following Machiavelli's advice, which is as follows." "If an injury has to be done to a man, it should be so severe that his vengeance need not be feared." "I kind of like that quote, don't you, after all you inflicted terrible injuries to so many people." Gwen voice was calm as she made her statements of fact, "and that leads to our next quote, you should love this one." "No enterprise is more likely to succeed than one concealed from the enemy until it is ripe for execution."

"Welcome Darcy Shanahan to your execution." "And yes, that removes the threat of your vengeance."

Unable to move and unable to speak, all Darcy could do was go over everything in her own mind and realized that her time was running out, but why, at least have the decency to tell me the truth.

Again, as if reading her mind, Gwen spoke, her very thoughts, "so you want to know why and you feel that you deserve an explanation, what you would say, oh yes, please have the decency to tell me why." Gwen was now mocking her.

Then Gwen began to tell her about what was going to happen, to Darcy her voice sounded like she was doing a lecture for an audience, but she realized that she was the audience.

"Darcy let me explain, what is happening, you have been found guilty of high crimes and misdemeanours and sentenced to death." "After four years I have reviewed all of your crimes against humanity, you have committed and I have presented it to a jury of twelve, and they have condemned you to death." "But we will hold a complete trial, with witnesses and then you will be found guilty, and I will have the great pleasure of passing the sentence." "After all, you are entitled to due process and to hear your accusers in a court of law."

With such incredible calm Gwen switched topics and continued on a new path of facts.

"Let me describe the room to you, it is completely covered in plastic, that is maybe why you feel so hot, the windows are open, but don't worry, no one can hear you." "On that note, don't you just love duct tape?"

"We have two rows of six chairs, they are for the jury, and by the way, they are also the witnesses at your trial. Very neat and compact, on the other side is the judge's bench, that is where I will be seated." "And you, alas dear Darcy, are in the prisoner's box, or in your case the execution box as we have already strung you up on your cross."

Horrified by what she was hearing, Darcy was screaming in her head to herself, "this woman is insane, surely someone will come to save me."

Again, Gwen read her mind, "No Darcy, I am not insane, and no one is coming to save you, what can you expect when all you left in your wake was a trail of destruction."

A trail of destruction you say, yes definitely, lost hopes, broken spirits, individuals left with the complete sense of unworthiness. Yes, you alone did this to your staff, no remorse for what you did to them. Each person being labeled and added to your catalogue of redundancy.

You took away their sense of worth and declared them redundant to themselves and the world.

SHAME ON YOU! DARCY!

Chapter Fifty-Five

The music had been turned up and it continued on its loop, driving Darcy into a mental frenzy.

Between hearing the same music over and over again, the sweat crawling along her skin, not being able to see anything, Darcy was beginning to feel tears welling up in her eyes. Her arms and legs were dead weight, she could not move a muscle, and to herself she asked what they are giving me to cause all these sensations.

As abruptly as the music had started, it stopped, the silence was now deafening, and then a new piece of music began to play, a sense of deep sadness and sorrow came over Darcy, she knew that piece, Moonlight Sonata. This is not a bad dream, but her reality.

The music played on and on, leaving Darcy to remember so many things about her past. She had always been selfish, difficult to get along with and yes, she had to admit it, she had been a very cruel individual.

Could she had done better by her staff, yes. Calling them redundant was cruel, she realized, but surely that was the terminology used when staff was no longer required by the company. "I had no idea that the power of that word could be so damaging to individuals, redundant fine in the dictionary. But as an individual was faced with that word about their own existence and life, it was so cruel and unfeeling. I had been the head of human resources and yet I now was seeing I was anything by humane.

With those thoughts passing through her mind, she turned her attention back to what was being said by others. As Darcy listened for any indication of what was happening, she heard Kathleen call the court to order, what did she say, "Court is in session."

Then Kathleen explained that there were twelve witnesses, who would testify and give their impact statements, the jury would decide her guilt and then the judge would pass judgement and state what would be the punishment.

After her opening remarks, the twelve ghostly witnesses came into the cabin single file and silently took their seats, waiting for their instructions from the judge. And with that pronouncement the judge called on the first witness.

Chapter Fifty-Six

Gwen realized that at any time, they could be discovered, so she had thought ahead of time of how to move the proceedings along. Using those ideas, she stated to the witnesses the following, "Each witness will give evidence of the injustice committed against them, by the defendant, the witness will speak of only one, the most insipid act and how it impacted their lives. She had planned ahead of time also to group them together based on the music piece they had requested be played while they spoke.

The first group up had requested that Chopin's Nocturne #20 in C sharp be played, these included Rebecca, Giselle, Everett, and Claudia. Thinking to herself as the music began to play, "this music has a haunting sound, which speaks of separation, loneliness, and moments of hope only to return to its haunting sounds that speak of a quiet desperation of man." Left with those disquietly thoughts, Gwen moved ahead with the proceedings. The music playing gave Darcy the creeps, it sounded so withdrawn, she could not relate to the sounds, but then she began to hear the first person and she understood that she was on the losing end of this proceeding. Thinking in her mind, "you cannot win against deep seated hatred, you can only endure."

It was at this point Gwen made a change in the scenario; she removed the duct tape from Darcy's mouth. Knowing that no one would hear her speak, she decided that this would send Darcy into a fit every time someone spoke, but they would ignore her words.

The Gwen spoke to the group, "I have removed the duct tape from Ms. Shanahan's mouth, so she can breathe more easily, however no one is to reply to her questions or statements." "She has had her say for the last twelve years, now it is time for her to listen to her catalogue of the redundant." "She needs to know that you are living people who had goals, dreams and hopes." "You are not redundant to mankind, but you are children of God." "Do you understand that Ms. Shanahan, they are not redundant, they are all God's children." "Something you forgot about on your quest for power, while we are here to remind you now." The Gwen spoke, "I call upon Ms. Rose to give her statement."

And with that, the witness came forward and began to speak, "You found out my sexual orientation and used it against me, you told me you loved me during those times we were together, yet you continued to sleep with others."
"You stole my dignity and left me friendless; no one would associate with me at work, because of you." "You made me

one of your spies and then you discarded me like yesterday's newspaper." "I have lost my will to live and will never get it back." "I am too damaged to go on living." Then Rebecca left the stand, sobbing quietly for she knew she would end it all when this was over.

Darcy screamed out to Rebecca, "I did love you in my own way", but it was met with silence.

Waiting a moment for calmness Gwen called the next witness, "I call Ms. Vander to testify."

And with that, Giselle came forward and took her place at the stand. "You saw my weakness, you manipulated me into shameful acts, and we became lovers." "We committed adultery, the result was I lost my husband and my children, you destroyed my life, and I was stupid enough to allow you to do that to me, because I was afraid of losing my job." "Rot in hell Darcy." And with that brief statement Giselle returned to her chair.

"Wait Giselle, I did feel for you, you know your husband was not for you, I just helped you realize it." Darcy's outburst was met again with silence.

As if nothing horrible had been said Gwen called the next person, "I call Mr. Brown to give his statement."

Then Everett spoke, "you knew my secret, and used it against me, you created a work environment that was filled with hatred and prejudices." "I gave up all of my personal life to keep my job." "And for what, you prevented me from ever advancing in my chosen career."

"Thanks to your cruelty, I became a heavy drinker and smoker, now I face my diagnosis of pancreatic cancer, I will not survive, but neither will you." And with those emotions Everett left the stand and returned to his chair.

"Everett, I did care, but you were drinking long before you knew me, so you cannot blame me for your drinking problem." Again, the silence was deafening to Darcy's outburst.

As if she was an automated machine, Gwen continued with the proceedings, "I now call Ms. Gordon to the stand."

Claudia walked to the stand using her walker, she made a point of dragging it along the floor so Darcy could hear the noise. "Yes, Darcy I use a walker, all those times I needed to go to see the doctor, you said I was faking it, guess what Darcy I was not, I have a form of MS, and had I done what the doctors had told me, maybe I could have slowed it progression." "You made my life at the board a living hell, my only consolation is that you will soon be in the real hell. Slowly and with purpose Claudia made her way back to her chair making sure that Darcy heard the walker scrapping along the floor as she went.

Darcy screamed, "lies, all lies, none of you are being truthful." Again, her outburst was met with dead silence.

Gwen called for a five-minute break now that the first group of witnesses had said their piece.

During that time, the cabin was completely silent, Darcy wondered what was happening. Were they having second thoughts, did they not see the insanity of their actions?

Praying to herself, begging for forgiveness, here she was bargaining with God, "I promise God, if I live through this, I will change my life around, I will try to make amends for all the hurt I have caused." "Please God, I am begging you to rescue me."

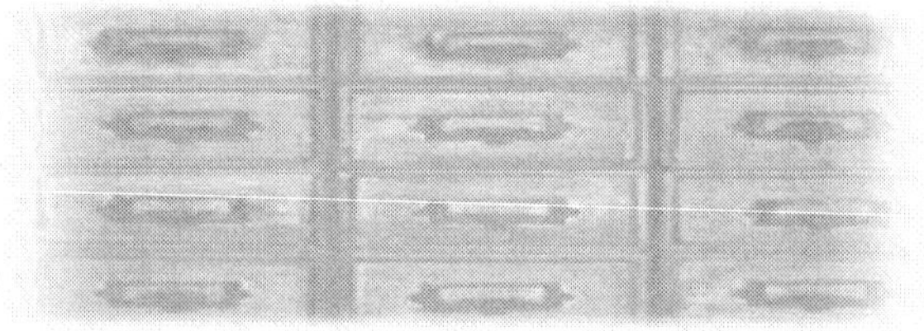

Chapter Fifty-Seven

After the five minutes, Gwen called everyone to return to their chairs, "please return to your chairs as the proceeding will continue shortly." She told the group that the next piece of music requested was Barber's Adagio. As the music began a solemn silence went through the group.

The music for this group of individuals spoke of sadness, the end of life, reflections of the past of the individuals, with an acceptance of their fates. Some of the notes spoke of a glimmer of hope for the future, life in the hereafter, the need for a person to lay bare their soul to the universe.

Gwen now called up the next person who was to bare their soul and speak of their heartbreak, "I now call Ms. Gregory to the stand."

Cecilia made her way to the witness stand, a broken woman, but when she spoke it was with a passion, that she had never used before. "Darcy, you knew that a horrible thing had been put in my personnel file, and you did nothing about it, you left me to doubt myself throughout my whole career." "Why could I never get a full-time position, and then to find out a false accusation of child molestation, which everyone knew was false, but you never corrected it?" "How could you leave a person to live their whole life with a false accusation and never make an effort to make it right?"

"Your answer was to condemn me to the basement of the building, with no windows, nothing."
"And to make it worse, I had to watch you destroy one of my only friends." "Your actions left me empty and void of the will to live." "No one should have the right to destroy another human being." And with her direct comments to Darcy, Cecilia left the stand and returned to her chair.
Darcy did not speak to Cecilia at this time, finally she was feeling guilt.

Without missing a beat, Gwen called the next person, "I call Ms. Strange to the stand."
"Emily moved to the stand swiftly and with propose, she quickly took her place and began her tirade against Darcy. "Yes, I slept my way to the top, but I put up with a lot of abuse in doing so, more than you could ever imagine, but then you took Melvin away from me." "I made one mistake, so you took away my career." "I am not proud of how I got ahead, but I never pretended otherwise." "You used my personal failings to persecute me and then you took away my job, and then you sent me to the hell school in the city." "I am now an alcoholic, it's the only way, I can cope." "How I wished you had seen my problems and my potential, and moved me to a better career path, but your jealousy prevented you from coming to another woman's aid."

"Shame on you Darcy, shame." And with her emotions at the boiling point Emily left the stand and returned to her seat.

Darcy spoke, but no one replied, "I did try to help, but you were to blind by your own guilt, that you failed to see the purpose in my actions.

Gwen was beginning to feel the need to speed up the process, so she called the next person, "I now call Ms. Michaels to the stand."

Dolores came to the stand, but was flustered, her anxiety was getting the better of her, but she finally spoke up, "Darcy you knew I suffered from anxiety, you persecuted me for it every day." "You would not allow me the sick time I needed, now I will be financially challenge until the day I die." She had so much more she wanted to say, but speaking in front of any group made her so nervous, so she simply left the stand and went back to her seat.

Again, Darcy remained silent, lost in her own thoughts about what her own fate.

Keeping to her timeline, Gwen called her next witness, "I call Mr. James to the stand."

Heath came forward, stumbling as he walked, when he got to the stand, he leaned on it to hold himself up. "Darcy, I became your lover to keep my job, I can say I never

loved you." "All those times it was for my career, and then when you no longer needed me you cast me aside."
"The consequence of my actions in trying to keep up with you, was simply, I became a total alcoholic, and to make you happy I did cocaine with you." "My body is that of a person twice my age, I can never have a family like regular people." "I will die alone." Stumbling Heath made his way back to his seat.

When Darcy spoke to Heath is was with anger, "You never love me, you bastard."
Heath never responded to her outburst.

Gwen left the angriest person for the last from this group to speak, "I call upon Mr. Carson to take the stand."
Carson came forward, took his place, and began his rant. "You made me out to be a boorish imbecile, you never backed me up when we were dealing with difficult students." "You falsify the accounts of Jerome Smith, so that he was not expelled from school." "Why, because he was your drug source?" "You put the entire school community at risk to feed you own drug habit, you are a selfish bitch." "Then you did everything you could to get me fired, so I would lose my pension." "The union saved my pension, but no one could save my good name and reputation." "This is the only

satisfaction I will get out of life is seeing you killed off."
"Rot in hell bitch."
And with those profound words Carson made his way back to his seat.

Darcy's respond to Carson was swift and to the point, "you can rot in hell yourself, you old bastard."

Nine people had spoken of their difficult lives and how Darcy had impacted them. Gwen sensed that they needed a rest, so she called for a five-minute break.
To Darcy, her life was flashing in the front of her mind, and all she could say to herself, "Lies, all Lies." In her mental rant of her own, Darcy called them all liars and losers.
"You are all liars, losers, the redundant individuals of the human race." "It's a proven fact that people who need all this understanding, will take their own lives eventual. So, take yours and let me get on with mine."

What so angered Darcy was that this group of losers would hear her thoughts and words but refused to respond. It was like they were not listening to her; it was like they were not even there. Here she was tied to a wooden cross, her body exposed, her dignity invaded, and they are feeling sorry for themselves. Speaking to herself out loud, "At least when I did things to you, I did not take away your physical dignity."

"Your decisions to be weak, were yours and yours alone." In her thinking Darcy still had not recognized that her actions towards other had brought her to this time and place. Denial was all that could be said regarding her circumstances.

Darcy was now moving between anger towards the group and still trying to bargain with God for her life.
"Please God, make them see reason, and get them to realize that they are wrong, I can make it better." "Oh, just give me the chance."

Chapter Fifty-Eight

Gwen had put on the next piece of music and called all to return to their seats. The piece that these final witnesses would hear while they were speaking to Darcy, was Albinoni's Adagio.

A musical piece that spoke to the deep sadness and sorrow of the assembly. There was a sense of frustration, deep emotions, almost an end-of-life story. Also, to the assembly listening to it created the sense that they would stay in a state of non-stop mourning, going about their days like robots until death called them by name.

Gwen's sense of urgency was building so she quickly called the next person, "I now call upon Ms. Pesto to take the stand."

And with that request Livia came forward to take her place. Not one to stay in the background anymore, she started right away, "for ten years I was Melvin's secretary, not only was he a complete asshole, but you were his enabler." "I thought when you came to the school, you would sort him out, and instead you turned your back on all the staff, particularly the female staff by becoming his lover." "How could we ever get justice; the odds were against us." "When you thought I was a threat, because I knew too much you made me, your secretary at head office." "It was like

jumping from the frying pan into the fire." "I kept so many of your secrets, but you abused me daily." "Every day you found fault with my work; nothing was ever good enough for your royal hinny." "Every day I came to work was hell, I became so unpleasant that my marriage collapsed."
"All of my family could not deal with who I had become, so I was left a lonely bitter woman." "I spit on you; hell is too good for you." Knowing that she was losing control, Livia stormed back to her seat, with not another word towards Darcy.

Darcy had so many things she wanted to say to Livia, but she knew they would fall on deaf ears, so she remained silent.

Gwen called her next witness, "I now call Mr. Jones to take the stand."

With that pronouncement Mark walked to the stand. A big, towering man, who had frightened everyone over years not because of his size, but because of his unpredictable behaviour. Your friend one day, your enemy the next. Mark had been diagnosed as a manic-depressive in earlier years, his was fine when he took his medicine, but that was not every day, and those were the days you avoided him like the plague.

Then he spoke, "Darcy I know that this trial is for you but there are others in this room, who should be right there beside you in the prisoner box, but I am told it is you we are dealing with today." "You abused me because of my disability, you made me the laughingstock of the school, your actions and words isolated me from the other staff." "But for me the worst thing you did was destroy my one good friend Kathleen O'Hare, why, I can only imagine, jealousy." "When you destroyed my friends, you made a bitter enemy out of me." "Some enemies need to be terminated." With that proclamation, Mark returned to his seat.

Darcy, remained in shocked silence, she knew it was Mark who had planned all this, he was the only one who would have the physical strength to do the manual work required.

Keeping with her timing, Gwen continued, "I now call our last witness Mr. Kirkpatrick."

Melvin made his way to the stand, avoiding Mark and Livia. Surprisingly to everyone, for what can only be assumed a first in his whole life, Melvin kept his speech short and to the point.

"Darcy my affair with you made me the laughingstock of the entire board, I lost all credibility with my staff." "I lost my life and my sense of dignity." "I lost everything for absolutely nothing." "My mistake, but this time I will make no mistakes." Finally turning towards the group, but not looking at them, he spoke to Darcy as if she was somewhere in space. "If they thought I was a narcissistic asshole, then they truly never knew you." "You took narcissism to a whole new level of depravity." "And when I no longer served your purpose, you sent me to the hell school." "The end result was I lost my wife, my children, my whole existence." "Your very existence destroyed my existence."

And with that proclamation of his life, Melvin returned to his seat, looking at no one, why because he knew every one of the other twelve witnesses hated him to their very bones.

"Speaking back towards Darcy, he yelled, "You have left me an empty shell, to be discarded when the time comes."

Darcy yelled out to the room, "well it takes one narcissistic bastard to recognize another narcissistic bastard." "Yes Melvin, bastard to bastard, you were the bigger narcissist," and with that proclamation Darcy went silent.

It was at this point Gwen stopped all the music and let the room go silent.

The silence overpowered all present, Darcy, the orchestra of the disenchanted and Gwen.

Gwen had now turn over the cabin to nature, to let the natural sounds envelope it and its inhabitants. A symbolism of purification for the entire scene, both the living and the non-living. This was to prepare the cabin for what was to come next in the procedures of Darcy's trial.

Gwen had collected dry sage and started a small fire in a pot. She let the sage burn; the aroma filled the cabin. This was part of Gwen's purification process for all the living and the dead.

Chapter Fifty-Nine

Turning off all the music, the only sound the entire assembly heard was the rain hitting the roof of the cabin, and the sounds of the wind blowing hard outside. The wind was blowing through the open windows, cooling the room, and adding relief for everyone. The wall of plastic had made the room stuffy and uncomfortable for all. The smell of human sweat was making everything horrible and disgusting. The burning sage had added to the stuffiness of the room, making breathing hard for everyone. Gwen now wanted to bring this entire proceeding to a rapid end.

After what seemed like and eternality to Darcy, Gwen called for a vote from the jury, "I ask now that each member of the jury give their verdict at this time, I will call each member, one at a time." "Your answer will be either guilty or not guilty" "Thank you and now we will begin." Gwen had called on each jury member, "How does the jury find the defendant?" To which each reply "Guilty"

It was after the call for the vote of guilty, that Gwen replaced the duct tape back over Darcy's mouth. She knew that she could no longer stand the sound of Darcy's voice. She needed to silence it now, although within the hour it would be silenced forever.

Darcy heard the pronouncement, but in her head, she was pleading not guilty, but she realized that no one could hear her. “Was this a true trial or a kangaroo court, does it matter, I am still going to die, but how?” were Darcy’s thoughts to herself.

Again, Darcy tried bargaining with God, but she was beginning to feel that it was too late for her.

“I am sorry, please forgive me!”

Chapter Sixty

And then there was a break in the proceedings, the room went completely quiet. Darcy was so thankful that the dreadful music had been silenced. In her mind, she began to speak to each one of her accusers, she knew they could not hear her, but it all had to be said.

"I am in no physical position to help myself and I know I am not leaving this room alive, but for my own mental peace before I die, I will tell the universe in my head how I feel."

"Melvin, you called me a narcissistic bitch, and yes, you are right, I am all that and more, but I did care for you, if only for a fleeting moment in time." "That being said Melvin, you were a piece of work too, and your whole world revolved are you." If others did not do your bidding, you persecute them, look at how many of your staff are in the room, at this very minute." I bet none of them spoke to you, did they?" "That being said, Melvin the greater narcissistic bitch is Kathleen O'Hare, she had manipulative all of you to do her bidding, regardless of the consequences to all of you." "I could see over the years, that I worked with her that she was changing, her mental outlooks be becoming more perverted, she became more distant and colder." "Reality for her was becoming blurred, if I could have diagnosed her, I would say she suffered from Dissociative Identity Disorder.

Letting loose in her head, Darcy began to eviscerate the rest of the witnesses, her anger and venom came out, had anyone heard her actual words, they would be shocked. Such cold bitterness towards others, no empathy, no compassion, just pure unadulterated hatred.

Darcy began her mental monologue, "and now for the rest of you pathetic losers, there is not one of you worth a moment of my time, actually the only person I could really connect with was Kathleen, smart, beautiful, and a worthy opponent." "Rebecca, you say no one talked to you because of me, no one talked to you because you had the most repugnant antisocial personality I had ever encountered." "No one talked to you, because of you!"

"So, Mark, I made your life difficult, you were the most dangerous person, I ever dealt with, when you tampered with the Freon line for the school air conditioner, and the contractors said it was done deliberately." "You could have caused major damaged, but I covered for you and said that school had been dealing with a lot of vandalism." "The Board bought my explanation, and you kept your job." "You're welcome."

"Now to my eternal victims, it's not my fault you had terrible childhoods, so did I, but I didn't let it interfere with my goals." "Instead of trying to get everyone's sympathy, you could have used those energies to do a better job."

"Claudia, you have health issues, who doesn't, you had the summers off, to see doctors and get yourself on a healthy tract for life." "You had full medical benefits, so you could have gone for any therapy you wanted." "But not you, you took satisfaction out of complaining, it was your way of drawing attention to yourself, the attention you so desperately wanted.

"Dolores, my pill popping friend, was there ever a pill, you did not like." "Stop complaining, anxiety my foot, the pills were candy to you." "Well others on staff turned to alcohol and hard-core drugs, you fell in love with prescription meds, why not your drug plan covered it all." "At lease the alcoholics paid for their pleasures out of their take home pay." "Dolores you were a leach on the system, and all I did was make you take responsibility for your own pleasures."

"Alas we come to Heath, always the victim, your mommy did not give you enough attention, because in bed, you were a very demanding baby." "Did you ever wonder why I always had to do a line or two of cocaine before sleeping with you, it was to kill the urge to suffocate you." "If that was not enough, your paranoid behaviour would drive a sober person to drink." 'Oh, what was it now, yes, I remember, everyone is watching me, no one likes me, and the best they are all trying to sabotage my work." "No, Heath, you sabotaged your own career, you cannot blame anyone else but yourself."

Not sure if it was the heat in the room, or Darcy's cravings, she became more vicious in her internal rant. "And now to my paranoid individuals, your downfalls were of your own making." "Being so paranoid, you never truly took the time to understand what was happening to you." "It was always someone else's fault that your lives fell apart." "No, my dear friends, your paranoid personality disorders are what destroyed you."

"Everett, everyone knew you were gay, no one cared, and really we all called you the dancing queen." "Who did you think you were kidding?" "No, your career did not advance because of your sexual orientation, but rather that you just were the worst teaching assistant on the payroll." "Most of the classes you were assigned, complained, they said you spent so much time on the computer, and you never assisted the students." "The very reason for which you were hired, but we could not fire you, because we could not trust you, and we did not want a lawsuit."

"Giselle, who are you kidding, you came to my bed, because your husband was not meeting your needs, don't blame me for that." "That decision was all yours, so the failure of your marriage is your fault not mine." "And the fear about your job, bullshit, you were good at your work, but it was your own self-doubt that was responsible for your failures."

"My precious Livia, you are a backstabbing bitch, you spent every working day trying to bring down Melvin, because he was not interested in you." "I saw those quick side glances, when you thought no one was watching." "It obviously made your blood boil when you found out the Melvin and I were having a fling." "Did you really think Melvin would ever think of you in those terms?"

"A frumpy middle-aged woman, with a husband and two children in tow, not likely."

"By the way, I moved you to head office, at Melvin's request, you gave him the creeps and he wanted you out of his sight." "I am not the reason your marriage fell apart, look in the mirror bitch, the only person responsible for that disaster is you."

"Finally, my passive aggressive what a piece of work you two are, stabbing in the back while being polite to people's faces.

"Mr. Carlton, oh yes, Carson, you are a boorish imbecile." "If we had ever you placed in a school where the parents knew better, you would have cost the school board millions in lawsuits." "You physically and mentality abused our students, and you got away with it for years." "I would like to take credit for the removal of Jerome Smith's internet history, but it was not me." "That being said, I am glad he did not get expelled, because of you, I would never have let you have the satisfaction." "You are the very definition of a monster, kind and passive in front of others, but when alone with the vulnerable, you were a sadistic aggressive fiend." "I would have done anything to stop you." Darcy's final respond to Carson was swift and to the point, "you can rot in hell you old bastard."

"And last, but not least Cecilia, Miss nice to everyone, Miss Congeniality, Miss 'the biggest' Backstabbing Bitch ever. Always a passive person, agreeing with everyone, but what those saps did not know was that the other side of you, 'Miss Aggression', ratted everyone out to me." "You would be the last person, I would leave in charge of a classroom, so no I would never remove that accusation from your file." "If I had children, in no way would I let you teach them, not because you molested a child, but because of your sick twisted priorities."

"I wonder how, my jailer and our esteem judge would feel, if she ever found out that you told me everything that went on in library services." "No, I don't think you would want her to know, otherwise the next person on trial would be you."

Getting it out of her system, gave Darcy temporary relief, but she realized it had not changed her current circumstances.

"And to all you idiots, everything that happened at the board, was determined the higher ups, I was merely their tool to carry out their wishes.

"The blame for all your misfortunes lies with not only your own shortcomings, but with the Shanahan's."

"I was forced to reduce the work force to cover up for their financial decisions that were a disaster." "You are condemning an innocent woman; it should be Grandmother Shanahan here not me."

With that mental excretion, Darcy felt drain of all energies. She merely let her head hang and closed her eyes behind the blindfold. Darcy knew she had won many battles, but in the end, she lost the war.

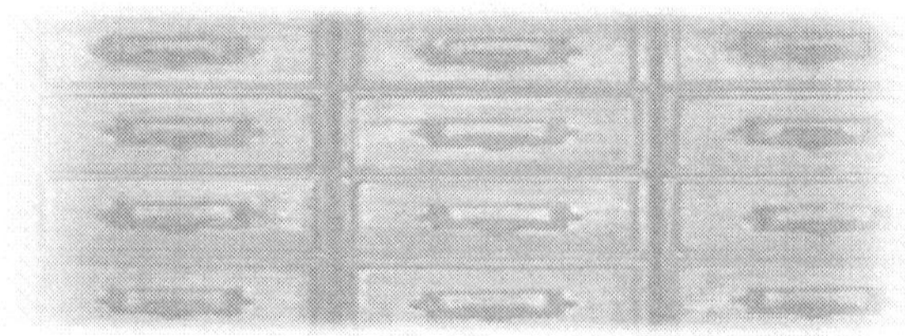

Chapter Sixty-One

After a ten-minute break Gwen called everyone to return to the court room. Gwen took about another ten minutes to do a summation of all evidence that was submitted. Speaking to the room Gwen said, “All the evidence shows that the defendant is guilty beyond a reasonable doubt.”

“The sentence is death, and the execution will commence immediately.

Gwen then called each executioner to come forward and exact their due. “I will call each individual who had presented evidence today to come forward, take one of the weapons on the table to cut the prisoner.” “The prisoner’s execution will be death by exsanguination, so I ask to you to cut into the body, but not the main arteries.”

As Darcy’s was hearing those words, a new horror filled her mine, “what type of monster cuts a person to death?” “This is something out of a horror movie.” “I cannot believe these people are capable of do this to another human being.” “Kathleen what kind of sick psychopath have you become?”

Gwen stated, “I ask that the women form a line in the following order, Dolores, Cecilia, Giselle, Claudia, Livia, Emily and Rebecca.” “Each one of you may make between five and ten cuts." "When you have finished, please return to your chairs."

Each one of the women followed Gwen's orders, some were very weak, and their cuts hardly drew blood. Gwen was thinking, thank God, I have Heparin going through the IV-line, so her blood will not clot. In what seem like an eternity the women finally finished.

In Darcy's mind because of the drugs, "I am not feeling a lot of pain, but I can feel the fluid flowing across my skin." "It feels warm, oh no, it's my blood."

Then Gwen called on the men, "I now ask the gentleman to continue the execution." "Everett, Heath, Carson, Mark and Melvin when you're ready."

The men proved to much more effective in opening up Darcy's body to let the blood out, Everett and Heath added some wounds, but when their time came, Carson, Mark and Melvin were much more aggressive with their cutting. To Gwen a good description would be almost animal like, it was like wild animals tearing apart their prey.

Darcy was screaming in her head, "stop, please stop, please God take me soon."

Forty minutes later they had completed their task and awaited their next instruction. Gwen waited five more minutes, then stated, "Ladies and gentlemen of the jury, you are now relieved of your duties, the court thanks you for your time."

And with that the twelve ghostly figures left the room in a single line in the same complete silent manner in which they had entered the cabin.

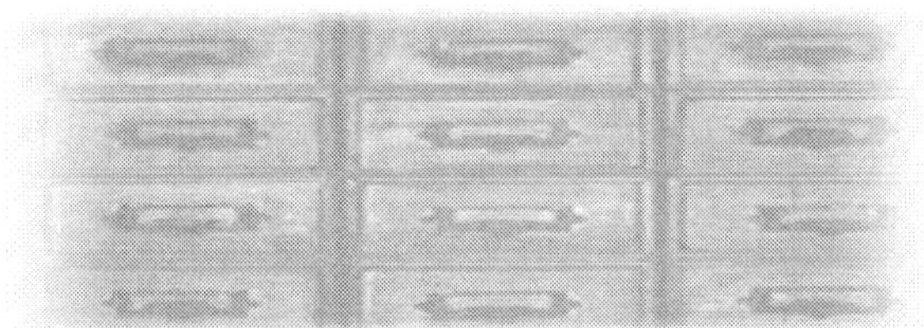

Chapter Sixty-Two

In what were to be Darcy's final moments, she heard in her head Puccini's La Boheme, the only opera she ever liked. Darcy could feel her life slipping away. Again, she reviewed what was said to her, she proclaimed her innocence to the universe, for only the universe could hear her.

"I am innocent, I was merely the tool for others, I carried out their wishes, yes for selfish reasons, but for my own survival." "I never really meant to harm anyone, but I did not know of any other way to protect myself and my family."

Darcy could feel a hand cup her head as she opened her eyes for one last time, the blindfold had been removed. Darcy was looking directly into Kathleen's eyes. In them was sorrow, joy and for a fleeting moment Darcy detected regret. Kathleen was holding her head gently, did she hear her saying a prayer, and it was so faint, that she could not tell.

Her final thought "I am the victim here; everyone was always against me."

And with the final thought Darcy slipped into the sleep of death.

Chapter Sixty-Three

As silently as they had come into the cabin, the twelve ghostly witnesses left in a single file, gone into the darkness of the night, the rain falling on them and from the cabin the haunting sounds of Beethoven's Claro De Luna. However, there was no moonlight to light their path away into their own worlds, only complete darkness for both the body and the soul.

Inside thc cabin was the scene of the court and the execution room as one. Darcy tied up, her head slumped down and the basin filled with her blood. There was no moonlight in this room either, just the glare of spotlights, which laid bare the horror of what had taken place in building. There were no soft moonlight beams to remove the image of death only bright lights that showed the reality of the day's work.

Gwen sat at her bench and looked across at Darcy, studied her and how she was positioned. Then she got up and walked over to Darcy, gently lifted her head, and watched as Darcy's pupils dilated, then she allowed the head to fall back down.

Gwen returned to her bench and congratulated herself on a job well down, a moment later she recognized that she had crossed over to the dark side and was no different than Darcy. Then she spoke out loud to the empty room Machiavelli's quote, "The end justifies the means." But in her mind, she now questioned that statement, maybe the end could never justify the means?

Then quite to her surprise, Gwen broke down in tears and cried so loud, that had anyone been near the cabin, they would have come in, to see if she was alright. But lucky for her, no one was around for miles.

Gwen recognized that her tears were for so many things, a loss of innocence, that her actions would forever change the course of her life. There was no going back, why had she not listened to Micky, he was right, this action did not make her feel better. After an hour or two, Gwen realized that she still had work to do and so she went about her actions as if in a trance. Giving thanks for the programs Forensic Files and Dexter, she went about the disposal of Darcy and all evidence with little or no thought as to the details, they were automatic.

Chapter Sixty-Four

In the wee hours of the morning a single boat went out into the middle of lake using a trolling motor. The rain coming down had created a curtain of darkness, so that if someone was on the shore, they would not see what was taking place on the lake.

As items went overboard, there were small splashes on the surface of the water, but with the winds and rain, they were soon lost from hearing and vision. As quietly as the boat had entered the water and moved across the lake, it was returned to its dock. A lone figure emerged from the boat and tied it up to the dock, checked every detail, so that nothing looked disturbed, then the lone figure headed into the woods.

Several properties later along the shoreline the lone figure came out of the woods and checked the dock at this property, also to make sure there was no evidence on it. After ensuring that everything was secure, the ghost figure walked through the woods into the cabin.

Still very early in the morning with the rain still falling, the lone figure started a fire in the wood burning pit, once it was very hot, they began adding items to the fire, bloody clothing, plastic and whatever else had been in the room, the twelve wooden chairs had stoked the fire so that it burned hot and efficient.

Two hours later everything that did not belong in the cabin was reduced to ashes. However, the ghost figure added more wood to the fire, they knew there was more to burn. On a normal day the smell of burning plastic would have alerted the neighbours to something odd, but nobody was around because of the bad weather. That bad weather had given cover to the smell, between the rain and the blowing winds; it was dispersed and lost into the atmosphere.

Chapter Sixty-Five

Then the lone figure, crushed glass medicine bottles to small fragments and dumped them off the dock to be lost forever into the sands at the bottom of the lake. Finally, they dragged the pail of blood and poured it over the soil, the blood mixed with the rainwater was being absorbed into the soil, by the end of the rain, the blood would be so diluted, that almost all traces would be removed by nature adding nutrients to the soil.

Then the lone figure walked to the car in the woods, removed the branches that covered it and carefully spread them back to the areas from where they had been collected. The individual took a moment the make sure the cellphone was still beside the car, it was, totally covered in debris and what the naked eye could see very damaged by the elements.

Soon the winter snows would cover everything and then it would be invisible until the spring. The silence in the woods was eerie, but the ghost figure was quite at ease, relishing the peace that came with that silence.

Returning to the fire pit, the person took off the hazmat suit and gear they had been wearing the whole time and placed everything into the fire. After all the remaining items had been burned, including the twelve mini recording tapes that had been used during the trial. Then the lone figure entered the cabin, checked around to make sure all was in place. The smell of bleach was very strong, but it would dissipate over the winter months. The jar of Hydrochloric acid with its dissolved items was emptied and the contends disposed in the depth of the woods. Also, the container was buried deep in the woods. One last look at the kitchen counter revealed and empty carving knife block, ‘no one will notice that’ thought the lone figure. Then the lone figure quietly closed and locked up the cabin, and walked back through the woods two miles to where their van was parked.

Leaving quietly from the area the stranger made sure that there was no trace of their presence or of their deed.

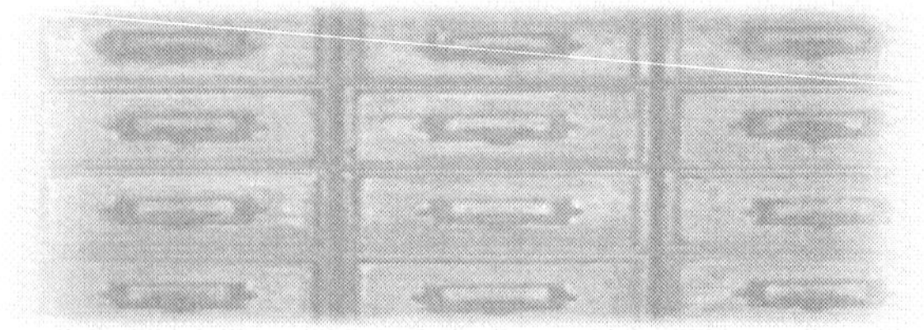

Chapter Sixty-Six

On the morning of October 10th, the lone figure boarded a bus in Philadelphia heading south, the final destination known only to themselves, was Dallas.

On the morning of October 12th, Gwendolyn Wahl boarded a plane in Dallas heading to Puerto Vallarta, Mexico, by five o'clock she was on her cruise ship heading south towards Peru.

Sitting quietly by herself on the deck and watching the setting sun, she spoke quietly to herself, "It will be wonderful to experience a second spring and summer in the same year." And then again to herself, "I cannot change my past or that of my past actions, I can only hope that I can make my peace with God and maybe someday make peace with Micky."

Later that evening sitting quietly on her balcony, Gwen sat thinking about her orchestra of the disenchanted. She remembered back to how she had brought them all together. It had been well planned out and had taken four years of cultivating their friendships, spending time which each and every one separately and sometimes as small groups. During those years, she had systematically work towards Darcy's demise.

Some had been easy to get to know and work their minds around to her plan's others were a bit harder, but in time they had all agreed to her plan. She had spent time getting to know the personal favourite activities, likes and dislikes of each of her instruments. With this knowledge she had set about preparing them for her final revengeful act.

Each and every one had their story, Gwen listen, never found fault with them. Gwen had become their sympathetic ear, their confessor, and their free psychologist. She allowed them to vent, never a criticism, just a gentle nod of the head a few kind words, she was slowly getting them to completely trust her. Only after she had their complete trust, could she trust them to help, her carry out her plan.

Sitting there and thinking back, with her cup of tea, Gwen had given up drinking after the killing of Darcy. Those past four years of preparations and planning could now be reviewed. Then Gwen would file them away forever in the back of her memory bank.

As she sat back thinking and reviewing how each person had been cultivated, she remembered that she had bought each one of them something special. Whether it was an antique piece, tickets for a favourite play or sports team, Gwen had made sure that each birthday gift was individualized. Something special for that individual, it was her way of letting them know she understood their circumstances and was sympathetic.

One thing that made it easy for Gwen to do all of the activities with each person was that she took the time to understand their particular interests. Whether it was shopping, going to the theatre, or taking in different sports events. She took the time to educate herself about each and every aspect of the activity. She knew the best shopping areas for each category of shopping interest. Also, she had taken the time to learn about Philadelphia's different sports teams and learn as much about the games, so that she could carry on intelligent conversations with each individual.

Those had been very interesting years, Gwen had learned so much about her own city that she was unaware of, even though it was her home city.

Chapter Sixty–Seven

Gwen had switched between spending time with the men and spending time with the women. It made sense, to her to switch up activities, so as not to become weary. She knew she needed to get the whole group on her side, and it would take time to get them to work together. In a way she was blending the ingredients to make a cake, but she was not planning on baking a cake, but the removal of a pest.

She started with Rebecca; a teacher who was going nowhere fast. Inviting her to coffee and chatting, she found out that Rebecca, played tennis. So did Gwen, so they made of point of playing tennis every two weeks and then going out for lunch and girl chat.

One year for Rebecca's birthday, she bought her the most up-to-date tennis racquet.

What a way to seal the deal!

Gwen brought up about Rebecca's sexual lending's. Rebecca talked about how her parents first responded to her coming out. Her mother had been kinder to her, but her dad just could not accept it. She told Gwen how until the day her father died, he never acknowledged her lifestyle.

Gwen was sympathetic and shared how her mother was angry when Gwen refused to marry. She explained how her parent's marriage was a disaster, and she just did not want to go through the same hell that her mother had experienced.

Two women, sitting, sharing cups of coffee, and speaking about the troubles they had endured with difficult parents. Gwen was right; sharing painful family experiences was a bonding tool. She knew eventually that when the time was right, Rebecca would be on her team one hundred percent.

One of Gwen's favourite sports was playing golf, so Melvin was to be her next project. Her time spent with Melvin would have to be a secret from everyone else, as they all despised him. Spending a day on the different golf courses, sometimes Cobb Creek, then on to Walnut Lane. Walking the course with Melvin, Gwen managed to get him to open up about his life. He had married young, had two children and the usual; a house, with the big backyard and of course the oversized dog. He had worked hard to become a principal, but even he admitted that he was a narcissus. When they were playing a round of golf, he would always insist that Gwen tee off from the women's tee, while he teed off from the men's tee. To Gwen it was stupid, as she was just as good a golfer as Melvin. However, she played along to his ego, always letting him win by a few strokes.

When the time came, Melvin's birthday gift was a top-of-the-line putter. Melvin was thrilled, one thing Gwen learned about golfers, they always love a new putter.

In those times while they were walking, he talked about meeting Darcy and how it started his life on a downward spiral. At first, his wife was clueless to what was happening at work, but then someone sent her pictures. That proved a very messy divorce, which almost cost him his job, but of course Darcy saved the day. Then he admitted that he always thought Darcy was responsible, but he could never prove it or take actions against her.

Over the four years, they had golf at different courses in the city, John F. Byrne, Juniata, and a few others. Melvin sometimes ask Gwen about her family, but he always turned the topic back to himself. Slowly over the four years, Gwen spoke about how better everyone's life would be if Darcy no longer existed. In time, Melvin agreed with her, as a matter of fact he said it would be better if she was never born. To Melvin somehow having Darcy die, was like an early Christmas gift. Gwen knew it would take time to get him on board, but eventually he was prime for the picking.

Gwen switched between the men and the women, she was becoming so busy going to museum, sport events, pubs, diners, coffee shops and playing sports, she barely had time for her doctors' appointments. Thinking to herself, the psychiatrist had told her to get out and about, but she probably did not expect Gwen to be forming her own hit squad.

Switching things up she had got some of the ladies together for trips to the museums.

Claudia loved going to Independence National Historical Park, so Gwen got Livia, Emily and Giselle go along. Walking around the park and viewing the different points of interest, Independence Hall, and the Liberty Bell, they ladies talked about work. Each of them spoked about the problems with Darcy and compared notes on how she had treated them. Each had their own story to tell. They spoke about their personal lives and how their job had affected their home lives.

The stories were painful to hear, but Gwen encouraged them to talk freely. Those quiet conversations were the building blocks of building friendships that would allow someone to follow another into the forces of hell. Gwen over time quietly and successfully convinced the women of the need to see an end to Darcy.

Gwen, however, also spent time with the ladies pursuing individual activities. When she wanted to visit museum, Claudia was the lady. Gwen was sure that over the four years, they had visited at least thirty museums and art galleries. It was in those quiet times, that Gwen worked on Claudia. She also knew that several of the ladies had coffee together and Claudia would wear the others down.

Eventually they would agree to Gwen's plan for Darcy. When Claudia's birthday came around, she made sure she had purchased a replica of an artifact from one of the museum's gift shops.

Each one of the ladies had difference interest, so Gwen had made sure her special gifts to each of them, match their likes.

Emily love the different art galleries, so Gwen's gift to her was a copy of a famous Monet painting. Emily was so thrilled, it turned out Monet was her favourite impressionist. She gushed over it and said, "I have a special place to hang this in my living room." With this act of kindness Gwen had sealed the deal with Emily.

Livia was an antiques enthusiast; they would spend hours just the two of them poking through the shops and looking at different items. Livia loved antique glassware, so when her time came Gwen bought her a beautiful vase of cranberry glass, hand-blown. It was just the right size for the centre of her dining room table. Another piece of the orchestra delivered in Gwen's mine to be available when the time came to carry out her plans for Darcy.

Giselle also love antiques, but her favourite items were silver serving dishes. There was one beautiful cover serving dish that she fancied, but it was out of her price range.

The day that Giselle opened her birthday gift and there in the box was the serving dish she loved, Giselle became an instant musical instrument for Gwen to play.

Chapter Sixty-Eight

Everett proved to a difficult partner in crime, the biggest problem was that he was seldom sober. They went to the Flyers games, which was fine as Gwen enjoyed hockey, but she could not even imagine, trying to keep up with Everett in the drinking department. Every sports event they went to Gwen was always the designated driver.

The 76ers' games were the worse, Everett would suggest that they go to the pub before the game and then he would continue to drink all the way through. Getting him on board for anything would be a huge challenge. Thinking to herself one day, "will I ever get the chance to talk to Everett about Darcy, or is he simply a lost cause?"

Gwen was persistent and after three years of basketball and hockey games she got him interested. Even when he was drunk, his hatred for Darcy came through loud and clear. Gwen realized that getting Everett involved would be easier than she thought.

So, when the time came, Gwen bought him a sixty-ounce bottle of eighteen-year-old scotch. It was the perfect candy for Everett. Bought and paid for!

And so, Gwen continued with the orchestra building. In Heath and Dolores, Gwen found kindred souls, they both like to drink, and they both loved the theatre. So many times, it was the three of them going to the theater and then a late dinner. All of course compliments of Gwen. She made a point of buying the tickets for the different events as birthday gifts. There they were the three musketeers enjoying the theatre and then later enjoying, drinks, food, and chatter. These times had brought the three souls together and eventually over time they both agreed that Gwen was right, Darcy needed to take off the face of the earth.

Carson prove to be a more difficult person for Gwen to recruit, however, he loved having someone attend sporting events with him. And though he would never tell anyone else, it sure was nice to have a lovely lady at his side. Gwen fit the picture perfectly, plus she was knowledgeable about the games. Carson was a big Flyers fan and Gwen had studied all the stats on hockey so they could have intelligent conversations about the games and the team's players. It was during these times together that Carson told Gwen about his difficulties with Darcy. He had been brought up old school, so he had little of hug a thug mentality. Spare the rod and spoil the child was more his credo.

Carson's mentality no longer belonged in the twenty-first century school system, but he could not afford to retire. He talked about his dead wife and his children. They were all away now in different parts of the country, so he was on his own. Gwen realized the reason, he continued to work was that he was lonely and work in its own way was his social life. How sad for Carson, Gwen was thinking. So as time went by, their quiet chats and shared interests, Carson began to see Gwen's points about Darcy. Carson liked Gwen and he wanted Darcy punished for what she had done to Gwen. However, it did take time for him to warm to the idea. What brought him around was his heart attack, it was from all the stress of work, caused by Darcy.

Carson's birthday gift was Flyers' sweater. He just loved it and told Gwen that she was the most thoughtful person in the world.

What turned out to be one of the easiest recruits was Mark the caretaker. Mark was a big Eagles fan and wanted them to win the Super Bowl, so Gwen learned everything there was to know about football. Sitting watching the game at the local pub, Gwen would cheer and say that they needed to see the game live. Then she would surprise Mark with a set of home game tickets. To Mark, Gwen was the big sister he never had. When they would sit and talk, he told her about his childhood. It had been tough; his dad was a drinker and beat his mom and then him. His dad died when he was young, and his mother had to work two jobs to keep the house going.

He told her how his anxiety had started when he was young, but no one paid attention. Then after leaving school at the age of eighteen, he got different jobs, but he could not decide what he wanted to do with his life.

Then, he started drinking like his father did and he became abusive. He told her how he could never keep a girlfriend because of how crazy he was towards them. Eventually he was hospitalized, and they found out that he suffered from bi-polar disorder. He talked about how his life became a series of hospital stays and eventually someone got him a job at the school board. Mark talked about his medicines and how he hated to take them, but when he didn't, he got sick.

He said he became violent. Gwen was so kind and listened to his every word and when the time was right, she manipulated his thoughts to the removal of Darcy, and he saw no problem with her idea at all.

Gwen got Mark, the Eagles jacket he wanted, and she promised that they would win the Super Bowl.

The last person Gwen needed on her side was Cecilia. Gwen knew about all her troubles at the school board and how Darcy had manipulated Cecilia files.
Gwen was sympathetic to her and listen with great patience.

But she could not tell Cecilia her complete plan as she was a rat, who reported everything back to Darcy. Cecilia would be brought along for the ride at the very end, when she could not resist the urge for revenge.

Cecilia just loved brand name merchandise, so when the time came, Gwen bought her a Louis Vuitton clutch purse for her birthday. Cecilia was thrilled and promised to help out Gwen anytime she needed some information about what was happening at the board.

Gwen said she appreciated Cecilia's help, but in her mind, she knew the least amount of information she requested from Cecilia the better. Gwen had other contacts, she could get information from, and they would not reveal to Darcy, that she was making inquiries.

Well four years of building and foraging relationships had paid off, Darcy was history and not one piece of evidence pointed to her. Gwen's orchestra of the disenchanted had supplied the DNA evidence to confuse the authorities for years.

One very important detail, she had not overlooked was that she had convince each of the twelve to record what they would say to Darcy if she was dying. However, the recording part was Gwen's secret. Gwen decided to throw a dinner party, she invited everyone except Cecilia, she could not be trusted to keep a secret. During dinner they had discussed many things, mostly sports for the men, but surprising to Gwen the women were also big sports fans. She was amazed how everyone followed the football and were hoping for a Super Bowl win. After dinner Gwen suggested a game, she had heard about. It was called “Mock Trial”, each person would give their testimony about the defendant and then decide on that person’s fate.

Being ever the master manipulator, Gwen turn the conversation about having a trial charging Darcy with crimes against humanity. Eventually they all bought into the idea, so they held a mock trial where Darcy was the defendant. Each spoke freely about what Darcy had done to them and why she should be punished. When it came to the verdict, they all said she was guilty. At times, tears were shed, but in the end they all agreed that it had been therapeutic to get it off their chests.

What the group did not know was the Gwen had recorded each person individually to use at a later date, a date that would be her choosing.

After that evening each person went home, feeling better for expressing their anger and saying what they really felt. To all of them, Gwen was their best friend.

The only person she had to record separately was Cecilia, but that came up easy one day at a dinner. The two ladies had gone to the theatre and had seen a murder mystery. When they were talking at dinner Gwen asked Cecilia what she would say if the victim had been Darcy. After three glasses of wine, she did not hold back her anger and she let out all of her animosity towards Darcy. Gwen secretly recorded the whole thing.

After collecting all of the testimonies, she worked them into a master tape to be used when she needed their thoughts to be spoken. This was important, because you never knew when someone would unexpectedly die and change all your plans. Gwen was always planning for the future.

Gwen had convinced them that it was a therapeutic devise to let go of their negative thoughts and would open them up to a bright and new future. Little did they know, she would use those secret recordings for Darcy's private exit from earth.

Gwen work on the principle of need-to-know bases, they did not need to know she was recording their thoughts and statements. She just needed them to talk freely, and they did, not knowing to what end Gwen would use their statements. It was all just harmless fun.

The private conversations with each member of the group had been much harder for Gwen to handle, but handle she did, like a professional. The angry, the frustrations and the tears had been overwhelming at times for Gwen to listen to, but she did. That's what a good therapist does. Some of them went on at great length the others were short and to the point.

Some no doubt went home and drank themselves to sleep. Others merely went for long walks to think about how Darcy had truly affected their lives. It was their reality, to live and eventually die with.

To Gwen it was a time to gather all the information need to continue with her plans, with the full knowledge that each and every participant in her scheme would not let her down.

Cecelia was her only concern, but time and circumstance would remove that problem also!

Part Four

"ENDINGS (so many)"

Chapter Sixty-Nine

Hurricane Gaston had done a lot of damage to the island, and it took months of hard work and everyone working together to get the repairs done. Not only had the storm overwhelmed Father Michael but surviving his time with Gwen and hearing her terrible story had set his health back months. All the good that had taken place during the summer was eliminated by that one afternoon. Even though, he tried to pretend everything was fine, Isabel noticed his health had declined. Isabel encouraged him to get back to sailing on Captain Joe's ship.

Going to Mass that terrible night had paid off for Captain Joe, his ship survived the storm with no damage. Others were not so lucky, but everyone came together to help each other. The Island community had the one for all and all for one attitude, it had developed over years of overcoming difficulties. This was the philosophy of the island, after all they had endured many hurricanes over the years, so every so many years they would do rebuilding.

It was the same for everyone around the world that faced terrible weather. You traded having warm weather all year, knowing that at least every ten years or so, you would be doing major repairs.

To Micky who was used to heavy snow falls, his thoughts, where it looks great on Christmas cards, but wait to you must shovel it and drive in it, can change one's attitude.

The parishioners had cut up all the downed trees and broken branches on the church property. They cleaned up the gardens and had done the repairs to the roof of both the church and the presbytery. Father had used the money he had received over the summer from visitors to cover the cost of materials, so again he avoided using the insurance company.

Most of the resorts and other activities were getting back to normal by mid-October, the tourist season would be starting shortly, and it was all hands-on deck, to get ready. Tourism was the main economic engine of the island, so they needed to be ready for the snowbirds. Its predictions were for a harsh winter up north, the snowbirds would definitely be flocking south for warmth. Sunshine and days on the beaches enjoying the aqua blue waters of the Caribbean.

By the end of October, Father Michael was beginning to get back some of his health and he threw himself into the daily life of the island. No longer a priest to be seen only Sundays, Father Michael was now part of all the daily activities on the Island, for the first time in his life as a priest he really did feel useful to his calling and his sheep. He realized that he had now truly become their Sheppard. He had kept his promise to God to become a more dedicate Sheppard to his flock. If anything, that was the one good thing to come out of his encounter with Gwen. He was thankful to be alive and thankful for his everyday life as the parish priest.

Sometimes in the evenings when he was by himself, he still remembered that day with Gwen and wondered if in fact she had committed a crime or was she merely rabbling on to release her boxed up anger and grief.

Would he ever know if she had done something so terrible and would she finally go to the police, if not for herself but for the victim's family? They would need closure.

Thinking to himself, maybe I should go to the library and do some searches on the internet to see if in fact she had committed a crime. So, on days when he was not as busy, he would spend a few hours searching for crimes, but nothing of the nature Gwen describe showed up. Why would she lie about something so horrible, maybe she was just so lonely that she needed to seem important, if only to herself?

Then he would think back to 1973 and his love and friendship with Kathleen, speaking to himself, "I imagine that she turned out to be a fine lady, with a caring husband, probably children and grandchildren." "I pray that was the case, I could never see her becoming like Gwen." "What a revolting thought."

Chapter Seventy

As far away from the island as was possible, Gwen was found sailing in the southern hemisphere on a wonderful cruise ship. Months had passed since she had last been in the United States, and the way she had set up her finances, she might never return. She had removed her enemy, but the emotional cost had been more than she had bargained for, episodes of depression, anger and a sense of complete lost. Again, she realized that Micky was right, you could not kill off your problem you had to face it and deal with it in a civilized manner. Well, she had taken the uncivilized action of killing someone and she would carry that burden for the rest of her life.

There was nothing for her now in Philadelphia, every person, she had ever known was dead. She would now have to find a new purpose in life, but for the time being she would enjoy seeing the world during her sabbatical year.
And what better way than to be sailing the high seas in first class luxury. This was in fact the only time in her life, she stopped worrying about money and was truly enjoying life.

Speaking quietly to herself one evening on the deck, "it will be spring in a few months up north, I wonder when the shit will hit the fan." And with that lone thought about the past, Gwen focused her thoughts on the future.

What had become so uncanny to Gwen was she had lost her moral compass and could detach herself from her reality, almost as if was a bad dream and not reality at all.

Chapter Seventy-One

The spring thaw for some reason always reveals what the fall leaves and winter snows hide, and on a deserted wooded property in the Poconos, an abandon automobile was found. Alas the folly of young teenagers, they just loved to go out and explore. The more dangerous the landscape for some, the greater the adventure and for three young teenage boys, their experience of the spring thaw would be changed forever. Traipsing through the woods and not using trails that had already been blazed, they decided to create their own pathway.

That pathway would lead them to Jerome Smith's car, deep in the woods, the tires sinking into the soft ground, the car cover in dirt and debris. At first, they thought it might be a stolen car, but when they finally were about to look in the locked car, they saw a body. Like rabbits being chased by a fox, the boys took off in a flash back to the county road. It was amazing how athletic they were, as they ran more than two miles into town to find help. After they encountered one of the townspeople, they told their story of the body in the car, and then they were driven to the police station and there they told their tale to the sheriff.

Putting in a call for his deputy to return to the station, so they could ask the boys where they had seen the car.

Then the two adults with the three teenagers left the police station and went on the search for the car with the body. Three scared teenaged boys were going to show the sheriff and the deputy the location of the car. When they all got to the new pathway the boys had created, the boys froze and said that they could not go on, they remained standing beside the car, with the sheriff. The sheriff then sent his deputy to go and look for the car. Ten minutes later the sheriff got the radio call that yes there was a car about seven hundred feet into the woods, from where the sheriff was parked.

And yes, there was a body inside the vehicle. Knowing that he was not equipped to deal with this problem, the sheriff made a call to the state police.

Hours later after the car had been towed away by the state police with the body still in it; the boys were reunited with their parents. The parents were informed that the state police would want to talk to the boys, but for now they needed to get them home safe and sound.

The only information released to the press at that time was that a body had been found in a car and it looked like an apparent suicide.

What the police did not release to the press was that the vehicle and licence plates were from a stolen car report out of Philadelphia in early October 2016. They also did not release details about the corpse, male, black approximate age mid-twenties or about the syringe in the person's arm. They wanted to keep everything under wraps until after the autopsy was completed and given that the body was partially decomposed, it in fact would be a couple of weeks.

Three weeks later, the autopsy confirmed the identity of the person as a Jerome Smith out of Philadelphia.
It was revealed to the state police that he had an extensive rap sheet, for thief, and he was a known drug dealer.

The autopsy also revealed that he had died from a drug overdose of heroin that had been cut with a large quantity of fentanyl. The investigators thought it strange that a drug dealer would accidently overdose himself, but thinking to themselves, who knows, what goes through the minds of these individuals. Driving a stolen car and quite a distance from Philadelphia, perhaps he was on the run from his drug suppliers who were higher up the food chain of the industry. Maybe it was what it original looked like, a suicide or accidental drug overdose. If it was written up as either or it would save a lot of police resources.

Several days later the Sheriff look at the report again about Jerome's death, reading through it he realized that there was no report of a cellphone on his person. It listed his wallet, keys, and other personal effects, but no cellphone.

Speaking to himself, "that doesn't make sense, everyone has a cellphone these days."

Calling in his deputy he asked the question, "can you check the list of Jerome Smith's personal effects and see if it lists a cellphone. Also check the evidence boxes."

One hour later the deputy returned and said that there was no record of a cellphone. Then the sheriff said, "Let's go out to that property and check around." The Sheriff and his deputy drove out to the lake to search for the cellphone. After about a ten-minute search, they found the weather damage cellphone cover in leaves and soil. They brought it back to the station, but the lab boys said it was too damaged by corrosion to get any information off it or search its database. Another dead end!

Thus, the final decision was to list it as an apparent suicide from a drug overdose remained the same.

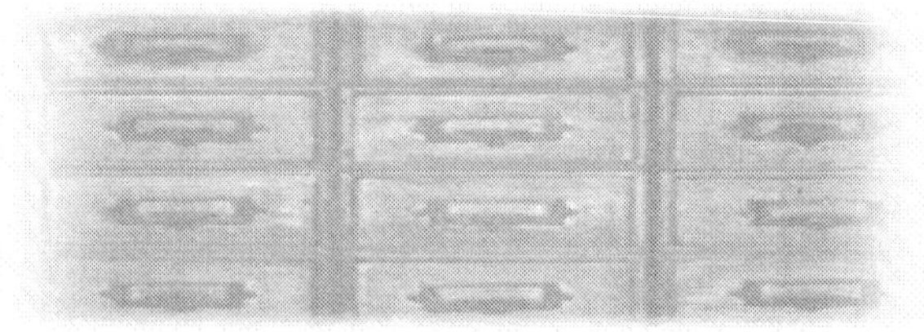

Chapter Seventy-Two

Just a week after Jerome was identified, an enthusiastic fisherman was trying out his new fishing boat. The gentleman took his boat out to the middle of the lake and began checking all of his gear. The new high-tech boat had lots of gadgets, which he wanted to try to get the hang of how they worked. For a fishing boat it was quite advance, but one of the main selling points to the gentleman was the ability to have a powered winch line to bring up the anchor.

When he was younger, he didn't mind pulling the line up by hand, but somehow reaching late middle age, he wanted things more convenient. He dropped the anchor, knew when it hit bottom and then he turned on the motor that controlled the winch line. Strange it seemed to be going slower than they had said it would, but when it broke the surface of the water, he could see why.

Not only had the anchor pulled up some seaweed, but also attached to it was a parcel wrapped in black plastic. The gentleman pulled the plastic parcel aboard, dropped it on the deck, and then cut it open. The shock of what was inside almost gave him a heart attack. Wrapped up in the black plastic was a hand, which had a thin cover of cement over it. The man took a deep breath, radio his wife that he was coming in and that she needed to call the sheriff's office to come out to the lake.

The sheriff met the man on his dock, the man showed the sheriff what had come up on his anchor. Telling the man to relax, he would be calling his deputy, the sheriff left the man standing on the dock. The gentleman, George stood on his deck staring out over the lake, he felt sick to his stomach and faint. That last time he had send a dead body was in Vietnam, which was expected, by not here in the Pocono's. As the sheriff was was walking back to his car, he called back to the man, who looked like hell; "George, you go inside now, we will take it from here." "Also, George could we ask your kind lady Mary to put on the coffee pot."

The sheriff knew the couple for over thirty years, they would take this very hard, but he needed them to stay focus on the problem. An old trick the sheriff had learned over the years was to give someone something to focus on after they have had a shock. Making coffee for everyone, 'God knows how many people', should do just that; refocus George and Mary's thoughts.

The sheriff got on his car phone and called the state police, "Sheriff Thane here, I think, I am going to be keeping you boys real busy up this way again, one of the locals just pulled up a body part from the middle of the lake." "How long before your boys get here?" "Fine, I am at George and Mary Jones' place" "Ask the locals, they will give you directions." "And don't worry about coffee, I have Mary making lots of coffee for your boys, more than likely she will do some baking before you are finished."

Several hours, just as Sheriff Thane had predicted Mary Jones had made lots of coffee and muffins to go around for everyone.

She had even put on a large pot of chili for the searches as the temperature was still on the cool side. What a lady, she even made homemade buns, hot from the oven to go with the chili.

These country folks really know how to treat people, thought one of the lead investigators.

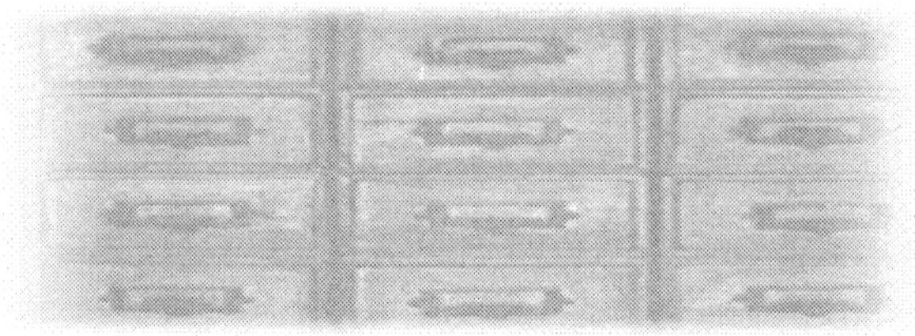

Chapter Seventy-Three

Within two hours, the area was swarming with the state police, they had brought in their own boat, large for the lake and had divers with every type of equipment you could imagine. They had commandeered boats from the locals around the lake to set up a search perimeter. However, dusk was coming in and the lake always had a thick mist in the evening during the spring. At six o'clock, they broke for the day, with a secure perimeter, they would all be up and working on the lake after breakfast.

Sheriff Thane made George and Mary's home, his command centre, it turned out to be a good idea, George and Mary were so busy being host and hostess, that George began to forget the horror he had seen. The state police were so impressed by the Jones' hospitality, they showed them great respect, by not simply brushing them aside, when things became more intense.

By the end of day two, the divers had brought up twelve packages that were wrapped in plastic, everything was photographed and then placed into the forensic evidence truck. The packages were of different sizes and weight, the biggest which they guess was the torso, weighed the most. The decision was that nothing was to be opened until it reached the coroner's building.

Three days later, the state police had wrapped up everything after finding no more packages, they removed all security perimeters and let the small community try to return to normal.

They did ask the sheriff to get a list of all the people who owned property around the lake and if possible, their city addresses if they were summer and weekenders only. And with that they were gone, however nothing was returning to normal, a week after all the excitement, George Jones died from a heart attack, leaving Mary to decided what her future would be, Mary an innocent and hidden victim because of someone's terrible crime. Close friendships were being strained and people began to lock their doors, even in the daytime. Yes, life for this community would never be the same again, because of strangers, or were they strangers. The community as a whole was now made up of hidden victims of the crime, not because of physical injury, but because of the psychological damage that had been down.

That day when Gwen dumped Darcy's body parts into the lake, she never imagined the whirlpool of victims she would create.

Chapter Seventy-Four

It was the middle of May, when the coroner called the head of the investigation to the coroners' office to discuss what the press were calling it, 'The Concrete Corpse' or 'The Lady of the Lake.'

He asked the team to come to the building, as he had his written report, but there were a lot of irregularities he needed to bring to their attention.

So, the next day at nine o'clock, the homicide team arrived at the coroner's building. They were ushered into one of the examinations rooms and laid out on the tables were the twelve body parts.

Then the medical examiner began his summation of his report. "As you know ladies and gentlemen, when the body came to us, it was wrapped in black plastic bags, we had to slit the bags and then allow each part to soak in cold water, so that we could remove the plastic and leave the concrete coating intact." "We were able to lift fingerprints off all of the black plastic bags, and there was only one set of prints on each bag and those prints were the same for each bag." "The fingerprints match those of Jerome Smith's, so it looks like he is the only person to have wrapped up the body parts."

"That is part one; now part two; we had to soak each body part multiple times to soften the cement, so that it could be removed and not disturb any evidence that was on the body parts themselves." "However, we did not get Jerome Smith's prints on any of the cement, not surprising." "He would have worn gloves while covering the parts with the cement, otherwise there would have been burns on his hands." "I went back and checked his autopsy report and there was no mention of skin burns on his hands."

"After we got the cement off of the skin, we carefully looked for fingerprints and other samples of DNA."

"We found thirteen samples of different DNA from the victim, not including theirs's of course." "One common DNA sample we got from each part was DNA from Jerome Smith." "The other twelve samples are of twelve different people, from what we have so far, is that the DNA is from seven women and five men." "And to be quite clear, no two pieces contain the same DNA of our mystery persons." "Jerome did not do this himself, but I am not sure how the others helped."

"One question Doctor James, what was the source of Jerome Smith's DNA," asked the one of the detectives.

The doctor's reply was, "the source of Jerome Smith's DNA was sweat and salvia, not surprising given the amount of effort to cut up the body."

"Also, on the bags were samples of his DNA, the source being, sweat, salvia and some blood, he must have cut himself." "Now I will continue with my report."

"Also, quite unusual, is that the body had been exsanguinated, there was no blood in the body."

The Captain asked the next question, "how do you explain that?"

"That can be explained by the fact that there were over sixty cuts to the body, some very superficial, others quite deep, almost ruthless in how the person or persons cut the body." "I think I am safe in saving that it was not a quick death, this person was definitely tortured." "There are ligature marks on the body parts that are the arms." "I believe the victim was hung up and then cut, and then allowed to bleed out, there was some pooling of the blood, but only in the feet, there were bruising signs, but then someone cut the bottom of the feet open, and the remaining blood flowed out." The medical examiner continued with his lecture about the body and the victim.

"We did some samples from the liver, and found traces of heparin, pavulon and ketamine in the liver tissues."

“The victim was alive long enough for some of these drugs to enter the blood system and make their way into the liver.” “Also, there were needle marks on both arms, the type made by IV-line needles, there was bruising around these puncture wounds.”

“Also, folks, you will be surprised to know that our victim was a long-time user of cocaine, there were traces throughout her system, plus and examination of the brain tissue, show the damage we usually see with long time drug abuse.”
“I have no idea who the other twelve DNA samples come from, sorry for that.”

“But we do have a name for our victim, it is Darcy Shanahan, who was reported missing last November out of Philadelphia.” “I hope this helps you.” And with that the coroner was finished and went about his way.

Now the police had a name for the victim and a suspect, except he was long dead. Who were the twelve mysterious people?

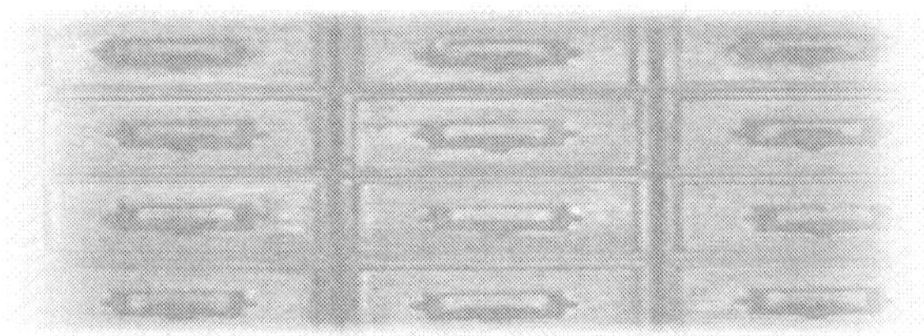

Chapter Seventy-Five

It was almost the end of May when the information came in about the other twelve DNA samples. These had gone to the FBI headquarters in Quantico for analysis and blood typing. What was really strange to the police was that the DNA was from twelve people who had worked with the victim over a fourteen-year period at one of the Philadelphia school boards. The FBI had found out this information as apparently each on the strangers had been blood donors when the blood drives were done within the board.

The Captain was now addressing the team, "What is so strange is that all twelve suspects were dead before the suspected time of the victim's death." "Jerome Smith was the only one still alive when she disappeared, and we can assume that she was killed shortly after being taken." "We can pinpoint the time she was taken to Friday, October 7th, because she was supposed to leave on a trip to the Bahama's, but she never made her flight." "As was her custom, her car was left in the underground parking of her office, but there is no record of her taking either a cab or Uber to the airport."

"Also, there is video surveillance of a grey panel van leaving the underground about two o'clock, but neither the driver nor licence plate are visible on the video." "The van had tinted windows and the licence plate was covered in mud." "Yes, we checked there are no video cameras inside the parking garage only at entrances, so the whole garage is not covered." "So, no help on that end, it looks like Jerome covered his tracks well." "Also, there are no reports of stolen vans, to follow up on."

"It doesn't mean, it wasn't stolen, but if it was only used in say an eight-hour window for transportation, it may never have been missed." "Unless someone noticed more miles on the van and noted it, it's a dead end."

"Hey Captain, wasn't that the weekend we were dealing with a lot of rain because of Hurricane Matthew, so traffic would be light heading up to the Pocono's." "Maybe we should be checking traffic cameras on the highway?" One of the officers stated.

"Good point Thompson, we did check the cameras near the building, but the vehicle turned off on to side streets, five blocks away from the board building and it never showed up on any other cameras after that time." "We will assume, the driver knew every back way of getting around the city and the back-county roads to get up to that lake."

"That methodology fits Jerome to the tee, low level drug dealer and criminal, knowing how to avoid detection." "To add to his freakish behaviour, there was a note found in

the victim's car, that simply said 'Sorry Miss'." "Jerome's fingerprints were on the note."
Also, Darcy's purse, luggage and cellphone were in her car. The only thing taken from her wallet was any cash, the credit cards were still in it. The only thing really missing was Mrs. Shanahan.

The Captain continued in his reporting, "We have video surveillance of Jerome purchasing, items that include rolls of plastic, saws, wooden folding chairs, bags of cement and boxes of black plastic bags." "He paid with prepaid VISA cards, instead of cash, strange but true." "Also, we were able to get a warrant to check his laptop, the FBI is handling that for us, and in their report is the fact that he purchased all the medical supplies online." "We are still waiting to hear what he purchased, so far they have information on drugs that were found in Ms. Shanahan's system, but there are a lot of other items." "Due to the fact he bought a lot of stuff on the Dark Web, it will be hard to determine what was used in this murder, and what could have been used in other criminal activities."

"Do we think it was a contract killing, what about the husband," another officer asked.
"Yes, we have interview Mr. Jonathan Shanahan extensively, but he was out of the country in Vietnam, at the

Asian Beach Games from September 24th to October 3rd." "It seems the Shanahan's had a very open marriage, each did their own thing, no children to worry about."

"According to him, he got back home around October 20th, which has been collaborated with airline passengers' lists."

"He says he knew his wife was going to the Bahamas, he expected her to return home on October 25th, when she did not come home that day, he figured she changed her plans."

"Apparently it was not unusual for his wife to do this on short notice." "Also, apparently it was not unusual for her to fail to inform anyone of the changes she made to her schedule." "He says he called and made a missing person's report on October 30th." "We contacted the Philadelphia police to confirm his statement; they said it's still an open investigation." "We informed them, they can close that investigation, and she's not missing anymore."

Then one of the officers spoke up, "what about the DNA evidence from twelve dead people."

To which the Captain replied, "Our next level of the investigation, how did the DNA from dead people end up on the victim?"

"Oh, and one last thing, Jerome's mother died early on the morning of October 7th, apparently she fell down the stairs at her apartment building." "Her family buried her; Jerome was not there and never seen again after the seventh.

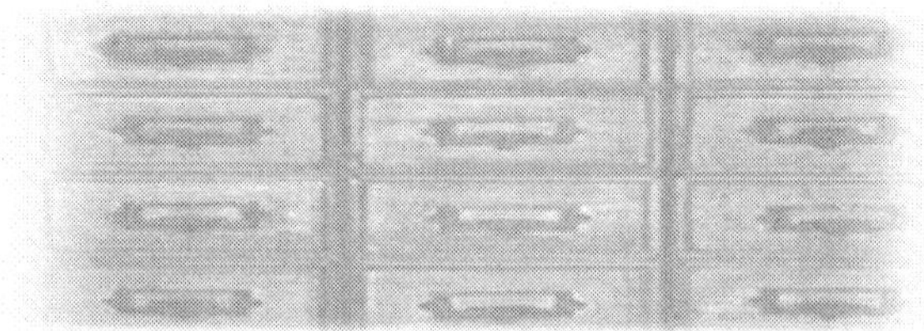

Chapter Seventy-Six

One week later the team met and reviewed all of the information on the twelve.

"Okay everyone, tell me what you've got," said the Captain.

Sargent Smyth started, "Melvin Kirkpatrick, school principal, died in August 2016, car accident, brakes failed." "The history is that he had a long-time affair with the victim." "Also, it ended badly, his relationship with her ended his marriage and almost ended his career. Then Smyth continued, "Mark Jones, caretaker at Melvin's school, died also in August 2016, heart attack, died instantly, by the way in his office at the school." "According to idol gossip, he hated everyone, particularly Melvin and Darcy." "Also, according to records he was being treated for bipolar disorder. Apparently, he did not take his meds all the time and he proved to be very anger person to deal with, everyone was terrified of him." "Some even came close to saying that he sabotage things in the school building to make people's lives difficult." "Quite a disturb person."

"On that note my last person, I looked into was Livia Pesto, and by the way both Melvin's and Darcy's secretary." She committed suicide in May 2016." "From everything I learned, she was a very unhappy person, apparently blamed Darcy for all her troubles." "Her marriage ended badly, and her husband got complete custody of the children, very bitter woman."

"Okay, Detective Brown, what have you got?" "Thanks sir, you gave me the female staff, hopefully not because I am a female." "Anyways that aside, there were six other women and all of them hated the Ms. Shanahan."

"Up first; Dolores Michaels, an elementary teacher, off sick a lot; was given a bad time by the victim." "Apparently, she suffered from anxiety and Mrs. Shanahan didn't believe her, so she was losing a lot of pay, she was in a terrible financial mess." "Ms. Michaels died in July 2016 from a drug overdose, prescription medication.

"Our next person of interest is Cecilia Gregory, killed in a hit and run in June 2016, bad thunderstorm, and the driver was never found." "Ms. Shanahan had put very unfavourable comments in her file, which prevented her from ever getting a full-time teaching position." "However, what is strange is the gossip mill says she was Mrs. Shanahan's lapdog, told her everything about everyone on staff." "This could add a different dimension to the investigation, but I just cannot connect the dots yet."

"My next person is Emily Strange, made her way up the ladder to become principal, screwed up big time, was demoted by the victim." "Also, the gossip says she slept her way to the top, but no one will give names." She also died in a hit and run accident, she was knock off her bicycle, died two days later that was in late September 2016." "Driver never found, no arrests."

"My fourth lady is Rebecca Rose, a teacher and a lesbian." "According to gossip she had an affair with the victim." "It seems according to gossip that Ms. Shanahan was a switch hitter." "Ms. Rose apparently committed suicide in early September 2016."

"Our fifth person is Giselle Vander, early childhood educator, married, but according to sources had an affair with the victim." "Her marriage survived, but in name only, it seems the husband had been stepping out the whole time." "A very vulnerable lady." "Mrs. Vander committed suicide in early June 2016."

"And my last lady is Claudia Gordon, teacher's assistant, heavy drinker, fell off her balcony, died on impact, again in early August 2016." "It seems her greatest interests where museums and anything to do with the history of our country." "She had an annual membership to the Independence National Historical Park." "That's all for my group, Sir."

"Thank you, Brown, seems like that school board was an unhealthy place to work,

"Well Detective Cartwright your up next," was the Captain's way of addressing his staff.

Then Cartwright started his narrative, "My first person of interest is Everett Brown, a teacher's assistant, according to gossip, he was a closet gay man, and apparently Ms. Shanahan had him as her personal spy." "Mr. Brown committed suicide on October 1st, 2016." "According to friends which were few, he had a major drinking problem, so no one was surprised about the manner in which he died."

"My next person is Heath James; he was second in command in HR at the board." "Apparently Ms. Shanahan's long-time lover, and a very heavy drinker." "He died in June 2016 from a drug overdose, he also had a heavy cocaine habit that he shared with the victim according to sources."

"My last person is Carson Carlton, a teacher, and older gentleman, close to retirement, and was being treated for depression." "His autopsy revealed an accidental drug overdose of his prescription medicine." "His death took place in September 2016." "Too bad he was a big Eagles fan; he didn't live long enough to see his team win the Super Bowl."

Then the Captain spoke to the team, "you mean to tell me, out of all these people, they either died from accidents or suicide, with only one person dying from natural causes."

"How strange is that, was an autopsy done on the caretaker, maybe his was death was not natural after all."

"Actually sir, there was no autopsy done on the gentleman, apparently, they figure because of age and other health problems, the attending doctor wrote on the death certificate heart attack."

"And before you ask Sir, we can't dig him up, he was cremated," was Smyth's reply.

Then Inspector Brown spoke up, "strange thing Sir, all twelve suspects were cremated." "And another thing Jerome Smith had contact with all of the victims as he attended both elementary and secondary schools in that board." "Also, Sir, you are going to love this, Jerome Smith was Ms. Shanahan source of cocaine."

"What the hell." Was the Captain's reply and then he went on further to state, "Something smells rotten in all of this."

He then continued, "We need to find out who owns that property were Jerome's body was found, maybe there is a connection."

"Also contact all the families, find out why they were cremated."

After the team left his office the Captain, sat reviewing all the reports, and then asked himself the question he wanted answered.

'How did the DNA from twelve dead people end up on a corpse of an individual who died, after they did?'
This simply does not make sense, there has to be another answer, and the Captain realized that the answer would be very disturbing.

Why when he was so close to retirement did this case come up, would it be solved before, he retired? Or would he be like so many of his friends and always have that one case that you could not solve. Would this become a cold case?

Chapter Seventy-Seven

Two days later, Cartwright came in with the answer about who owned the property. The Captain called his team into his office to hear the details, "okay Cartwright you've got the floor, details please."

Then Cartwright began to give the details, "the property in question was acquired by a Michael Kennedy in 1925, he built a summer home, when he died the property went to his son Michael Kennedy JR." "He rebuilt the place in the late 1950's, and when he and his wife died in a traffic accident in the late sixty's the property went to their only child, Mallory Kennedy." "Then sometime in the early 1990's the property was transferred to a Kathleen Kennedy, not sure of the connection, probably a niece." "We assume it was a niece as there are no records of marriage for a Mallory Kennedy in the state of Pennsylvania."

"The property expenses are covered by a trust account set up by Michael Kennedy Jr., a Law Firm in Pittsburgh handles all the arrangements." "When I called them, they were not very helpful, all they would say is that Ms. Kennedy checks in with them once a year, about account balances and with instructions for the caretakers of the property." "She also communicates about what matters are to be attended to and timelines for the work to be done."

"We can assume from that information, that Ms. Kennedy is still using the property on a regular basis."

Then the Captain spoke up, "actually Cartwright, we cannot assume anything, who's up for going for a ride into the Poconos, and poking around, sorry for the pun." "Anyone?" "Okay we head up tomorrow, we will take two cars, so I can spend some time with Sheriff Thane, sometimes these locals know details, and you just need to get them talking, casual like."

And with that statement he dismissed the group and said they would leave at nine in the morning.

Cartwright came back in to speak to the Captain, "Sir, I called all the families about the cremations; it seems that all of them had changed their wills in late 2015 and had added the provision that they be cremated." "The families stated that each had stated a friend suggested it as a way to save money and then they would be able to leave more for their loved ones."

"A very thoughtful friend indeed." And with that Cartwright left the office.

The next morning at nine o'clock his team headed up to the Pocono's in two cars, the Captain loved to play classical music, so the rest of the team went in the other car.

Thinking to himself, how can such intelligent people be so devoid of culture?

Three hours later the team were meeting with Sheriff Thane and the contractor who was the caretaker for the Kennedy property. Each one of them had questions for both people.

The Captain asked the first question, "Have either of you met with Ms. Kennedy?"

The sheriff said no, but then the contractor replied, "Yes, I met with Ms. Kennedy in person about fifteen years ago, as she wanted to make made major changes to the property."

"You do realize that we are talking ten acres of land."

The Captain asked, "What kind of changes?"

To which the gentleman replied, "When her father had the land, he had large parts cultivate with gardens and lawns, very high maintenance, no wait a minute I mean her grandfather." "However, she wanted the land returned to its natural state, she had us widen the driveway, then instead of asphalt, she wanted pea gravel." "Then the area around the cottage was reduced, walkways and patio area were also to be pea gravel." "Then the lawn area down to the lake was narrowed down, with perennial borders, plus a new dock."

Another question from the team, "Did she own a boat?"

The answer was, "No."

Next question asked by one of team members was, “Then why a new dock?” The contractor replied, “That’s easy, safety, the other one was a hazard.” “Then over the next fifteen years, we have been working to restore the forest area, she wanted it returned to a habitat for wildlife.”
“Ms. K. was big on nature and protecting the habitats for as she said, ‘God’s creatures.” “Any more questions?”

“Yes, who does the winterizing and spring cleaning of the exterior and the interior of the cottage?” One of the detectives asked. “Also, did you notice anything unusual when you did the winterizing last fall?”

“We do Sir, we usually open up the place about the beginning of April and usually do the winterizing after Thanksgiving, most seasonal places are used right to the Thanksgiving weekend, and then they close up.” “The only thing that was slightly unusual was that there was a smell of bleach, but then we just assumed, that Ms. K. was doing some heavy-duty cleaning.” “The ammonia smell helps keep the mice out, one of her natural methods, Ms. K. did not want to use poisons.” “If that is all Captain, I have to get back to another job site.”

Captain replied, “No, that’s all you been a great help, one more thing, how did you communicate with Ms. Kennedy?”

The reply was simple, "She always called once a month, with questions and instructions, and since there never seem to be any problems, I never had to contact her, she always calls me."

"Well thanks again," was the Captain's reply.

After everyone had left, the Captain sat by himself, looking out over the lake, he sensed that something terrible had happen here, but there was no evidence, just a gut feeling. In the distant were the sounds of birds and other sounds of nature. As he walked down to the dock, he heard the sounds of the waves splashing against the wood. If only this dock could talk and tell him a story, a story of how the body parts of a woman made it to the middle of the lake?

Standing looking out over the lake, a sense of complete silence filled the Captain's mind, it was like he was in a void. He felt the presence of something or someone, but he could not determine what it was or who. The deathly silence was unnerving to the Captain, it was like someone was trying to reach into his subconscious, but his analytical mind was preventing him from receiving the message. What secrets did this land hold onto, what did the trees witness, what did they see? These thoughts races through his mind. Who was trying to speak to him from the other side? Speaking to himself, "Eugene get a grip on yourself, you

follow the evidence and the facts, there is no magic genie to help." "My Mary would say listen to the surrounding noises, if you give yourself to them, the answers will come."
"That's Mary, maybe not always practical, but so filled with love, she was opened to the universe."

Without warning the sounds of the area returned to Eugene, the void was gone and so was the connection to the universe. Turning around the Captain headed back from the dock to land, maybe the water was intoxicating and led a person to imagine the impossible.
Then continuing in his thoughts and throwing out a question to the atmosphere,
"How did not one person see anything?"

Then looking around, he decided that if this was his property, he would definitely cut back the forest, it was so gloomy and it made the place feel eerie. Speaking to himself; "Okay Gene, you are letting your imagination get the better of you, you really are a city boy, let the naturalists have their jungles, I like a nice, manicured lawn." And with that thought he got back into his car and headed back to the city.

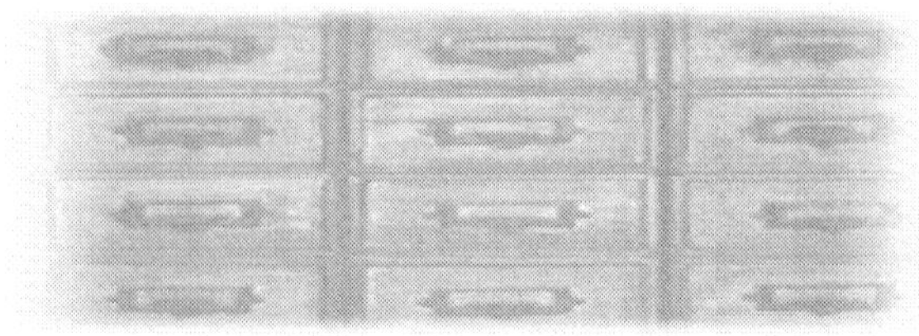

Chapter Seventy-Eight

Driving back to the city, it hit the Captain, he said granddaughter, but Michael Kennedy only had one daughter, which was Mallory, who had never married. Thinking to himself, well the rich really do cover their tracks. Then out of the blue, the Captain spoke to himself, "Was it my imagination or did seem like there was a sense of sadness, despair, and evil about that property?" As he continued driving as sense of loneliness filled the car, and he wished he had one of his team drive back to the city with him.

A week later, one of the team asked the Captain to call everyone in, they had some new information on the Shanahan case. Later that afternoon the group sat in the conference room to hear the details.

Smyth spoke up, "Sir, I went back to the board, talked to the current head of personnel and found out something unusual, there is another staff member no one has seen since February 2016."

"Her name is Kathleen O'Hare, and she was the head librarian for the school board, but that being said she has been off on medical leave since sometime in 2012."

The Captain asked another question, "Medical leave, did they say why?"

Smyth continued, "No Sir, but from the gossip mill, it sounds like she had a nervous breakdown." "Also, she was at odds with Ms. Shanahan and was good friends with the other twelve persons of interest."

"Anything else Smyth?" the Captain asked.

Smyth came back with a quick reply, "Yes Sir, you will like this bit of information, it seems Ms. O'Hare was helping out Jerome's mother, neighbours said an older white lady brought groceries to Mrs. Smith, once a week and then a month or two before Thanksgiving 2015, they overheard her yelling at Jerome, about how his life choices were destroying his mother's health."

"No one saw Ms. O'Hare after that date, and no one reported her missing as she had no living relatives." "They are still paying her monthly salary."

"Can we check with her bank to see if the accounts are active?" the Captain asked.

Smyth replied, "Not without a warrant, and so far, I have not got a judge who believes she is a missing person, and who will issue a warrant."

"Okay folks, we have a person who has not been seen in close to two years, it looks like we probably have a fourteenth victim, we need to prepare for a news conference," was the Captain's statement. In his mind, he was thinking can this get any worse.

About an hour later while the Captain was listening to one of his favourite pieces of music, Moonlight Sonata, it came to him out of the blue, 'Kathleen Kennedy – Kathleen O'Hare were they the same person' no can't be he thought, but if in fact the two were one, it would explain a lot. However, it would also create a whole new set of circumstances that might offer answers and then maybe lead them down a black hole with no resolve to the mystery.

Then speaking to himself, "Yes, we do need that news conference, and the boys need to get the most up-to-date picture of Kathleen O'Hare, plus maybe a photo that was taken fifteen years ago.

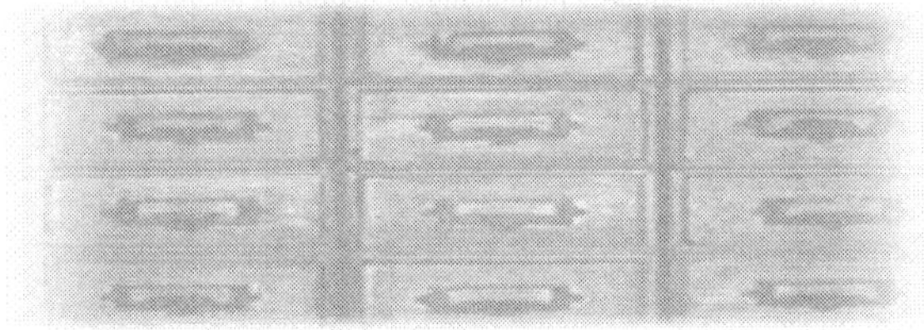

Part Five

“Final curtain (shock)”

Chapter Seventy-Nine

Two days after the state homicide team had met, they were getting ready to do a national news conference on the case. The Captain was in his office, adjusting his uniform, he wanted to look properly presentable for the press he was about to address.

As the Captain was adjusting his tie, he began to think back to his past, looking at the mirror and starring back at him was Captain Eugene Collins, a university grad, who had spent ten years in the US Marines, then he switch to the Pennsylvania State Police, starting as a highway patrol officer, finally after thirty years, here he was the Captain of the state police's major homicide division. He had handled a lot of cases in his career, but he admitted to himself, that he was stomped. However, he would never admit that to anyone else.

Ten minutes later, he was looking into the press conference room and could see reporters from FOX, CNN, MSNBC, as well as all the other networks. The press were just like bloodhounds, he was thinking to himself, ready to cover anything sensational, with stories like 'The Concrete Corpse and The Lady of the Lake' they will eat this story up alive, like vultures. Then still to himself, it will be interesting to see the different spins put on the story, I wonder who will report it, just as it presented to them. No, every outlet will have their own spin, he had witness that over the years as so many of his fellow officers had shared their stories.

Then speaking to himself: "Okay Gene get through this ordeal, then it's time to retire." Again, to himself: "Two more weeks, then in goes the retirement letter, things are getting too bizarre, and it's time for the younger ones to handle the insanity." "I'm sixty-two, time to enjoy life, I've got my garden and I love to paint." Perhaps I will make that my third career, artist extraordinaire."

"Plus, my wife Mary will be so happy, no more sleepless nights worrying about me."

"I know she will not miss, my brooding about crimes that seem to have no answer, some that were so terrible, that at times I could not eat." "The worse crimes where those that involved children, twice I had gone to the company shrink, just to function in my everyday activities." "Mary will be happy when those days are over, sometimes when things were tough, I thought our marriage would fall apart."

"However, Mary was the strong one, strong enough for both of us." "We will celebrate another anniversary together, maybe this time we will take a trip. No work to prevent us this time." "We had missed many times away, just when Mary would everything planned, something would happen, and our plans were cancelled." "What a mother she is, so many events I missed, but she never did, she never complained." "Mary never allowed the children to find fault either, or even if they did, I was never told." "If my children were successful, their mother was the reason, however I did at times put in my two cents worth."

And with those closing thoughts the Captain walked in the conference room.

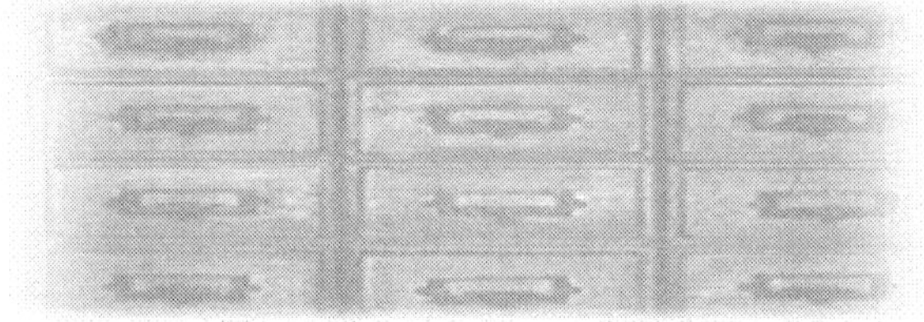

Chapter Eighty

June – The News Conference

The Captain took to the podium, addressed the assembled press core by first thanking them for their time and they would take questions after all pertinent information was given.

"Ladies and gentlemen, welcome to our news conference, we ask your patience and that you hold all questions until my team has presented the complete details of the crimes in question."

"The first part deals with the discovery of a body in early April in a wooded area in the Poconos"

"The body was discovered in a stolen car from Philadelphia, the car was stolen in early October 2016."

"Inside was discovered the partially decomposed body of Jerome Smith, a low-level drug dealer and petty thief from Philadelphia." "The autopsy of Mr. Smith showed that he had died from a drug overdose of heroin cut with fentanyl and was probably dead a least six months when his body was found." "His body was found on a piece of property owned by the Kennedy family, there is no apparent connection to him or the current owners." "It is believed that he picked that piece of land to park because it looked deserted." "And then by accident injected himself with the fatal dose of heroin." "We are not ruling out suicide as it seems from reports, we received from the Philadelphia police department he had made some dangerous enemies with the several street gangs."

The Captain continued speaking, "I will now hand over the next part of the press conference to Inspector Brown, and she will give you the details pertaining to the body found in the lake." "Inspector Brown, please." And with that statement the Captain stepped aside to give the podium to the Inspector. It had been agreed upon before, that the press would not be given anything that was sensational, and the details were to be scarce.

Also unknown to the press, but know to his team, the Shanahan family had got a court order sealing the autopsy report of Darcy Shanahan. Thinking to himself; money and political power can surely buy anything. And with those thoughts in his head, his female inspector began her narrative.

"Good morning, ladies and gentlemen, the information I am relaying is surrounding the death and ultimate discovery of the body of Mrs. Darcy Shanahan, the wife of Jonathan Shanahan, the son of one of Philadelphia's more prominent families." "Mrs. Shanahan's body was found at the bottom of one of the lakes in the Poconos in early May of this year." "It is determined she died from blunt force trauma." "At the request of the family, no other details will be released." "Thank you!" And with that statement Inspector Brown left the podium returned to her seat at the table and the Captain again was the speaker. Inspector Brown sat stone faced, imagining what the press would say if they knew all the details from the autopsy, eventually it will leak out, but not by her team.

Then the Captain started again, "We also have found that twelve other members of the same school board, who had contact with Jerome Smith died in unusual circumstances over a one-year period. "Jerome's mother died from a fall on the same morning that we believe he kidnapped Ms. Shanahan, and the evidence is that he killed her for some reason, that we have yet to determine."

"Our next concern is for a fourteenth staff member who has not been seen since she was overheard having an argument with Mr. Smith about his treatment of his mother."

The lady in question has not been seen since that day in September 2016." "We will now show you a picture of Ms. Kathleen O'Hare who was the head librarian for the school board." "We are asking if anyone has any information as to the whereabouts of Ms. O'Hare to contact us here at the Homicide Division of the Pennsylvania State Police."

"Thank You."

The large picture of Kathleen was displayed for the press, one in colour and the other in black and white. It was hard to get a picture of the lady as she was notorious for avoiding a photographer's lens. It showed a middle-aged woman, with her hair pulled back, nothing fancy.

Plain clothing, suit and shirt with a neck scarf, no jewelry was evident in the photograph, there was nothing note worth at all. You could pass this lady on the street and not even realize it was her.

Captain Collins spoke to the press assembled in the room, "Now we will take questions and answer those that we have confirmed information about."

Twenty minutes later the team had answered the questions, they planned on answering and nothing more. The last thing they wanted was the State Attorney General on their case. Another problem with wealthy people, they were always highly politically connected, so you always had to watch your back, and in this case your front.

The team returned back to their desks, tired and wanting to get away for the rest of the day, but already there were other cases on their desks to deal with, but nothing that was as horrible and bizarre as the case they had put to bed today.

They all realized that someday the body of Kathleen O'Hare would show up, but not today.

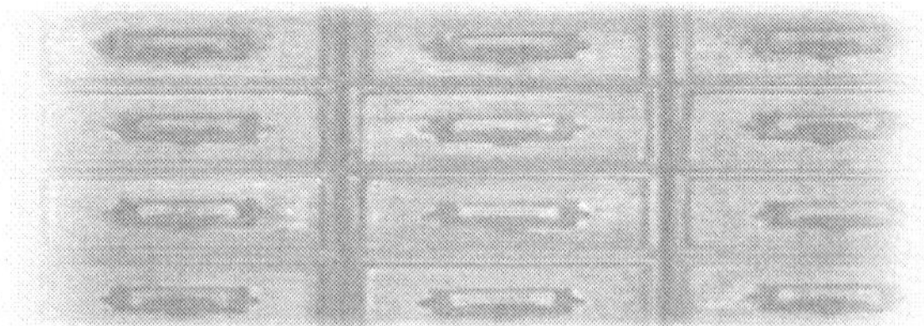

Chapter Eighty-One

June – The Caribbean

While the newscast was showing the live press conference from Pennsylvania, three people were sitting in the kitchen of the Presbytery of Father Sweeney's church. When they had finally finished eating their lunch, they turned on the telly to watch the news while they had their coffee.

Across the bottom of the screen were the words 'Breaking News' but the reporter was talking about the newscast that had taken place early in the day from Pennsylvania, it was about multiple deaths and a missing person. The three people sitting together and watching the tale unfold were Father Michael, Isabel, and Captain Joe. Captain Joe turned up the volume to hear everything, the TV news were replaying the entire press conference.

The three friends listened to all the information and commented how horrible it was, they showed a close up of the photograph of the missing person. Micky remembered seeing that person on the island last year, then Isabel yelled, "Father that's Ms. Wahl the lady I took care of at the resort." "How can they say she is missing, and the name is not the same?"

As Father Michael looked closer at the screen to study the photo, the long auburn hair and deep blue eyes caught his attention, take away the years and he was looking at his first and only love Kathleen O'Hare. The shock was making Micky feel dizzy, his heart was pounding, he knew the truth, the woman he had love was a somehow wanted by the police.

Either she was a missing person or the person of interest. The shock was beginning to set into Micky's mind, and it was having a terrible effect on him.

The room was now spinning, and he could hear both of his friends asking him if he was okay, he could hear Isabel calling for an ambulance, he could feel Captain Joe holding his body and yelling stay with us Father, don't leave us. Then he was travelling, everything was white, he could see the confessional and hear Kathleen telling her story, then she was there on a dock, but not in the Caribbean, but in the Mediterranean, the architecture of the buildings told him was the Greek Islands.

He could see Isabel crying, the ambulance people working on him, the oxygen mask, the man pounding on his chest and then back to Isabel crying uncontrollably. Then out in front of him was Kathleen standing in a sea of blue, she was speaking directly to him, "Sorry Micky, but you are too young to die." While all of this was happening, he could hear the music of Debussy, his lighthearted piece called Claire De Lune, it was like he was travelling through time and was being carried through it by the music. Then the music stopped, and he was back, the relieve faces of everyone made him so overwhelmed, that he started to cry, he had never cried in his whole life, but now he bawled like a baby.

Thinking to himself and speaking in his mind, “The medical staff are assuring Isabel and Captain Joe that I am going to make it.” With that they left for the hospital, Micky was in the ambulance with Isabel and Captain Joe was following.

Micky spoke to himself, “I knew they would always be there for me, but I could never tell them the true story of Gwen, that I will take to my grave.” “Why did I see her on a dock calling me back, was it possible that true love travelled through time and people were able to reach out to their loved ones.”

“If that be true, then Kathleen never stopped loving me.” “A new sadness entered Micky’s heart and mind, but one he could never share with another living soul.”

As the ambulance raced to the hospital, Father Michael thought back to Gwen, Kathleen, whatever, she was a true pragmatist. One pragmatist that she always mentioned was Machiavelli. It came to him as he was fighting for his life in the back of the ambulance, one of Machiavelli's quotes, 'the more sand has escaped from the hourglass of our life, the clearer we should see though it.' And then to himself, "I now see through your hourglass Gwen, and it is only filled with darkness."

Those thoughts were causing him problems, the ambulance person and Isabel pleaded with him to stay with only positive thoughts and focus only on himself.

Again, Micky thought, "They know I am travelling back into the past and revisiting a dark space, I need to send the thoughts of Gwen to the winds and forget about her completely." As if he heard his own wisdom, Micky focus on the people who were with him now, and let the past fly out the window.

For a brief moment in time, his thoughts went out to the love of his life Kathleen.

What happen to you, I am so sorry I didn't go to find you over Christmas that year. If I had maybe everything would have turned out differently.

And then his thoughts turned to the present, please Kathleen do the right thing and turn yourself in, make your peace with everyone.

Once at the hospital and stabilized, Micky was left with his owns thoughts, Gwen had confessed to him in

August, but the news said that the woman did not disappear until October 7. Almost two months after Gwen had confessed to murder that had not even happened. Perhaps she was fantasying about she wanted to do, and in fact had not done anything wrong. Maybe his words had reached her, and she had done nothing.

Perhaps it was this Jerome Smith and Kathleen was innocent.

Yes, the Kathleen I knew could never hurt a fly, let alone kill someone.

I pray God, that I am correct, and Kathleen is not involved in this terrible crime.

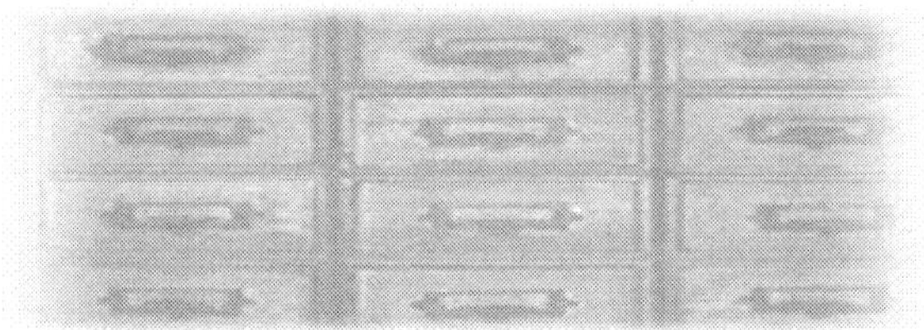

Chapter Eighty-Two

July – The Poconos

One month after the news conference and two days after his official retirement, Captain Collins decided to take a trip to the Pocono's. He had contacted the contractor who was the caretaker for the Kennedy property to meet him at that location. After the usual pleasantries the Captain showed the fifteen-year-old picture of Kathleen O'Hare to the gentleman. Captain Collins did not identify the person in the photograph.

The contractor looked at the picture and stated that that was a picture of Kathleen Kennedy. "That's the lady I met with all those years ago, strange how you got a picture of her, she would never allow anyone near the property if they had a camera, I would say she was totally camera shy."

The two men talked some more and then they said their goodbye's, when he was almost at his truck the contractor called back to the Captain, "just one more thing Sir, Ms. K. called me about two weeks ago, she said she is still on her extended world tour." "She also told me to close up early this year as she will not be using the cottage again this season."

The Captain called back to him, "thank you for that information, have a good day."

Speaking to himself, the Captain said, “So Kathleen Kennedy AKA, Kathleen O’Hare is alive and well and touring the world.” “We won’t be finding her body any time soon.”

Captain Collins sat in his car for about another twenty minutes and then decided to head back home. He realized he could never tell his wife he was chasing a ghost, not if he wanted his marriage to last. Listening to his music he went over all the details of the case, and he concluded that there was so much more to the story, but he had reached a dead end.

It was while he was sitting waiting for a red light, that a flash of a detail overlooked came to him, “The woman’s body had been cut up badly, but no one has ever mentioned what weapons were used.” They had got a search warrant for the cabin because the car with Jerome’s body had been found its property. Thinking back to the pictures of the car, he remembered that there were scratches on car, possible from tree branches, but there were no branches on the car.

He remembered the void and emptiness he felt on the dock that day, but that was his imagination, at least what he planned as accepting as the answer. The cabin was fine except that it was a little dusty, it was in perfect order, actually quite neat for a country retreat.

Nothing about this place spoke to anything relating to the lady of the lake. Sitting at the light a thought surfaced, he was thinking back to the interior of that cabin. Nothing came to mind.

Then in a flash, going back in his mind, he was back in the cabin looking around, and there on the kitchen counter was the block for carving knives, but it was empty. "Shit, how did we miss that, and where the hell are those knives?"

Then again to himself, "is this case really a dead end, or is there more to come, but when?"

Until I hear the Kathleen Kennedy is back in the United States, and I can get the team to talk to her, it's a closed case.

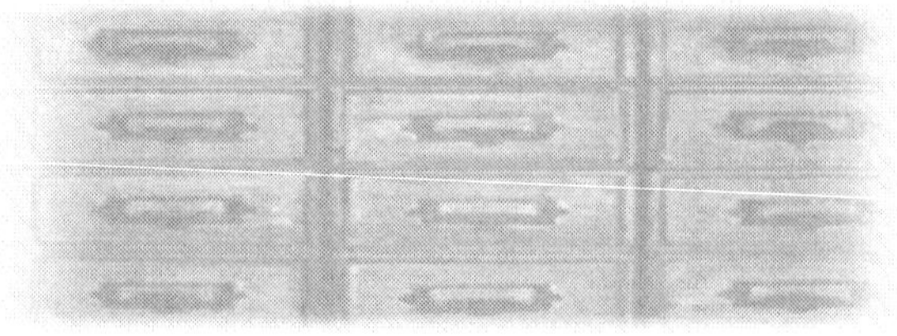

Chapter Eighty-Three

June – The Mediterranean

On a beautiful day in June, Gwen was on the docks in Crete, where they were having a stopover on her Mediterranean Cruise. She was enjoying the sunshine, the beautiful scenery, and thinking quietly to herself, that it was a good thing she had acquired two passports over the years, one in her mother's family name Kennedy, and one in her adopted name Gwendolyn Wahl.

Then she stated to herself. "Jerome's connections had come in handy in a pinch, when it was safe to return to the States, she could use either" The past year Gwen had done some major overhauls of her outside appearance, she had lost some weight, also she had toned up her body, "just love cruise ships, you can use the gym every day and no one cares, actually they are encouraged when the passengers do use the facilities." But not only had she improved her body and health, but she had also changed her hair, gone was her auburn colour, now it was a soft silvery-gray and much shorter than she had ever had it before.

It felt liberating knowing that she no longer resembled her photograph that was being showed worldwide on the news, she was betting that even the people from the resort would not recognize her now.

Yes, she was happy, her task had been completed and the crime rested solely on Jerome Smith. It had taken years to plan and years to complete, but it was done, and she felt rejuvenated.

Back on the ship and sitting on her balcony, she watched the sunset over the Mediterranean, the yellows, oranges and reds blending with the ever-darkening blue colours of the sea water. Her thoughts travelled back to the past as a young girl and then she called out to the universe, "Next up, is justice for you mom!"

"I am not sure how or when, but I will bring it about, but no one will die by my hand."

Sitting there quietly, she put on her CD player and for the first time in many years, she played a light hearted piece of music, she knew Micky loved this piece, so she played it for him, Debussy's Claire De Lune, "Micky I hope you hear this" Then a closing thought was spoken into the wind "I will always love you Micky Sweeney, may your God watch over you always." "I am so glad you survived." "Yes, I know the bad news gave you a heart attack, but your faithful servants saved you. For that I will be ever in their debt."

"Did you see me that day on the dock when I called out to you, telling you to live."

“I believe that true love transcend time, and we can reach out to our loved ones in their time of need.” “Micky you needed someone to reach you that day and you responded.” “For that I give thanks.”

As the sun set, Gwen acknowledged, that Micky was right, you could not kill your enemy, you had to move above such thoughts.

As the breezes off the Mediterranean caress her skin, Gwen promised never to take justice into her own hands. “I will spend the rest of my life God, trying to make amends.” “Fifteen lives lost because, I failed to listen to reason and to Micky.”

“Never again, God, I promise!”

Fingers crossed: I HOPE!!

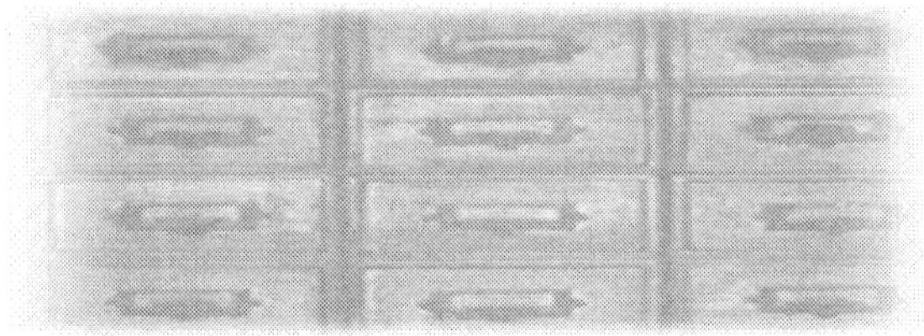

Epilogue

Kathleen had spent the last year travelling the world on cruise ships, she had circumvented the planet and had been able to say she had visited six of the seven continents. She had learned so much about the world and had seen things that she had only read about over the years. Some of the materials she had read were accurate in their information about different places, she also realized that many books published were more fiction than fact.

It was now time to return to the United States, but would she arrive as Gwen Wahl or Kathleen Kennedy. That decision had to made quickly as she is booking passage on the Queen Mary II, once that was done, there was no turning back.

Kathleen spent the last month when she was by herself thinking about everything that had transpired during the last two years. Recovering from her mental breakdown, building her orchestra of the disenchanted. It had been hard making friends with that group, but it was a necessary evil, she needed them to fulfil her plan. Yes, it had been hard work, but the result had been success in defeating her enemy.

What that group of friends did not know was that she had been paid handsomely by Grandmother Shanahan to get rid of their problem. Ten million to be precise, that was why she was able to travel the world in luxury. The family had promised they would give very little help to the police and block all information to the press. Following the news stories, they had kept their promise.

Kathleen now had to decide what to do with her life. When she had finally closed up the storage compartment that contained the items from her mother's apartment, she found a box of her mother's diaries. Kathleen was surprised, she did not realize her mother had document all of her life experiences, the highs, and the lows. In between her time spent with her friends, she read her mother's journals.

Some of the stuff broke her heart, her mother had really loved her dad and had married him against her family's wishes, for so many reasons, but the big one was his religion. Kathleen's family were Catholic, her dad was not! In the sixties, marrying a Jewish person was a social no-no for a Catholic.

This information surprised Kathleen, as her father had been very active in their church belong to the Knights of Columbus, plus other groups, to everyone dad was a devote Catholic.

Mother had certainly never revealed that information, that would explain why there was no wedding album. Mom had eloped with dad in Las Vegas.

However, someone knew the truth and caused mom grief throughout her life, things got bad for mom when we moved to New York, she felt like an outcast. So that explained her starting to drink and eventually dying from alcohol abuse. Some of the information had become so painful for Kathleen to read, that she took the box to the Pocono's so she could stay focus on the Darcy problem. Remembering those days, Kathleen knew she could not do justice to both problems, so Darcy took first place and her mother's journals came last.

A week later as Kathleen was approaching the dock of the Queen Mary II, where she was listed as Gwendolyn Wahl of New York City. Gwendolyn fortunes had allowed her to book a room on the Princess Suites level. Expensive but exclusive. The first evening in the dining room she was shocked to see Teddy, an off and on-again travelling partner for the last year on the ships. Nice guy, same age as her and he was from Boston, but somehow, he just did not fit in to the scene. Gwen knew very little about him, only that his uncle was big shot in Boston.

Teddy never revealed his name, and she did not ask. Strange though, whenever Teddy went ashore by himself, we would here about a killing one to two days later.

Gwen had enjoy having a dance partner on the different ships and Teddy was always there for her, but he was always vague about his work. Given Gwen's circumstances, she did not ask to many questions.

Gwen would sit quietly when the chance arose, and she would think about all the stories she had heard form different passengers over the past year. The happy stories and the stories of those trying to escape their trials by travelling to distance lands. Teddy had talked about being an altar server and said that was why he quit the church. Others spoke about failed surgeries, criminals that had harmed their families and where never prosecuted.

Those individuals blame politics for their troubles. One theme that emerged from those sad stories was that corruption ran deep in the government and they felt lost.
All of these stories haughty Gwen, she felt she needed to help them, but how?

During her time away, Gwen had signed up for and completed an on-line course to become a PSW, she didn't know why, but she had done so, after all she would not be going back to working in libraries in the near future. Also, being a PSW, would put her in places to do some good, if she so desired.

For a brief, moment in time Gwen could also see how being a PSW could put her situations where she could perhaps bring some justice for suffering souls.

Maybe that was her calling, to help bring justice in an injustice world. Only time will tell was Gwen's thoughts as she landed on US soil in Brooklyn six days later.

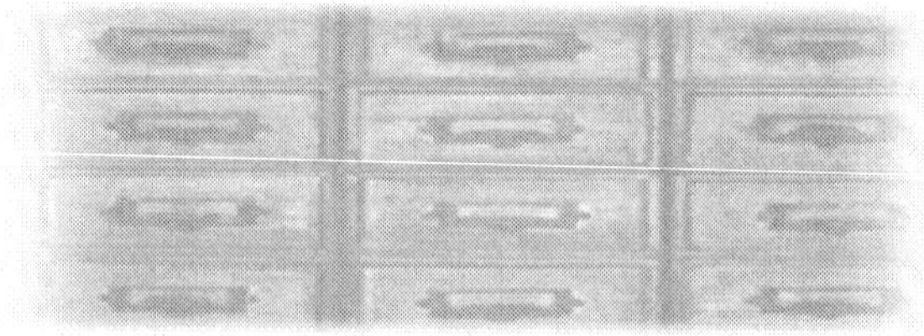

Manufactured by Amazon.ca
Bolton, ON

34784646R00217